CAM

CAMEO

a novel

by Rob Doyle

WEIDENFELD & NICOLSON

First published in Great Britain in 2026 by Weidenfeld & Nicolson,
an imprint of The Orion Publishing Group Ltd
Carmelite House, 50 Victoria Embankment
London EC4Y ODZ

An Hachette UK Company

The authorised representative in the EEA is Hachette Ireland,
8 Castlecourt Centre, Dublin 15, D15 XTP3,
Ireland (email: info@hbgi.ie)

5 7 9 10 8 6 4

A CIP catalogue record for this book is
available from the British Library.

ISBN (Hardback) 978 1 3996 3107 5
ISBN (Export Trade Paperback) 978 1 3996 3108 2
ISBN (Ebook) 978 1 3996 3110 5
ISBN (Audio) 978 1 3996 3111 2

Typeset at The Spartan Press Ltd,
Lymington, Hants

Printed and bound in Great Britain by Clays Ltd,
Elcograf S.p.A.

www.weidenfeldandnicolson.co.uk
www.orionbooks.co.uk

To Lara, Evan, and Constance

Because we all have been for all time: I, and thou, and those kings of men. And we all shall be for all time, we all for ever and ever.

— *The Bhagavad Gita*

I do not know which of us has written this page.

— J.L. Borges, 'Borges and I'

Prologue

The Last Interview

To start with, let's go back, if not to the very beginning, to a beginning. I've been reading some of your press interviews from the period when you were just commencing what would become the phenomenally prolific – and successful – Ren Duka novel cycle. It strikes me that words like 'transition', 'transformation', and 'chrysalis' peppered your contemporary reflections on where you were in your work and your life. What did those words mean to you then, and what do they mean to you now?[1]

Well, I began writing the Duka novels, as you know, shortly before I turned forty. That's a landmark age, perhaps *the* landmark age, for a man at least. Turning forty clearly heralded the onset of a new, perhaps disquieting phase of life. On the other hand, the notion of the midlife crisis had always seemed laughable to me, for the simple reason that there'd hardly been a minute in my life when I *wasn't* in a state of crisis. What could middle-age inflict on me that youth hadn't already inflicted? Of course, this was a spectacular delusion. As the middle of life as traditionally conceived drew near, I began to see that there *is* an inevitably brutal transition that must be endured. I knew I was in for a rough time of it, and

[1] Interview by Li Wei, published in the *South China Morning Post*, August 2032

I knew too that it was a question of mutate, evolve, grow or face annihilation. The stakes suddenly seemed perilously high. The publication of the first Ren Duka novel was my response to the emergency.

Bearing all of that in mind, I want to ask you about a subject which may or may not be delicate for you.

No subject is especially delicate. Ask away.

Well, what I want to ask you about is your productivity, this explosion of energy that went off when you began writing the Ren Duka novels and you became so remarkably prolific.

Why would that be a delicate question?

Because it suggests a related question, concerning stimulants, your narcotic intake. Some have suggested that your suddenly accelerated rate of production was linked to that.

I see. Well, sorry to demystify, but the fact is, the commencement of the Ren Duka cycle coincided precisely with my decision to *quit* recreational drugs, rather than take more of them, if that's what you mean to imply by your question. The secret to my profuseness in creating the Ren Duka cycle is no secret at all, and in fact it *is* psychopharmacological or whatever the word is: caffeine. Balzac, who was significantly more productive than me, a real writing machine, is famously said to have drunk fifty cups of coffee a day. He's the kind of writer I used to hate, the kind who just kept flooding the world with his pages and never paused to consider that sometimes silence might be both noble and golden. Funny how things change. Ren Duka made me a whore.

It's curious that Ren Duka's Seen a Few Things, *the novel that began it all, concerned the ordeal of a young, drug-dealing poet.*

I wrote that novel as I was in the process of leaving that life behind, in part to make sense of the feelings of self-recrimination I was going through with regard to my various self-destructive habits – but also more generally as a decadent Westerner, a hedonist in a burning world. If we can be Kierkegaardian about it, I was trying to transition out of the aesthetic stage of life ...

Into the ethical stage.

Yes. Though actually it's misleading to say I was renouncing an aesthetic attitude to life. I've never really understood Kierkegaard, truth be told.

But all of this loops back to the question of midlife. I decided I would absolutely not permit myself to become one of those dismal males who grow inflexibly sad when they're past forty because they can't properly mourn and move beyond an earlier – and, in certain key regards, better – phase of life. My extremist method of ensuring I wouldn't succumb to such a defeatist attitude was to pare my life back, rid it of the last vestiges of enjoyment in anything other than work, which is the one thing that's always made me happy. I mean, what else was there? Chase around after younger women and get high all the time? Don't get me wrong, I'd probably have been up for that if it was remotely feasible, but I could feel the walls closing in. So I decided I would create a new character, Duka, who was both me and not me, and through him I would make myself into a beast of incessant writing, a true meaning-wallah. And for a decade now that's what I've been. Others might have turned their thoughts to having children, but it's both ridiculous and true to say – as I had myself say in *Ren Duka's Extinction* – that Ren Duka is my child. He's my survival, my surrogate self.

And yet, the unforeseen popularity of the Duka novels certainly brought about whole new crises, even catastrophes, in your personal life. Critical studies have begun to appear that explore these very connections. With this in mind, I'd like you to tell me about the first Duka novel, and in particular about the interplay between your life and that of your creation, beginning when that novel was published. Tell me about Ren Duka, Paulie Sheehan, the film adaptation, the scandals, all of it.

Okay. I think we'll be on firmer ground there. Well then, let's see...

1. Conception

Ren Duka's Seen a Few Things (December 2023)

And so it was that, as he was approaching the milestone of his fortieth birthday, the author who would become known to the world as the creator of the Ren Duka cycle took stock of his life so far. Measuring the books he had written against those he still hoped to write, he conceived of a fresh means of attack, a whole new raid on the temple. While he could not have known it then, the project whose outlines he began to discern would consume his creative energies for a furiously productive decade – and totally upend his life.

'I felt like Zarathustra coming down from the mountain,' the author would later say of this decisive phase, in which the invention of a new on-page persona catalysed the process by which literature and life bled inextricably into one. Eschewing the stylistic rigour of his previous work, the reborn author of *Ren Duka's Seen a Few Things* adopted a freewheeling narrative rhythm that was at once intimate and expansive, playful and cryptic, timeless and contemporary.

The inaugural Ren Duka novel begins in a loosely anecdotal mode before morphing into something darker. Ren Duka, a writer living in his native Dublin after long years of wandering, announces that he is going to tell in full the story of his life – to describe the titular *few things* he has seen. However, like Tristram Shandy, he never quite gets to the point. A ship on the horizon, a robin alighting on the terrace next to him, or some feature of the south Dublin coastline will catch his eye and prompt a digression, with the promised autobiography postponed for several more pages. In never quite managing to tell his own story, Duka collaterally tells an embarrassment of *other* stories, thus presenting a vivid social topography of contemporary Ireland. Eventually, as if conceding that a pilot episode must have a plot, he alights on a single story – and spends the remainder of *Ren Duka's Seen a Few Things* telling it.

For the past half decade, Dublin has been the battleground in a vicious conflict between two rival drug gangs whose power and reach have expanded far beyond the nation's shores. In a series of flashbacks, Ren Duka recounts how a kid from the house next door to his childhood home, Joey Flynn, grew up to be a lieutenant in one of the warring cartels. As Duka's literary reputation had begun to rise in his late twenties, Joey Flynn already sat at the high table of a crime empire that spanned Europe, Latin America and the United Arab Emirates. Flynn's dramatic assassination in 2019 shocked Ireland, made headlines around the world, and instigated the gang war that would deluge the capital with blood and bullets.

Ren Duka chooses not to think too much about his complicity in the carnage by way of the drugs he consumes at book launches, literary festivals and prize ceremonies. 'People have no idea of the sheer volume of narcotics that circulate in the publishing industry,' he tells his friend Matt one night while they're drinking in a pub on Westmoreland Street. 'In Ireland, the entire machine is virtually run on cocaine.' Generally Ren is able to suppress his guilt and look the other way – until he meets Paulie Sheehan.

Paulie is a talented internet poet in an age when poets occupy the lowest rung on the cultural ladder. Duka gets to know the younger man at Dublin book events. He likes Paulie, seeing in him an integrity that sets him apart. At the launch of a debut novel about a young feminist obsessed with a rich and cruel man, Paulie tells Ren about his creative struggles. By now he's had poems placed in several literary journals, but getting a collection published is proving a challenge. 'And even if that happens,' Paulie says, 'it's not as if it will be the making of me. Just getting by enough to keep writing will always be a dogfight, a lost cause.'

'Not lost,' says Ren. 'Underground. Samizdat. Remember, you write for posterity.'

The next time Ren sees him, Paulie is handing plastic baggies to a trio of novelists in the corridor of a Christmas party at a publishing house in north Dublin. As Ren approaches, the novelists move off in unison towards the bathroom. Shaking Paulie's hand, Ren grins and says, 'Don't tell me you've become a drug dealer?'

Paulie shrugs, looking past Ren at some short-story writers dancing to a rap song. 'I need the money,' he says. 'Poetry isn't paying the bills.'

'Couldn't you get an honest job?' asks Ren, feeling foolish even as the words leave his mouth.

Paulie laughs. 'Whatever. I just sell a bit of bag at launches, readings, literary festivals. There's a market there. It's low risk. I'm not an idiot.'

Later that evening, Ren buys a gram from Paulie and together they inhale some lines in the toilets. 'Just take care of yourself, Paulie,' he says, daubing a nostril with a little finger. 'You weren't cut out for this lifestyle. Be careful.'

Walking home that night, Ren's thoughts circle around his young friend. Paulie grew up in the inner city, and, when he was twelve, his mother moved with him and his two sisters to Salthill in County Galway. Although he was well liked at school, good at football and precociously knowledgeable about music and films, Paulie was an introvert who enjoyed staying in his room with a book as much as he did hanging out with the lads on a Friday night. When he was nineteen, he moved back to Dublin to study German and English at Trinity College. It was during his final year that he and Ren Duka met. By that time, Paulie had begun publishing his poems online, building a reputation. Keeping up with his work, Ren was frequently amazed by the creative leaps Paulie made between one published poem and the next.

For several months after the Christmas party, Ren sees nothing of Paulie. He has not been turning up at book events and his social media accounts have gone silent. One evening, Ren attends the launch of the new issue of a literary magazine. He is among the issue's contributors, with an essay about a cult New York novelist whose work, according to Duka, was as luminous and urgent as her life was violent and depraved. He reads the first few pages to the sizeable crowd of mostly young people. When he finishes, a woman replaces him at the podium to read her poems. Ren weaves through the crowd to refill his wine glass. At the drinks table, a tall, slender, golden-haired woman in her early twenties is sipping a glass of prosecco. She smiles at him in a manner that suggests they have met before. He greets her, then confesses he can't remember where he knows her from.

'Oh, we haven't been introduced yet,' she says. He can't place her accent. Is she English? Irish? She comes from wealth – that much is clear. 'I enjoyed your reading,' she says. 'I like your books, you know.' Then she tells him that they have a friend in common – Paulie Sheehan. He asks her where Paulie has been, admitting he's been concerned as Paulie hasn't responded to his DMs. The tall woman watches him for a moment, as if deciding on how much she ought to say. Then she places a hand on Ren's arm and leads him into an adjacent room where the sound of the ongoing reading is muffled. 'Easier to talk here,' she says. Then she tells him about Paulie.

The day after Christmas, Paulie had decided that, if he was diligent, he would be able to shift enough cocaine on New Year's Eve that he wouldn't have to worry for a while about the rent: January through to late summer he could devote himself to poetry. A few days before New Year's, he visited his contact – the guy above him in the supply chain who apportioned the product to the street dealers – at a flat in an inner-city high-rise. There were spotters positioned in the courtyard, on the balconies and at street corners. It was like walking into a fortress, Paulie said.

'And how do you know all this?' Ren asks, interrupting the woman's story.

'Because he trusts me,' she replies.

It's clear to Ren that she and Paulie are lovers. Or perhaps that's over and they've remained friends, which is Paulie's style. She continues her story. Paulie had asked his supplier for twelve times the volume of cocaine he usually shifted.

The guy looked at him for a long time before responding. He told Paulie that that was a serious amount of product, far more than someone of Paulie's status would usually be trusted with. Paulie was about to give up and leave when suddenly the supplier motioned for one of his subordinates to fetch the cocaine. While they were waiting for him to return, the supplier asked Paulie if he knew what would happen if he fucked up and didn't pay. Paulie nodded and said yes, he knew. But the guy shook his head and said no, he didn't know, he really didn't have a fucking clue.

On New Year's Eve, Paulie's plan had started out well. From early afternoon he cycled around the city, delivering cocaine to novelists, editors, short-story writers, and the occasional essayist. By 7 p.m. he had already sold more than he usually did in a fortnight. He knew that as midnight approached, the requests would accelerate, the city reaching a frenzy of appetite. He was living in a studio flat on Gardiner Street in the north inner city. Ren had visited him there once. It was the archetypal poet's dwelling: a spartan room strewn with books, wine glasses and rolling tobacco, Paulie's notebooks lying open on a lamplit desk. Each time Paulie made a delivery he left the bulk of the cocaine concealed inside a defunct toaster, carrying only enough to supply the next two or three customers. Around nine o'clock, after dropping off deliveries to Stoneybatter and Phibsborough, he returned to his flat to pick up the next batch. When he prised open the toaster, the stash was gone. For half an hour he pulled apart the tiny flat, overturning everything in the desperate hope that he had somehow misplaced the huge quantity of cocaine. When he got his wits together, he accepted he had been swindled. He packed a knapsack with some clothes and belongings. Then he took a coach – one of the last buses leaving the city on New Year's Eve – from Busáras station north to Drogheda. He told no one he was leaving Dublin. That night and for the two that followed he stayed with an old college friend. From Drogheda he texted his supplier, explaining what had happened and assuring him that he would pay in full very soon (he had no idea how this might happen). The supplier called him back immediately. The situation was made clear: Paulie owed twenty-two thousand euro, and if he didn't pay up within two weeks, the interest would quickly accumulate. As it did, very bad things would begin happening. 'Where are you?' his supplier asked. Paulie hung up.

By this point in the woman's story, the final reading from the magazine launch is in progress. She and Ren are quiet for a moment, listening to the muted voice. Suddenly she says, 'Paulie did the only thing he could do: he went on the run and stayed out there.' Meanwhile, he has been pursuing every possible means of rustling up the money. He doesn't know who ripped him off. All that matters, she says, is that Paulie pays the gangsters back, then cuts his ties for ever with the drugs trade. Thankfully, none of his family are in Dublin (one sister is in London, the other is in Galway with his mother), so they are not in immediate danger. Paulie told the woman not to talk about him to anyone. Their relationship was still new – Ren had guessed correctly – and still offline enough that his pursuers wouldn't know about her.

'If he told you to keep quiet, then why are you talking to me?' Ren asks.

She looks at him for a moment. 'Because he trusts you,' she

says. 'Because he asked me to. And because he hopes you'll do something for him.'

Ren is about to protest that he doesn't have that kind of money to spare – he'd spent his most recent advance before the novel even appeared on bookshop shelves. As if reading his mind, she tells him it's not what he thinks. Paulie's months on the run, she explains, coincided with what she describes as a 'volcanic eruption' of his poetic talent. While laying low and moving between Airbnbs and friends' couches in Louth and Galway, Paulie was amazed to find himself writing like never before: a new poem every day, or else more lines in an epic poem of urban squalor and transcendence that would become the cornerstone of the collection that emerged from this terrible period. 'The poems are ... Well, they're brilliant,' she says.

Ren watches her closely. 'You're in love with him, aren't you?' he says. She meets his gaze and replies with calm assurance that yes, she is, but that hasn't clouded her judgement.

'So what does he want from me?' asks Ren.

'He just wants you to read them.'

'That's all?'

'That's all. And, well, if you like them, perhaps you could write a few words of endorsement.' She reaches into her handbag and produces a sheaf of printed sheets in a binder clip. As she hands it to him, he reads the title page:

These Last Days Keep Dragging On

Poems by Paulie Sheehan

Uncorrected Draft

'He says it's important that I give you a hard copy,' she tells him. Ren smiles – he and Paulie had bonded over their belief that it's an insult to send someone a book in PDF form. A wave of affection for the young poet passes through him. 'My email is on the back,' says the woman. Only when he glances at it does Ren learn her name: Scarlett. 'If you like the poems, you can send any words of support there. If not, naturally he won't hold it against you.' Ren nods and gets ready to leave – he's not in the mood for the gossipy hobnobbing that will follow the readings. 'One more thing,' Scarlett says. 'He's publishing the collection soon. He's already signed a contract. With things as they stand, he won't be able to do so under his own name. His publishers know his situation is … delicate, and they're willing to publish him under a pseudonym.' Ren assures her that he understands.

As soon as he gets home, he pours a large glass of Brouilly and begins reading the poems. The epigraph is taken from the film *Sicario* – Ren recalls the lines being spoken to Emily Blunt by Benicio Del Toro's enigmatic assassin in the final scene:

> *You should move to a small town, somewhere the rule of law still exists. You will not survive here. You are not a wolf, and this is a land of wolves now.*

A few pages in, he realises that everything Scarlett told him was true. The poems are exquisite. He already knew that Paulie was talented – but this is work of a whole different order of magnitude. He finishes the collection then immediately turns back to the start and reads it again, enthralled by the abundant felicities of rhythm, the subtle gradations of tone, the almost scandalous assurance of metaphor. When he finishes reading it a second time, he crafts a paragraph of ardent praise. After polishing the endorsement for twenty minutes, he emails it to the address on the back of the printout. As he finally lies down to sleep, he tells himself that a master has emerged in their midst. Images swirl in the hypnogogic montage: Paulie on the run across Ireland; inner-city gangsters with golden crucifixes and inscrutable tattoos; books of poetry written in blood.

Two and a half months pass. Ren reviews a couple of books, begins and abandons a novel, gets into a particularly nasty online spat. He hears nothing about Paulie Sheehan. After thanking Ren for endorsing the book, Scarlett had gone quiet. Then Ren receives an email from a publisher inviting him to the launch of a debut collection of poems by one J.T. Fearey. He does not need to read his own quote (which is included along with praise from two other writers) to realise what this is. He sends a brief reply saying he'll be delighted to attend.

The launch takes place in the same Georgian building on Parnell Square where Ren had learned of Paulie's troubles. He arrives early and is heartened to find that a good crowd has turned out. As he picks up a glass of red wine, he registers a buzz in the air unusual for this type of gathering. Everyone here knows the score, he thinks. At that moment, he sees Paulie across the room, smiling politely as he listens to two young women. Paulie waves when he sees Ren. Excusing himself from the two women, he greets his friend with a warm embrace. Ren has to check himself while praising Paulie's book lest he embarrasses his friend. Paulie thanks him graciously, ever the soft-spoken gentleman. Then, in a quieter voice, Ren asks him how things are going. Paulie sighs, peers into his glass of sparkling water, and says it's been a difficult time – but things are looking up. He has managed to gather most of the money with the help of his sisters and brother-in-law. 'In a week's time I'll be able to pay off the gangsters and be done with that world for ever.'

'That's good,' says Ren. 'I'm sorry I haven't done more.'

Paulie waves away his apology. 'In a strange way, I regret nothing, apart from the burden on my family. I couldn't have written like this if my life wasn't in danger. I can't explain that, but it's the truth.'

The crowd is summoned to attention. At the podium, Paulie's editor, a woman in her fifties in a dramatic emerald-green dress, surveys the room. She thanks them all for coming, then declares that in thirty years in publishing she has never come across a debut collection of poems as impressive as that of Paulie Sheehan – she uses his real name. In her impassioned speech she alludes to the unusual circumstances of the book's publication and insists that literature should always make a stand against 'brute force, intimidation, cruelty, and tyranny in all its forms'. She then welcomes Paulie to the podium. A hush falls on the crowd as he takes her place. Adjusting the micro-phone, Paulie again thanks everyone for coming and apologises for the air of secrecy surrounding the event. He makes a joking reference to Ol' Dirty Bastard's legendary appearance onstage with the Wu Tang Clan in New York while he was on the run from the law. Then he reads several of his poems. During the first poem, Ren spots Scarlett across the room, a head taller than everyone around her. Noticing him, she grins and waves.

Ren decides that when the reading is over he will invite Scarlett and Paulie for dinner at his place later in the week.

In the hubbub that follows the reading, however, Ren is drawn into conversation with an editor and an intern. When he extricates himself, he can locate neither Paulie nor Scarlett. An acquaintance confirms what he has surmised: the couple left the building as soon as the reading ended.

In a gentler world, *Ren Duka's Seen a Few Things* might have ended there. But life is brutal, and thirty pages remain. Ren hangs around the launch talking to friends and rivals. Returning home after midnight, he goes to bed guilty at having compromised the next day's work by drinking too much free wine. His sleep is hot and fitful. He dreams that Scarlett is calling to him from the end of a dark, narrow corridor. Waking just after 7 a.m., he looks at his phone and sees three missed calls and more than thirty messages. Instantly he knows that something is terribly wrong. All the messages are from friends who attended the launch. Two of the calls are from Scarlett, at 3:02 and 3:15 a.m. The other is from an unknown number, at 4:01. By mid-morning he has established the basic facts – the rest is filled in over the days that follow. When Paulie and Scarlett left the building on Parnell Square after ordering a taxi, two men emerged from the shadows at the foot of the steps. One of them punched Paulie in the gut. When Scarlett screamed, the second man punched her in the face, breaking her nose. When she fell to the ground, her attacker stepped forward and kicked her in the ribs. The men forced Paulie into the back of a white van, which immediately screeched off into the north inner city. They drove around for several hours. Perhaps they drove to the Dublin mountains, or through deserted industrial estates at the edge of town. After taping Paulie's mouth shut and binding his hands behind his back, his abductors showed him photographs of his sister in Galway. 'We're being nice to you, Paulie,' one of them said. 'It's better you're dead before you hear what we do with her.'

The other one joined in: 'She's a fucking ride. How come you're so ugly?' The two men barked insults at him, and whenever he tried to speak they punched him in the head. Spluttering through blood and broken teeth, he told them that he had the money, he was going to pay it in a few days.

'You fucking liar,' one them said. 'You're lucky we didn't drag that lanky slut in here too. She's way out of your league, pal.' The same man held up a Stanley knife and gripped Paulie by the scalp. 'We're taking your bollocks, Paulie,' he said. 'Do you reckon that skinny blonde cunt will still want you when you can't ride her? I'm going to feed your cock to me German Shepherd.'

Paulie's muffled screams filled the windowless metal cabin. The man with the knife held up a chunk of pink bloody flesh: 'There you are Paulie.' Small mercies: it was not his genitals they had removed, but a piece of his ear. 'This is your one and final warning. Next time it's your cock we'll be taking, and we'll be paying your sister a visit too.' They dumped him on the side of the road in a business park in City West, his hands still bound. After some time – it could have been minutes or hours – he came to, pulled his phone from his pocket, and managed to call for an ambulance.

Over the days that follow, Ren Duka and his friends keep in close contact, sharing updates on a dedicated WhatsApp group. Paulie is in an emergency ward at Cherry Orchard

Hospital. The Guards visit him for a statement: he tells them he remembers nothing, has no idea who did this or why. After three nights he is released. His face is badly scarred, his mutilated ear bandaged over. Scarlett sends a message to his friends on his behalf: Paulie wants them to know that the worst is over and not to be alarmed if they don't hear from him for a while. By the end of the week, Paulie arranges to meet with a representative of his creditor at a Burger King in a suburban shopping centre. Sitting at a table surrounded by other diners and in clear view of a CCTV camera, he hands over in full the money owed, stacked inside an envelope. Without sitting down, the collector counts the bills as an associate looks on. Then he puts the money in an inside coat pocket and tells Paulie that their business is settled. 'That's it now. You won't be hearing from us again.'

'What about my family?' Paulie asks.

'I said it's settled,' the collector repeats. 'You don't owe us anything. Your family are of no interest to us now.'

The final pages of *Ren Duka's Seen a Few Things* are a statement of defiance and celebration. Ren Duka envisions a possible future life for Paulie Sheehan – free of violence and devoted to poetry, travel and friendship. In the closing paragraph, he honours his young friend's dignity and courage. 'Nobody reads poetry any more,' Duka concludes, 'which only proves that those who consecrate their lives to it are the last warriors, the carriers of the flame. Pasolini wrote that the mark of the true writer is that they place their bodies in peril to achieve their work. By this measure, Paulie Sheehan is the great Irish writer of our times.'

Ren Duka Bets on the Horses – US title: *Duka is Back* (May 2024)

Nobody – not the author, nor his editor or critics – foresaw the huge commercial success of *Ren Duka's Seen a Few Things*. Overlooked by the year's prize lists, it gained rapid online and word-of-mouth traction, first in Ireland and the UK, then everywhere. The author surprised those around him by appearing to take in his stride the overnight leap to bestselling ubiquity. Later, looking back on this vertiginous ascent, he told an interviewer for *Le Monde*, 'I was forty years old. By that age I'd seen so much, had so many ups and downs, been through every sort of abject crisis and personal upheaval. Sudden fame couldn't derail me the way it might have done ten years earlier. I didn't accord it any great respect. I did appreciate the new financial freedom, even if it hardly changed how I lived. I went to the same pubs, hung out with the same friends. What I mean to say is, when all that stuff happened – fame, riches – I regarded it as not really happening to me, any more than a film you watch, even a gripping one, happens to you.'

In her memoir *Selling Ren Duka*, the author's agent Laura del Valle recalled: 'For a while it was silly season. He went to bed one night with social media followers in the low thousands, where they'd plateaued years earlier, and woke up with six-figure counts across all platforms. Many have wondered why such an unlikely novel became a mega-bestseller, but to me there's no mystery. It was the TikTok kids.' A minor industry of profiles and think-pieces roared into life. 'It was like a presidential campaign,' wrote del Valle. 'All the envy and resentment came out alongside the adulation. Enemies emerged from the woodwork. There were scandals, stories, unearthed tweets – the kind of thing that might have killed other careers. But they were all swallowed up in the supernova of that first book's success. It became somehow impersonal, a chain reaction, a phenomenon that both he and I felt no longer had much to do with him and everything to do with an archetype or projection, a fluke of the *zeitgeist*, for which he was the figurehead. Crucially, the media circus never prevented him from writing.'

For the first time in a career that had previously unfolded to a relaxed rhythm, the author was subject to intense pressure to produce his next book. Intoxicated by spiralling profits, his publishers – like his readers – wanted more of the same. Whether cynically or in harmony with his artistic instincts, he gave it to them. The second Ren Duka novel is almost provocatively unassuming, a work that intrigues through its very mundanity. In *Ren Duka Bets on the Horses*, a newly famous Ren Duka weans himself off the platformer video games on which he has been frittering away his time and takes up an alternative habit: going to the bookies. He spends his afternoons hanging out with the gruff old-timers, labourers and taxi-drivers who frequent Superb Bookmakers in the Liberties area of Dublin's south inner city. Initially they treat him warily for his habit of dropping lengthy quotations in French (La Rochefoucauld, Chamfort, Joseph de Maistre), but Ren's way with a dirty joke soon wins them round. In what would become a hallmark of the Duka novels, there is little in the way of plotting, but very much in the way of *yarning*. The most celebrated passages are Ren Duka's comically precise, deadpan accounts of the horse races themselves. He narrates these contests with the precision and solemnity of an old monk chanting his prayers, his gaze roving around Superb Bookmakers to register the facial expressions, muttered curses, and gasps of the men watching the races alongside him. These racing passages have been compared to the *Nouveau Roman* as practised by the likes of Alain Robbe-Grillet, and to the hypnotic, mystically fervent music of John Coltrane at his most uncompromising. While detractors have objected to the novel's inverse class snobbery – proletarian subjects are glibly glorified or treated with cloying sentimentalism – readers who had enjoyed the first Duka novel were no less enthusiastic.

While insults or praise from regular readers tend neither to greatly sting nor elate, those of a writer's peers can rankle for a lifetime. Among the author's chief rivals was Kevin Mulvaney, whose debut novel *Sex Tape* had been published in the same year as his own. *Sex Tape* was a sizeable critical and popular success, but as the years passed Mulvaney had failed to follow up with a second book. During that period, Mulvaney was heard to insinuate that his rival's then modest sales indicated a deficient instinct for the passions of everyday people. Now that the first two Ren Duka titles had blown up beyond all expectations, Mulvaney was putting it about (sometimes in late-night posts deleted by morning) that his rival's outsized success was proof of his work's lowest-common-denominator populism. With consummate vengefulness, Mulvaney wrote a widely shared article wherein he eviscerated 'the new populists' who wrote not for the individual reader, but for the globalised masses of a homogenous late capitalism. In a precision strike that his wounded target might even have admired, Mulvaney quoted the author's beloved Schopenhauer: 'He who writes for fools always finds a large public.'

Ren Duka's Blues – US title: *Duka Rides Again* (September 2024)

There are those, Sigmund Freud observed, who are wrecked by success. For a time, it seemed as if the author's initial nonchalance around his sudden global celebrity was a false dawn. At least, that is the impression that arises from the third Ren Duka novel, published just nine months after the first. With his writing career gone stratospheric and the rest of his life coming along well too, Ren Duka sinks into an inexplicable desolation. Asking himself what it has all meant, and whether he has failed 'if not as a writer, then as a man', he takes a journey into his past via a series of encounters with former lovers and estranged friends whom he tracks down online. Over drinks, meals, or long walks along Dublin's canals and streets, he questions them about the Ren Duka they knew. It is as if he is trying to reconstruct a self he no longer recognises, or perhaps mis-recognised all along. After a string of increasingly intimate, late-night DM chats, he rekindles a relationship with an early girlfriend, Hannah Pelling, a lawyer in London who is now engaged to another man. The pair travel for a fortnight to Norway. On the flight to Oslo, Ren is overcome by dread. He realises he never even wanted to travel to Norway with Hannah, and if he had any sense he would fly directly home on arrival. And yet, as in an awful dream in which the dreamer marches towards a precipice, he obeys a will external to his own. Gloomily the couple explore the fjords and archipelagos near Bergen. They sleep in wooden cabins and wake under coastal skies of unblemished blue. Night after night they make love with demonic intensity, as if attempting to obliterate themselves with pleasure. Here, *Ren Duka's Blues* takes on the qualities of surreal, hallucinant pornography. 'I fuck life, I fuck death,' Ren gasps while penetrating his lover atop a mossy rock by a secluded cove.

'Come in me', Hannah cries. 'Give me all of it – the tongue of the serpent.' As they orgasm together, black ravens circle in the sky, spiralling above the couple's fused bodies in the contours of a vortex.

When they return to their respective lives – Ren in Dublin, Hannah in London – she learns that she is pregnant. After three tense phone calls – and a threatening email to Ren from Hannah's fiancé, a trader in the City – she decides to have an abortion. Ren's depression, which had briefly lifted following his return from Norway, returns with redoubled ferocity. He moves to a drab town in the Irish midlands, where he lives alone in a rented room. He sleeps late every day and spends his afternoons watching TV (sometimes he doesn't even bother turning it on). His thoughts circle endlessly around the prospect of suicide.

Months pass, then years. Having vanished from public life, Ren sometimes reads articles about himself online: 'What Happened to Beloved Storyteller Ren Duka?' (*New York Times*); 'Has Ren Duka Found God (and is that Why We Don't Hear from Him These Days)?' (*Vogue*); 'What the Silence of Ren Duka Tells Us About Modern Celebrity' (*Financial Times*). He consistently marvels at the factual inaccuracies they get away with printing, before chucking his phone onto a pile of clothes and going out to wander in the woods.

The truth is more mundane than the articles suggest. After a period of trial and error, Ren has settled on a course of medication that defangs his worst depressions – at the cost of piling on weight and nullifying his libido. Too vain to be seen looking bloated in public, he has abandoned the literary world and become a recluse (and a celibate). However, he hasn't stopped writing. Calculating that a pause will only whet his readership's appetite, Duka has held back publication of his new novel – the one we are reading – which covers his 'woodland hermitude amid the morning dewdrops, the song of the egret and the curlew, the poplar and the oak, the brook and the vale'. The long, contemplative passages of *Ren Duka's Blues* drew comparisons to Thoreau, Whitman, Kerouac and Dillard. As a scalding account of depression and social withdrawal softens into a paean to the forests and mountains of County Cavan, the customary, slapdash style gives way to a precise yet lyrical naturalist's taxonomy. By the novel's end, Ren Duka has quit the meds, left his woodland shack, and returned to urban life with its intrigues and temptations.

While reviews were generally favourable, *Ren Duka's Blues* was by a large margin the lowest-selling Ren Duka novel so far. The author appears to have taken heed. The instalments that followed saw him revert to – and update – the formula established in *Ren Duka's Seen a Few Things*, recounting Ren's adventures in sprightly volumes that eschewed ascetic contemplation in favour of yarn-spinning, amiable character sketches, and crude innuendo … but newly unshackled from the strictures of realism.

Excerpt from *A Cool, Dry Place*

Often in their autobiographies writers will take pains to emphasise a great childhood romance with books and reading. In this regard I'm an outlier – to put it mildly. My gloomy childhood was riddled with compulsions and phobias, not least of which was a hysterical fear of books. I've delved with more than one therapist into this enigma of why I've ended up devoting my life to something that used to irrationally terrify me. The consensus seems to be that my boyhood bibliophobia was symptomatic of a primal alienation: books frightened me because each one contained a parallel world potentially even more hostile and bewildering than this one. If I'd encountered books whose intention was to pulverise worlds rather than multiply them, say the various Jungians and Lacanians whose bank accounts I've inflated, then I'd have taken to them more readily. The only fictional worlds inhabitable to me – a skinny kid with bad nerves and night terrors – were the most horrific or the most fantastical. Comic books were something different: I could abide those. Once when I was ten, while helping an uncle clear out a spare room, I found some boxes filled with his old 2000AD comics. He let me keep them, and those retro future-shock dystopias became a source of paradoxical comfort, with Judge Dredd a sort of fascistic daddy-figure. This led, a little later on, to an interest in Japanese manga so intense it made me resent my parents for bringing me into the world in Dublin instead of Tokyo, where I was certain things would have gone better for me.

As for real *novels, I read fanatically and without phobia the cheap novelisations that expanded the universe of the* Alien *films. In those trashy paperbacks' vision of a cosmos ruled by chaos, horror and malevolence, I discerned something profound about life as I experienced it as a child in suburban, working-class Dublin. When I later encountered philosophers of the Void such as Schopenhauer, Cioran, Nāgārjuna and Chandrakirti, I found in them a more sophisticated exploration of the abysses that had transfixed me in* Aliens: Nightmare Asylum *or* Aliens: The Female War.

The first stories I ever wrote were baldly derivative of those Alien *novels, and of other Hobbesian 1980s action-movie franchises like* Predator *and* Terminator *– fan fiction, though that wasn't a term I'd ever heard. I filled multiple copybooks with gory spinoff stories about aliens colonising far-off planets, with terrified humans in catacombs being picked off one by one. Men, women and children would commit mass suicide rather than live in an unendurable hell. My favourite of these early stories was set on a planet where a deranged sect worships the xenomorph as a god of cruelty and suffering. They ritualistically sacrifice themselves to the monster on huge stone altars, believing that by being impregnated and destroyed by the alien they will be reborn in a pure land beyond fear and pain, reunited with the ancestors. I took great pleasure in depicting the sheer hopelessness that contorts their features in their final agonised moments as they realise that there is no pure land, no awaiting ancestors, no salvation.*

Initially I wrote these bullet-strewn stories in the third person. But one day, without premeditation I started writing a Predator *story in the first person. The bare fact that I could do this came as a revelation. It just hadn't occurred to me before that I could enter the sensorium of an extraterrestrial psychopath, describing each kill as if I was the one carrying it out. In school the next day I read the story to my friend Joseph Mooney; he called it an important work. After that I rarely wrote in the third person. Gradually the alien fanfic set in remote star systems gave way to more local but no less bloody scenarios. There were stories about serial killers at loose on ocean liners; tower blocks filled with paranoid schizophrenics in a government experiment; wars between biker gangs who vie for control of derelict fairgrounds. One night, after doing my homework, I began writing a story about a character who had no name. I wrote in a trance and only when I was several pages in did I realise it was* me *– and he was heading through the school gates, his red eyes crazed with lust. I had him sodomise a dozen classmates over their school desks. After he's fucked them all, he gets head from our real-life French teacher, Ms Rousse. Midway through the act, he stands up and Ms Rousse's head detaches, impaled on his erection. He struts through the school's corridors with his French teacher's severed head affixed to his phallus, as hundreds of boys take up a mysterious chant.*

I didn't show that story to anyone, not even Joseph Mooney, but I read it scores of times. I felt that with this story I'd broken through to a dimension of absolute freedom wherein there was no law – where I *was the law. I've always believed that my true life as a writer – and perhaps my damnation – began with that story.*

Excerpt from *Night Taxi*

The rain was coming down hard. Henry K. Dillon had started his shift at eight – already the streets were rivers. Now the windscreen wipers beat a rhythm as he waited for a green light by the IFSC. Two young black guys, both very tall, were laughing with a pretty white girl who stood between them sheltering from the rain, enjoying their attention. Henry wondered what the set-up was, who was fucking who. He clocked his reflection in the rear-view: creased, neutral, weary. Forty-seven years old. Driving his taxi six nights a week, he'd begun to feel that the city was becoming foreign, replaced before his eyes, everything familiar leeched away. But then he'd catch himself in the loop of such thoughts and realise that no, *he* was the one becoming foreign, strange, old. Dublin was what it had always been – mutating, churning – and now it was beginning to excrete him.

The lights turned green and he crossed the Liffey to the north side, leaving the young people to their laughter.

At the top of the hour he turned on the radio and took in the news bulletin. A wave of drones had attacked Paris, most of them shot down. The war was getting closer but he wasn't worried, not yet. There was a story about a refugee camp in the inner city that had been torched overnight, one woman and her baby severely burned. And: martial law in Sweden; fires engulfing Portugal; the president of Finland claiming she'd been contacted by an alien civilisation; a sect calling for accelerated climate change; cartel leaders in Mexico worshipping a new AI (twelve men were sacrificed in a deranged ceremony). There was a story about a hyped new cinema release, the tale of a superhero with the power to birth universes from her womb, promising sequels set inside each nested reality.

Henry turned the radio off, listened to the rain.

A fare brought him out of the city centre, into the fraying southern suburbs. On the way back in he picked up another fare. A tall, gaunt man probably in his late thirties, wearing a faded green military jacket and lugging a suitcase, got in the back. The smell of stale alcohol and musty clothes filled the car.

'Where are we headed?' asked Henry.

'Connolly Station.'

The passenger was silent as the taxi pulled out. He looked through the window at the teeming night, maybe at his own reflection.

As they passed the Coombe and turned north at St Patrick's Cathedral, Henry asked him if he was going on a journey. The passenger replied that he was taking the late train out of Dublin; he was moving away to live alone on the southeastern coast.

'You might get a bit isolated down there,' said Henry. 'There isn't much doing in that part of the country. Do you work from home?'

'I suppose I do.'

The taxi veered round at Christchurch and headed up Dame Street, passing pubs that belched out aggressive cheer.

'I'll have enough work to keep me busy,' the passenger said, watching a trio of drunk men singing arm over shoulder. 'I'll be living next to a beach where no one ever goes. It's at the end of the train line, next to the port. You're right, there's nothing there, just some houses, a derelict hotel, a bunch of refugees in a disused school. There's something… clarifying about living at the end of the line.'

They stopped at a red light in front of Trinity College. Two drunk girls staggered past as they crossed the road. One of them slammed a palm against the window, made a grotesque face.

'I'll have plenty of time to read', said the passenger. 'That's crucial. Reading in peace and quiet, by the sea.'

As they waited at the lights, Henry found himself telling his passenger that he was a writer, or rather he used to be: he'd written a novel in his twenties. 'It was a hit at the time, though not many people talk about it now.'

'What's it called?' the passenger asked.

Henry said the title.

'I'll look out for it.'

'It might be hard to find. That was a different life. I don't write any more. I've been driving this taxi for nine years.'

The light turned green and they moved off. The man in the back started talking about the book he was reading, which he'd found on a bench by the canal. He told Henry that the book had started getting into his dreams.

Henry glanced in the rear-view. 'Oh yeah?'

'It's… the most sinister book I've ever read,' the passenger said.

'What's it about?'

'Well, that's just it. That's what's disturbing about it. It's about … me.'

Henry said nothing. So, another crackpot – barely a night went by without one.

The passenger went on: 'I was thirty pages in before I accepted what was happening. Now I'm more than halfway through. All my fucking secrets are in there. All my shame. It's as if the book was written just to punish me.'

'What's happening now?'

'I'm dying slowly.'

'You need to read on.'

'That's why I'm moving to the coast. I have to be alone for this. I need to see how it ends.'

'What's the book called?'

'*A Cold, Dark Place.*'

They crossed O'Connell Bridge, passed the GPO. As they approached Connolly Station the streets were weirdly deserted. The passenger's eyes locked onto Henry's in the rear-view. There was an intensity about him now.

'Stop here for a moment,' he said. 'You can leave the meter running.'

Henry pulled over in a dark street with a railway track passing overhead. As he did, he suddenly understood that the man in his taxi was insane, dangerous and possibly armed. He had the impression, between panic and exaltation, of having lived out this precise scene, down to its minutest details, many times before.

Staring at Henry with terrible eyes, the passenger reached for his inside pocket. He said, 'Since you're no longer writing it all down, here's a fucking story for you.'

2. Expansion

Ren Duka in the Third Reich (December 2024)

The initial sequence of Ren Duka novels had cleaved to a realist template. The stories were plausible – and, in many aspects, true. And then, four novels into what readers had begun semi-ironically to call the 'Ren Duka saga', the series took an abrupt swerve into the fantastical. 'I figured that as long as I kept him – Duka – in the centre, as the narratorial anchor, then I could take the stories wherever I wanted,' the author told Lucia Vallejo in an interview for *Bookblitz*. 'His voice would keep things grounded, and this allowed me to indulge all sorts of wild plots and outlandish scenarios. I realised it didn't have to be realistic. I felt I was returning to my earliest inspirations – the cosmic horrors and lurid mangas I'd consumed as a fucked-up teenager.'

An entertaining if silly time-travel caper that was written in under two weeks, *Ren Duka in the Third Reich* sees Duka abruptly transported into the Battle of Berlin when the bumper-car he is riding at a fairground on Potsdamer Platz is struck by lightning. Adapting quickly to his new circumstances, he picks up a dead Russian soldier's PPSh-41 submachine gun and opens fire on the Soviet attackers, killing four young men. Amid the gruelling combat sequences that ensue, Duka seems to believe that if he can just survive for long enough, the German forces will repel the Russians and he can start figuring out how to get back to the twenty-first century.

After much extravagant violence – and a lyrical homoerotic interlude – Duka finds himself holed up in the Führerbunker. With the Reich in flames around him, he drinks up a storm with the remnants of the Nazi high command, downs shots of cognac with a frisky Frau Goebbels, dances the jitterbug with Eva Braun, glimpses a shaky Adolf Hitler shuffling between inner sanctum and lavatory, and sings along as a sozzled lieutenant general bellows sentimental Bavarian ballads.

Just as the Russian shelling reaches a deafening crescendo, Duka is wrenched back to the present day as abruptly as he was exiled from it. Instead of a bumper-car, he finds himself sitting in a Turkish barber's chair in Neukölln, having his beard trimmed. As the clippers move over Ren's face, the barber intones a moving, surrealistic monologue that covers many topics, including smiling girls in the first flush of youth, the mountains of central Turkey, the preference of having daughters over sons, the belief that any religion is better than none, and the transience of all earthly things.

Ren Duka in the Caliphate – US Title: *Duka's Jihad* (April 2025)

While some regretted the author's move away from familiar, relatable situations – what the critic Kristofer Larsen has called his early 'bookies and boozers' period – his turn to more far-fetched stories attracted readers who otherwise avoided 'literary fiction' in favour of less staid genres. To Larsen, it was as if the author was 'ticking off a generic bucket list the way a certain type of traveller might whizz around Asia or Europe determined to "do" as many countries as possible'. Set in the heart of the Islamic State during its period of rapid territorial expansion, *Ren Duka in the Caliphate* elbowed in on an unexpected genre: the geopolitical thriller.

Unlike previous Ren Duka novels, *Ren Duka in the Caliphate* is recounted in retrospect, its action taking place ten years before the period of its composition. On a promotional junket to Beirut in the spring of 2014, Ren Duka accepts an invitation to join a group of foreign correspondents on an overland expedition into Iraq via Syria. Among the group is the beautiful Inga Vaitkienė, who is writing a book about the fate of Kurdish Iraqi women since the downfall of Saddam Hussein's Baath party. No sooner have the group arrived in the city of Tikrit than the army that would soon become known to the world as ISIS, Daesh or Islamic State commences its uprising. Within days, black-clad fighters have swarmed across Iraq, sowing horror in their wake. When Tikrit falls to the fundamentalists, the foreign reporters are taken hostage. Inga Vaitkienė and the others are struck dumb with fear, but a quick-thinking Ren Duka immediately pledges his devotion to radical Islam. Amused by their prisoner's abject lack of integrity, his captors press him on his beliefs. Duka articulates some basic concepts from the Koran; then he denounces the West as an empire of drunkenness and harlotry, spits on the name Barack Obama, and offers to become the Islamic State's mouthpiece. Shoved in front of a laptop by his skeptical captors, he is able to point to quotations from press interviews in which he has expressed bitterness towards Western civilisation. The fighters confer and quickly conclude that Ren Duka believes in nothing. Deciding that this spineless infidel can be useful to them, his captors force him to wear an orange jumpsuit, then film him reading a menacing speech. The next day, the video beams around the globe. Audiences in their millions watch Ren Duka sitting in the half-lotus posture on a dusty stone floor. Flanking him on either side is an ISIS fighter in a balaclava brandishing an AK-47. On the wall behind them is the black flag of the Caliphate. One of the fighters waves a Koran at the camera as Duka warns his fellow Westerners that they will burn in hellfire for their iniquity, godlessness and imperialism.

Realising that they have seized a valuable asset in their propaganda war, the militants film more videos of Ren Duka denouncing the West. Each time they drag him from his cell and force him to his knees in some dusty room or godforsaken dune, he is sure his end is imminent. As he resigns himself to awaiting the blade pressed against his neck, one of the captors, a man with a deep, husky voice who speaks better English than the others, crouches beside him and talks in Ren's ear. He goes over the topics he wishes Ren to address and instructs him on how to speak for the camera ('With valour and much precision'). He tells Ren to orate each speech as if it is his last – 'Or else it will be.' Before one recording, the fighter places a hand on Ren's shoulder, squeezing it gently before withdrawing to oversee the shoot. The touch of the man's hand is all the human warmth Ren has felt in weeks; he is flooded with gratitude.

The videos, which are uploaded on jihadist social media channels and then broadcast on global news media, last between five and twenty-five minutes. In the first recordings, Ren sticks to the script. However, as new videos appear at intervals of three or four days, he seems to become more comfortable in the role. Rather than simply read his speeches, he begins to extemporise about the immorality of life under Western liberal democracy. Initially, it's clear that he is trying to ingratiate himself with his captors. In the later videos, though, he is less obviously insincere. Like an actor who vanishes into his role, Ren is eerily convincing as he issues harsh tirades against the civilisation that created him, insisting that it will fall before the wrath of the righteous. Among the targets of his rambling speeches are neoliberalism, the United States of America, the Irish political establishment (which is 'venal' and 'nihilistic'), drugs, NATO, feminism, cultural Marxism, social media companies, the World Bank, Benjamin Netanyahu, promiscuity, the decadence of Europe's creative elites, homosexual propaganda, and Kim Kardashian. Stunning audiences back in the West, he even attacks his literary rivals, including writers barely known beyond Dublin publishing circles. In a twenty-second passage that would be immortalised as a meme, he savages the writer Kevin Mulvaney's cult novel *Sex Tape*, which he'd read on the journey across Syria. The masked fighters seem content to let him rant about these extraneous matters. Gradually, we realise that their English is not strong enough to fully comprehend his monologues. At times the fighters appear uneasy, but whenever their captive utters certain phrases – Zionism, Great Satan, Barack Obama – they nod in approval.

After seven videos are recorded, the ISIS fighter with decent English visits Ren Duka in his cell. Speaking in a soft, fatherly tone, he tells Duka that he has done well – his words have blazed with the spirit of the Prophet, and paradise surely awaits him. The following day, Duka is taken from his cell. A hood is pulled over his head and he is driven to a cluster of dunes on the edge of the desert. This time he is certain he is being led to his execution. But when he is pulled from the back of the jeep and the hood is removed, he sees a gaunt and bedraggled woman standing alone at the centre of a ring of masked men. She is weeping and seems to be praying under her breath. One of Ren's captor's turns to him and says, 'She is adulterer. This her punishment. Allahu Akbar.' When the masked men begin hurling stones at the woman, Ren turns away. The fighter behind him grips him by the back of the head and forces him to watch. Afterwards, the woman's body lies broken on the blood-soaked earth. For some minutes the fighters stand gazing in silence. Then they turn away and board their vehicles.

When Ren is back in his cell, the fatherly fighter steps

in and closes the door behind him. In silence he watches his captive. Finally, he speaks. 'The woman you come here with ...' He holds up a photograph of Inga Vaitkienė. 'She is spy. Zionist whore. You are going to do her like you witness today.' Ren shakes his head. 'Yes, you must,' says the fighter. 'If not, we are doing terrible things to her. And *then* you are doing as we say. Better you are doing first. You have no choice. She is Zionist cunt.' The fighter smiles faintly – the first time Ren has seen him smile. 'You are become legend in your country. True famous. The writer who kills woman for the Daesh. Sell many books.' When the fighter leaves the cell, Ren falls to the ground, curling up like a foetus. Hours elapse before he sinks into sleep.

He is woken by chaos and noise. An explosion shakes the walls, spewing rubble and dust. Ren cowers in the corner of the cell as the air fills with rattling gunfire, the boom of stun-grenades, roaring voices. He hears a cry of 'Allahu Akbar!' followed by a deafening blast. Then everything goes dark.

The US special forces raid leaves all thirteen ISIS fighters dead. In the carnage, Inga Vaitkienė and one of her colleagues are also killed. Ren Duka is flown to a military base in Turkey along with the other rescued prisoners. There, he is interrogated by US officers. They suspect that he has been brainwashed. To reassure the Americans, Duka denounces Islam as emphatically as, in the videos, he had condemned the West. Eventually they believe him. After a period of recovery, he returns to Ireland. For two weeks he shuns the press, who station themselves outside his parents' home in the south Dublin suburbs to where he has retreated. Then he goes on national television to talk about his ordeal as a prisoner of the Islamic State. He tells the host of *The Late Late Show* that while making the videos he simply acted on instinct, relying on his storytelling gifts to prolong his stay of execution. In response to a delicately worded query, he confirms that he meant none of what he said about hating the West and wishing to see it burn. He has no problem whatsoever with Jews or Nigerians. He apologises to his peers in the writing world who he may have offended (by that point in his ordeal, he says, he had resorted to ranting about whatever came into his head). He makes a special apology to Kevin Mulvaney, whom he congratulates for *Sex Tape*, which has become a runaway success off the back of Duka's bizarre denunciations. 'The only thing I *did* mean in those videos was what I said about hating avocados and Liverpool Football Club,' he jokes, to scattered laughter.

Ren Duka Gets Remaindered – US title: *Duka is Yesterday's Man* (September 2025)

The backlash to *Ren Duka in the Caliphate* was severe. 'I'd had hostile reviews before,' the author told an interviewer for the *Shanghai Daily* three years later. 'But that was my first time at the bottom of a pile-on. Anyone who could hold a pen took a stab at me. The charge, basically, was that I had no right to go in there. That it was *not my story to tell.* The book was seen as an insult to the real victims of ISIS. Some even said it was offensive to ISIS themselves. Or maybe just to Muslims. What really set the whole thing ablaze was when the wife of an American journalist who'd been beheaded wrote an Instagram post attacking me. The reviews were brutal, but the critics were nothing compared to the internet. I began to feel like Jonathan Franzen, in how social media has always used him as a punching bag. But then *Franzen* came out against me! He said I'd trespassed, that I lacked decorum. No one would be seen anywhere near me. It's a lonely place, when the whole world despises you like that.'

Wounded by the novel's reception, the author took a month off, then dutifully returned to his desk. At first, he tried to silence the mocking voices in his head by continuing in the generically roaming vein he had opened with *Ren Duka in the Third Reich.* Intending to follow up the disaster of *Caliphate* with a novel of pure escapism, he set to work on a sun-kissed melodrama of romantic yearning (working title: 'Ren Duka on the Balearics'). Forty pages in, his motivation ran dry. For a week he acted as if nothing had happened and continued writing new scenes. But the spark was gone – at the end of each day he couldn't be bothered reading over what he'd produced. Having been in the game long enough to read the signs, he put the Balearics novel aside and began writing a BDSM erotic thriller (working title: 'Desire is an Arms Race'). He had his hero whipped, burned with candle wax, and stretched on a rack by a Slavic dominatrix, in search of the ultimate sexual high. After a few days of flow, his will to move the story forward evaporated. A day and night of gloom ensued – he feared that the Muse had deserted him. Then a dream told him he was going down the wrong path. The following morning, he banished the BDSM novel to the cast-offs folder and began writing what would be the most full-throatedly *meta* of the Ren Duka novels to date.

Telling a refracted version of the author's career so far, *Ren Duka Gets Remaindered* veers into fiction at certain key junctures. In the novel, Ren Duka's books enjoy unbroken commercial success until *Days of Jihad* which, despite being well reviewed, fails to find much of an audience. Thereafter he endures a series of flops. Writing through a depression while feeling spat out by the world, he condenses his experiences of declining sales and plummeting status into a brutally self-interrogating novel titled *Yesterday's Man*.

He is convinced that *Yesterday's Man* will put him back on the bestseller list, but on release it receives a smattering of lukewarm reviews and then sinks without a trace. A few months later, while browsing one afternoon in a Dublin bookshop, he comes across a stack of copies selling for €2.99. Impulsively he buys every one. Throughout this period, suffering from insomnia and anxiety, he takes long walks around the city in the small hours, contemplating literary failure and peer-gloating. Each moment of *schadenfreude* he ever enjoyed at the humiliation of a rival comes back at him tenfold. They are all inside his skull, all jeering at him. He convinces himself that some snotty kid working at the bookshop has posted CCTV footage of him buying up all his own books, and now it's gone viral and he is a laughingstock.

In a consummate irony that seemed to fulfil the novel's metafictional gambit, *Ren Duka Gets Remaindered* was itself soon remaindered. While painful, the experience galvanised the author's thinking about the direction he should henceforth take. It was clear: the reading public had even less time for his meta-textual ironies than they did for his nature reveries. They wanted sincerity, social realism, unpretentious storytelling – in short, the easy pleasures of the early Ren Duka novels... but with some new element to keep the formula fresh. To win back his audience, he would have to aim straight for the heart of relevancy. In the midst of renascent worldwide authoritarianism, he would abandon art for art's sake and imaginatively step into an unaccustomed role: the writer as activist.

Dina Tatangelo

I read those books while I was in rehab. Actually, I'd read some of them years earlier, when I was in film school – before I dropped out, I mean – but I really got into them in rehab. They were formative for me in the sense that they made visible certain possibilities, opened certain doors. I didn't like all of them. Some of them just fucking annoyed me. But some of them were cool. *Seventeen Suicides*, I liked that one. *Ren Duka's Violation* was probably my favourite. *Duka's Jihad, Ren Duka in the Third Reich* – they were kind of dumb, but they were fun too. *Ren Duka Does Time* was a good one, it had a warmth to it. But for me it was more about the template, the format. Rehab is a wonderful place to read, to watch films. You're delicate, wide open, sensitised. Art goes deep. I'm not anti-drugs, by the way. Not by a light year. I used to tell people that quitting drugs was the second-best thing I ever did – the best thing I ever did was to start taking them. Not that I've ever quit drugs for more than what, a few months. Drugs have been crucial in my creative life, my intellectual life. I liked them all, but heroin was my number one, the great love affair. Crack too. I saw those two drugs as a mark of seriousness. Most so-called drug users know nothing about the revolutionary nature of drug use. They don't *want* to know. They have no ethos. Gentrified narco-tourists and bourgeois hedonists. That kind of attitude is just not interesting to me. When

I decided to write serialised autobiographical novels of my own, I gave my alter ego, Zoe Zabarino, an appetite for hard drugs that put mine in the shade. She loves heroin the way Teresa of Ávila loves Jesus. Crack too, and coke and pills and everything else, but especially heroin. She's a fucking pig. That was my inspiration: to create a female pig, a depraved, amoral animal of pure appetite. Zoe Zabarino. She's a slut, a junkie, a criminal psychopath, a manipulator, and she's not above playing the victim when it gives her the advantage. But she's also a devout Catholic, she says her rosary at night and wears a silver crucifix around her neck that she kisses before she shoots up. She was a lot of fun to write. The novels were kind of an underground thing. I'm not what you'd call a household name, but the Zoe Zabarino books found their readership among the New York art crowd, the weird-music types, the bored transgressives. The whole series was published by Heavy Metal Bastard, a press in New York that had been set up by Nick Kassovitz, the guitarist for the Bullets of Transience. Each one sold probably a few hundred copies, a couple thousand at most. They get called cult novels and that's fine with me. My background, so there's no confusion, is solidly middle-class. I grew up on the Lower East Side. I played piano at an advanced level by age seven. My father was a violinist with the New York Philharmonic and my mother lectures in art history at NYU. As parents they were very permissive and liberal, but I rebelled anyway. I was wilder than they knew how to deal with. When I wrote the Zoe Zabarino books I found a way to express everything I hated about society, and my ideal of liberation through violence and excess. The first three or four novels wrote themselves. I didn't worry about

style or anything like that. Plot structure, character development – all of it was bourgeois. The Ren Duka novels lit the
spark, but the aesthetic I was creating owed more to the films
of Abel Ferrara or Pasolini, to no-wave bands and porn. I
wanted to create a shallow, violent world where I could explore
the deepest questions of spiritual truth, sin and damnation,
lust and depravity. Above all, I wanted to entertain. Art that
thinks it's above entertaining people can take a walk. If you're
boring us, you're in the wrong line of work. But it wasn't just
punk-aesthetics and sleaze. I was reading René Daumal,
Lautréamont, Violette Leduc, the Marquis de Sade. French
writers were always the ones who took it too far. George
Bataille, Octave Mirbeau. Intemperate, splenetic writers.
Vulnerable writers. I liked Baudelaire a lot. Rimbaud too, and
Verlaine, but above all Baudelaire. Most of my influences were
men – and yet my stuff routinely got described as misandrist,
which I suppose it was. I read French, by the way, I speak it
fluently. My mother was half French and she spoke it at home,
when she wasn't throwing plates at my father and calling him
a no-good Italian philanderer. Actually, she *did* speak French
when they were fighting, at least that's how I remember it
now. And he'd insult her in Italian – *vaffanculo* this and *cazzo*
that. He hit her sometimes – only once in front of me, but
hard enough to fracture her cheekbone. They were intellec-
tuals but he was the kind of intellectual who beat his wife. I
was maybe ten, eleven. I told myself that if a man ever hit me
like that, I wouldn't just cry and take it like my mother, I'd
cut his dick off and flush it down the toilet. But of course,
later on I did find men who hit me, and I never cut their dicks
off, though sometimes I hit back and once I broke a wineglass

over my boyfriend's face. I had to go with him to A&E to get it stitched up. In the hospital he kept crying and telling me he was sorry and he loved me and he was a piece of shit and he'd never hit me again. I cried too and told him I'd never meant to hurt him. We were a mess, all strung out. And of course he did hit me again, and eventually I left him. Anyway, films were always on a par with literature for me, at least as important to how my imagination worked. I probably shouldn't have dropped out of film school. I made a few short films there that I'm proud of. I still fantasise about making films. That was probably my real calling. I'm not talking down my novels, I'm just saying I probably would have made better films. But it wasn't to be. I'm difficult to work with. I'm less than reliable. I get impatient with people, and when you're making films you have to be patient. The Zoe Zabarino novels were essentially movies I saw in my head that I didn't have the skill or the resources to make. The first one, *Zoe Zabarino's Dream*, didn't take much longer to write than it takes to read. I wrote it when I was twenty-four, after my first stay in rehab, which got me clean for all of about five minutes. The plot was as follows: Zoe Zabarino, twenty-two-year-old model, artist, and unapologetic lover of heroin, is living with two men, Luke and Johnny, in an apartment on 10th Street. The three get stoned together and listen to records on a vinyl player that Luke boosted from a pawn shop in Harlem. Both Johnny and Luke are fucking Zoe, and sometimes they fuck her together. A girl called Britt, who Johnny is stringing along, occasionally comes over and joins in. Whenever they run out of money for heroin and crack, Zoe goes out and tricks. Sometimes Luke goes out and tricks, or else Johnny boosts a liquor store or mugs some suit in an alleyway. One day when Zoe goes out to trick, an older man takes her in his car to his apartment on the Upper East Side. It's so nice there that Zoe doesn't want to leave. So instead of going back to Luke and Johnny, she lives with this guy instead. He's in his late forties, maybe his fifties. When he goes out to work in the mornings she stays in his apartment reading Baudelaire and looking out the window at the Manhattan canyons. Sometimes when he comes home in the evening he'll have another girl with him, maybe a hooker, or just some girl he's picked up. Then the three of them will drink ice-cold vodka from the freezer, smoke crack, smoke heroin. One night the guy falls asleep and Zoe stays up with the pretty blonde he's brought home on this particular evening. Her name is Anastasia, she's Russian, twenty-four, a real beauty. Zoe is captivated by her and after they drink more vodka, Zoe eats Anastasia's pussy and makes her come six times. Then they decide that they don't need the older guy. Zoe goes into the bedroom and finds the Glock he keeps in the bedside locker. The two women watch him sleeping. Then Zoe puts the gun in his mouth and pulls the trigger. The first bullet doesn't kill him. She's never shot anyone before and she's fucked it up. He's making horrible sounds and gurgling blackish blood over his chin. Anastasia laughs hysterically. Zoe pulls the trigger again and this time his body jolts, spasms briefly, and then is still. I could have ended the novel there but I wanted to take it further and so I finished with a wild sex scene. The two women are excited because they've never killed anyone before, and they're very high. They kiss again and then Zoe hitches up her skirt and sits on the dead man's face in reverse, easing her pussy down onto the bloody hole where his mouth used to be. Rubbing her ass on his face, she leans over and unbuttons his trousers, opens his belt, pulls out his dick. It's hard like ivory and longer than ever – nine thick inches. Anastasia climbs up and straddles him, sliding his long dick inside her, facing Zoe. She grinds and rides him while Zoe bounces on his face, slipping her little ass over the blood. The two girls lean in and kiss. They both come at the same time, and as they do Zoe reaches down and unloads the pistol into the dead man's torso. It was the hottest scene I'd ever written and I was determined to film it, so I did, in my friend Steve's apartment in Hell's Kitchen. Steve was our camera-man. I played Zoe. My friend Christine – the hottest girl I knew – played Anastasia. Our friend Tommy played the dead guy. He was twenty-five years too young but it didn't matter. Tommy loved the idea of being filmed with two cute girls with their tits out sitting on his face and dick. We made him up to look like his jaw was all shot off. I didn't want to simu-late the sex, so I'd brought a viagra for Tommy so he could stay hard as long as it took to shoot, but when I tried to give it to him he laughed and threw it out the window, saying if he couldn't get hard with two hot girls sitting on his face and dick, then he may as well blow his brains out for real because it was all over for him. Tommy was sweet – tough but sweet. He's still handsome, charismatic, but these days he only has one leg – he lost the other in a motorbike accident three years ago. We shot the film in black-and-white. For the score I recorded a piano piece I'd written, 'East River Memory No. 3'. The film is still online. Steve told me it's on the porn sites now, which is funny because it's an art film about a dead body. It's strange to imagine people jerking off to it, but I guess people will jerk off to anything. I wouldn't want to watch it now though. It would make me sad, not just because Christine isn't here any more, but because we were all so hot then, and we had a kind of innocence to us. Christine was beautiful. So was I. Everything was upright, there was no slackness. And Tommy still had both his legs. I mean, I still look good naked, but I'll never look *that* good again. But what I was saying is, those first three or four Zoe Zabarino books were basically art-trash. Sex and violence, drugs and death, guns and heroin. I wanted to write books the way Abel Ferrara made movies: fast, cheap, brash. Exploitation movies where I was the one being exploited. I met Abel Ferrara once, by the way. He showed up at a party at a loft in SoHo. I was in awe of him but I was high on junk so I played it cool. I told him his films inspired me and he said he'd heard good things about my books and he'd check them out. But I don't know if he ever did. I don't know if he was much of a reader. During that party he picked up an acoustic guitar and started singing songs he'd written that sounded like Richard Hell or Lou Reed, songs about downtown pimps and uptown junkies, corrupt traders who see the face of Jesus on the stock ticker. I set the Zoe Zabarino novels in Abel's vanished New York rather than the one I knew, the post-Giuliano New York that's so safe and corporate and dead. Another idea I lifted from the Ren Duka novels was this whole deal of nested personae, this Russian-doll business. I thought it was cool that Ren Duka was the author's persona, but then Duka also invented his own character, who was this hard-boiled taxi-driver guy, and Duka keeps writing stories about him, so you've got these novels within novels, all the way down. Anyway, I decided that Zoe

Zabarino would have her alter-ego too. I had her dream up screenplays during her junk nods. In Zoe's screenplays (which she never even writes down, let alone makes movies from), the protagonist is a butch, middle-aged cop named Brody Flynn, a cynical lesbian who's seen it all and takes no shit from anyone. She's a casual racist and a not-so-casual anti-semite, and she's corrupt as hell too, but behind it all she's guided by a higher morality, a mystical sense of good and evil. I introduced Brody Flynn in the third Zoe novel, *Zoe Zabarino Shoots Up*. By then the notion of Zoe's religiousness, her Catholicism, was becoming interesting to me. While writing the first novel I'd decided on a whim that Zoe was a fervent Catholic, even though if you'd asked me at the time, I'd have said there wasn't a religious bone in my body. My parents weren't religious at all – there was no God talk when I was growing up. But the funny thing is, a decade later, I myself converted to Catholicism. In a big way. But like I say, those early books were just cheap entertainment. I had fun with them. Take *Zoe Zabarino's Sex Odyssey*, the second novel. That one was inspired by real life. When I was sixteen, with my friend Judy Schaubroeck – whose dad was a corrupt cop – I wrote a list of all the sexual stuff we needed to try before we could consider ourselves ladies of the world. The list got copied and passed around our high school, which made me and Judy instant celebrities, notorious sluts. We didn't give a fuck. We *were* sluts, or rather we had every intention of becoming sluts – that's what the list was about. Even now I've only done like a third of what we put on there (Judy has probably done all of it). But people are so literal-minded, especially in high-school. They believed or wanted to believe that there was no humour or hyperbole in that list. Anyway, whatever – the fact is, a few years later I used the list to write *Zoe Zabarino's Sex Odyssey*. The novel begins with Zoe and Anastasia wondering what they should do with their youth and beauty now that the old guy is dead. It's basically them rapping out as dialogue the list that Judy Schaubroeck and I wrote in high school. It starts with obvious stuff. Fuck an older guy. Fuck a *much* older guy. Fuck a black guy. That kind of thing. Fuck two guys at once. Fuck a girl. Fuck a guy and a girl at once. Fuck the best-looking boy at school. Fuck the ugliest boy at school. But then the list started getting freakier, more imaginative. Fuck a guy who's killed somebody. Fuck a drug addict. Fuck each other (Judy and I waited till we were nineteen to do this, at a party on Delancey). Fuck a guy whose political ideas you find disgusting. Fuck a teacher (Judy did this before me – she fucked our high-school maths teacher – but within a month of starting film school, I fucked my professor). Fuck a guy who looks like your father. Fuck a gay guy. Fuck a married man (Judy would do a *lot* of this, it was kind of her trademark). Fuck a really basic guy who's only into sports and beer. Fuck a guy in a band. Fuck all the guys in a band. Fuck a rapper (Judy in fact dated a well-known rapper for six months when she was twenty). Fuck an influencer with at least two million followers. Fuck a guy who's too drunk to stand up. Fuck an Irish guy, a Frenchman, an Italian, a Swede. Make a sex film. Fuck a priest, a Muslim, a Hindu, a Jew, a Jain, a Sikh, a Satanist. Fuck for revenge. Fuck for pity. Fuck a cop. Fuck someone in a wheelchair. Fuck an animal (we crossed this off the list because it was gross and illegal, but for the rest of high school, boys would make horny-animal noises and call Judy the dog-fucker). Do a gangbang. Fuck someone who's related to the Kennedys. Fuck a virgin. Fuck someone who's transitioning. In *Zoe Zabarino's Sex Odyssey*, Zoe and Anastasia do all of these things and more, a little mechanically perhaps – there wasn't much in the way of plot tension. I kept writing the Zoe books, acted in some films, did a little modelling work. When I turned twenty-seven my life started to get heavy. In some ways I was doing okay, people knew who I was, I was respected – in New York, anyway. I had a daily habit, but I wrote every day too. I'd written and published four Zoe Zabarino novels: *Zoe Zabarino's Dream*; *Zoe Zabarino's Sex Odyssey*; *Zoe Zabarino Shoots Up*; and *Zoe Zabarino and the Seedy Underbelly*. That last named is probably my favourite of all the Zoe novels. It's about how Zoe goes out to score one night and is led on an odyssey into the strangest depths of New York City. It ends with her acting as emergency midwife to a Guatemalan immigrant who's gone into labour in the back of a cab. I was living at this time with a man I'd fallen in love with when I was twenty-five. He was much older than me, thirty-two years older to be precise. I'm not going to say his name, but he's a man I had and still have a huge amount of respect for, a man I learned a lot from. After we were together less than a year, he started to become very controlling, very possessive. Maybe he was like that from the beginning, but you don't see it in that first flush when everything is magical. I've never been particularly jealous so when someone gets that way with me I struggle to understand it, I don't know what to do. He accused me of bringing men home when he was out of town, of fucking guys for money or junk. None of it was true – when

I'm with someone I'm with them, I don't find monogamy a burden like other people do, I guess I'm old-fashioned that way. But there was no conveying to him that I loved him and I wasn't out to screw him over. I think he was going through some sort of crisis. His latest film, which he was convinced was his masterpiece, had tanked. The only people who went to see it were New York art-world types who'd heard he'd made a turkey and wanted to laugh about it. There was one review in particular, in the *New York Magazine*, that he took really badly. I didn't understand it. He'd had plenty of bad reviews before, and this one didn't seem especially terrible to me. Things became intolerable. He was always either going on about this one review – how he was going to ruin the critic's life, humiliate him in public by exposing scurrilous rumours he'd dug up, or pay some gangsters to crush his testicles in a vice – or else he was accusing me of fucking other men. When I was high on junk it didn't get to me, but one day he came home after a meeting with a producer in SoHo, and he asked me to leave. He was cold about it, no anger or recrimination, he just told me he couldn't bear to live with me any more, he was sorry, but that's the way it was. So three weeks after my twenty-seventh birthday I moved to Paris, and that's where I lived for the next two years. My friend Clarice, a model from Chicago, was already living there with her boyfriend. When I first arrived in Paris I stayed with them, then I moved into my own place in Pigalle. I kept writing and I kept scoring junk. I wrote the next two Zoe novels: *Zoe Zabarino Turns Tricks*, and *Europe, Meet Zoe Zabarino*. Neither of them sold well, even by my modest standards. The Europe book in particular was not well received.

They felt I was tired, that the fire and flair of the first Zoe books had burned out and I was at risk of self-parody. I knew they were right. I was down on myself. During my relationship with the filmmaker, I'd built up an image of who I was, and now that image had been stripped away. In Paris I did some modelling work, helped by Clarice and some contacts from New York. On a shoot at La Défense I met Bruce – another older man, a photographer. He was born in the US, his parents were American, but he grew up in France and so it was like he had two worlds inside him, two cultures. With Bruce, the colour came back into my life. He didn't like that I had a heroin habit, but he said I was his muse and he took pictures of me all over Paris, which really is the prettiest city there is, I mean it's not even close. I was reading Baudelaire again, and Sade, Genet, Leduc, Daumal, Despentes, all those French writers I'd been so turned on by as a teenager. Bruce took me to orgies – high-society, invite-only affairs in beautiful apartments in the sixth or the first or the seventh arrondissements. Sometimes at these orgies I recognised actors, political figures, athletes, famous models. There was always cocaine, other drugs too. Bruce wasn't jealous like my ex, and it turned him on to watch me being fucked by other men. Sometimes we made films at his apartment in Belleville: me with him, or me with another woman while Bruce manoeuvred around us with his camera. He was a kind man and he was funny too, but I never loved him. Maybe it was too soon for me to fall in love. But I did get my zest for life back, and although I had a regular habit, heroin didn't control me the way it would later on. I wrote another Zoe book, *Zoe Zabarino's Daddy Issues*. When I sent it to Nick Kassovitz at Heavy Metal Bastard, he wrote me saying that in his opinion it was the best Zoe book to date. Maybe he was just being nice to me because the reviews for *Europe, Meet Zoe Zabarino* had been so bad and he wanted to keep my confidence up. But I appreciated it. And in fact I agreed with him – I'd gone deeper with this novel, there was more truth in it, more suffering. It's on a par with *Zoe Zabarino and the Seedy Underbelly*, in my opinion. All the Zoe books were more or less personal, and this one was a not very fictionalised account of my relationship with the much older film director. All the jealousy, the fear, the insults, the obsession. I didn't write it to hurt him and of course I changed the names. But I knew he'd read it and he'd find it difficult. I didn't send it to him to read before it was published in case he tried to make things hard for me. I never did learn how he felt about it. The day the book was published back in New York, Bruce took me for dinner to celebrate at a very old, very exclusive restaurant in the Marais. He was so happy and enthusiastic, like a little boy. That night he took pictures of me under streetlights, in front of boutique shops, on street corners and squares. They're probably my favourite photographs anyone's ever taken of me. I think I *was* in love with Bruce that night, but I didn't tell him and in the morning the feeling was gone, like a dream. I moved back to New York when my father got sick. I hadn't been close to him since my teen years, but the realisation that he probably didn't have a lot of time left shook me and I decided I needed to be near him. I'd broken up with Bruce. I let him down gently and we're still friends. He always invites me to his exhibitions even though I'm never in Paris. When I was thirty, my friend Christine died of an overdose. She'd been hanging out with this performance artist, Jude something, who screamed and shrieked in a noise band. The band played notorious shows in Brooklyn that always seemed to involve broken glass, attacks on the audience, fascist insignia, extreme sex acts. Everything about that guy was bad news, I could see it the first time I met him. Christine's death got to me in a deeper way than I initially realised. Life carried on, but I found that all the shit that used to excite me now just seemed sad and desperate. It was as if I'd lived my life in pursuit of an ideal, but as I approached it, the meaning of the ideal changed and everything I'd thought had been a victory turned into a defeat, a disgrace. For a whole year I wrote nothing. I visited my dad three or four times a week. He was living in the East Village (he and my mom had divorced when I was twenty-one). We got closer. He'd tell me stories that sometimes had me in tears of laughter, scandalous stories about the women he used to see before my mother, about his friends from the rougher side of town who he'd stayed in touch with after he became a successful violinist. My dad didn't know, or at least he pretended not to know, about my devotion to heroin, and he never showed any interest in my novels either. I'm not saying he never read them – maybe he did, maybe he didn't – I'm saying he never asked me about them or said anything encouraging or told me he was proud of me. I wrote just one more Zoe Zabarino novel: *Flowers for the Grave of Zoe Zabarino*. It was published when I was thirty-two. I almost didn't write it, I was going to let the series die off after *Zoe Zabarino's Daddy Issues*, but it didn't feel right to end it that way. It's like not saying goodbye properly when you're leaving someone or they're leaving you. You have to say goodbye the right way, you just have to. Before I wrote *Flowers for the Grave of Zoe Zabarino*, I tried reading the Ren Duka novels again, but now they seemed to me full of lies, like they were running from rather than confronting the plain facts of living and dying – facts that included my terminally ill father in his apartment in the East Village, with his unreliable memory and his dirty jokes. Facts that included Christine's perfect body eaten up by maggots in the fucking cemetery. Maybe I'd become cynical. Life had changed, I had changed, and the Duka books seemed to have changed along with me. I've heard it said that you shouldn't revisit the writers of your youth. Then again, Baudelaire has never let me down. Not in rehab, not in Paris, not after Christine died. Baudelaire is eternal. *Flowers for the Grave of Zoe Zabarino* sold maybe four hundred, five hundred copies. I didn't care how well or how little it sold. I was proud to bring the series to its conclusion, to be able to say for once in my life that I'd finished something I'd started. I especially like the final scene: the ghost of Zoe Zabarino watches her own funeral, insulting the mourners from beyond the grave. She mocks their bad shoes, their hair, their suits. She makes fun of the women who've gained weight, the men in their midlife crises who look at her coffin thinking they ought to have fucked her while she was alive. When the novel was published I was in rehab again, upstate. I've been in and out of rehab since I was twenty-three, but the truth is, I'll never quit heroin. I've accepted that. When I tell you I've found religion, you have to understand it's a form of religion that makes room for heroin. I do get clean for periods, weeks or sometimes months. I go upstate to Montauk, I read books and I just keep away from the stuff. But I always know I'll come back to it. Still, I do take religion seriously now. I go to church, I pray, I try to live in a Christlike manner, though frequently I fail. There's a fashion for Catholicism now, all these TradCath girls acting like it's an aesthetic affair, an accessory. To me that's worse than atheism, worse than no religion at all. The message of the Gospels is clear: you have to break open the heart, you have to let the light of Christ come inside you. People don't understand the revolutionary import in Christ's message of mercy. The same people may see a contradiction between my religious faith and my devotion to heroin, but I'm telling you, there's no distance at all between junk and Jesus Christ. People are suffering. The sorrow of the world is too much for me sometimes, it makes it so I can hardly breath, like the time I was in the L train and it got stuck under the East River and the lights went out and some maniac started screaming and everybody panicked. That was bad. I think of my father, alone in his apartment in the Village. Does he regret his life? Is he at peace? I can't ask him such questions, I just can't. Whenever I visit him the blinds are drawn and you can hear the guy in the apartment above screaming at his old mother like he's about to hit her. I think of Christine, dead at twenty-nine, and all the junkies I've known, the self-harmers, the crack-smokers, the losers. You've got to open up the heart, the suffering heart. All our pain will dissolve in the light of Christ. That's the message of the Gospels, but it's also what heroin means to me. One day our pain will be relieved, all our sorrows will come to an end. Heroin is a glimpse of the kingdom, the world to come, forever amen. Christ will return, he's returning already, but he'll return unfamiliar and maybe we won't recognise him because maybe we're not worthy to receive him. But he'll come to us anyway, undeserving though we are. That's what I believe, that's the conclusion I've reached from observing human life and reading what I could. In the meantime, we have to love each other. That's it, that's all there is. We just have to love each other.

3. Combat

Ren Duka Plays the Race Card (February 2026)

All writers recycle their own experiences. The novels that the author produced next exploited his various controversies in narratives that explored defiance, mass hysteria, internet politics, bad faith, transgression, shame and redemption at the ever-shifting frontiers of acceptable expression. A more broadly satirical novel than any the author had previously written, *Ren Duka Plays the Race Card* is set in 2017 and begins with the incident that would catapult Duka onto the culture war's frontlines.

Global society is in a frenzy. The unforeseen effects of worldwide connection and transparency have unhinged the human race. Reckless tech corporations have shattered mass culture into a chaos of rabidly warring factions. Bewildered citizens turn on one another in an orgy of outrage, and the mobs are on the hunt for easy targets – Ren Duka's friends are dropping like flies. Feeling backed into a corner by his heterosexual, white, cis-gendered identity in a period when the combination amounts to 'a royal flush of disrepute', Ren conducts a probe on his genealogy in hope of finding some mitigating factor. To his surprise, the research throws up inconclusive but strong suggestions of a distant ancestor from Algeria. One of his peasant forebears, he speculates, may have been impregnated by an Algerian pirate when the corsairs landed on south-west Cork in the seventeenth century, kidnapping hundreds of villagers to be sold as slaves. 'I'm a fucking raghead!' he exclaims in front of his laptop.

Ren's delight at his discovery is huge. In an instant, he has gone from being 'the most unfashionable entity on the planet' to someone with a claim, however tenuous, to immunity-granting victim status. Inwardly he already feels different. The idea of a swarthy *mujāhid* rapist swinging from the branches of his family tree puts a different cast on Ren's days, making him feel somehow more virtuous, more interested in himself. His budding ethnic pride, however, proves to be his downfall. No sooner has he moved to London, having once again grown weary of Dublin, than he writes an excitable opinion piece intended to publicise his genealogical discovery. The article that goes out one Tuesday morning on a popular centre-left news website bears the title 'How Discovering My Hidden Brownness Helped Me Understand Privilege'. By the end of the day it's the site's most widely read article – and the most ridiculed. In his column the following day, right-wing provocateur Mason Gould derides the article as 'sycophantic, slimy and downright sinister', while the left's culture warriors lambast what they see as Duka's attempt to win clout by aligning himself with a relatively oppressed ethnicity. 'This risible Ali-G crap ought never to have been published,' writes Suzanne Simmons in her hugely popular column that Sunday. 'The mendacity, opportunism and sheer wetness of Ren Duka's self-sanctification offers a case study in how bad actors can co-opt struggles that are not their own in a bid for status or approval.'

What ensues is nothing less than a sustained public humiliation. 'Every dickhead on the internet is lining up to throw a punch,' Ren tells his friend Fran in a pub in Bayswater, knocking back two Valiums with a double whiskey. He can't open a web browser without seeing his name speared to the end of an insult. He trends on social media over a two-week frenzy of hatred. Comedy shows lampoon him. Some four-hundred high-profile feminists sign an open letter published in the *London Review of Books*, denouncing Ren Duka and all men who seek to 'cynically exploit systemic oppression and anti-colonial struggle to boost their careers'. Hurt and angered, Ren draws up a spreadsheet in which he records the names of everyone who joins the pile-on, or even likes posts that mock him. Initially he vows to avenge himself on every single offender, but the sheer quantity of his detractors soon overwhelms him.

Appalled by what he has seen of the public's capacity to turn on its elected targets, Ren decides to make a stand. His opportunities to publish in mainstream outlets have dried up overnight, so he begins writing a twice-weekly column for the not entirely reputable website *Pugilist* in which he eviscerates the new moral-ideological pieties. His metropolitan critics smugly dismiss the column as appealing only to ruddy ale-swillers in Middle England and incest-ravaged aristocrats. However, it quickly becomes a cult favourite among cynical Londoners and contrarian artists who crave provocation in an age of performance ethics. To his surprise, Ren learns that he has an especially high quotient of readers among the UK's Sikh population. Investigating the matter further, he realises that his column has tapped into a conservative disdain among Sikhs for what they regard as a sloppy and depraved British culture – and perhaps for the West in general. T-shirts bearing the slogan Ren Duka's Seen a Few Things are already a familiar sight in England's cities and towns; now it is increasingly common to see young Sikhs in blue T-shirts emblazoned with the words Ren Duka is One of Us (an edgier, black, Muslim variant has the words printed under an Arabic squiggle resembling the ISIS insignia). Duka begins appearing on Russia Today and various right-wing platforms. Realising that his newfound role as caustic anti-liberal antagonist is good for ratings, mainstream media begin courting him anew. On TV panel discussions he is the reactionary fox in the progressivist coop. In these appearances, Ren's debating style is timeworn and simple: he bombards his opponent with mockery and sarcasm. Whenever an interlocutor, invariably in firmer command of facts and statistics, seems poised to get the better of him, Ren accuses them of racism. If he feels he is in a particularly tight corner, he accuses them of paedophilia. Suzanne Simmons and her cohort redouble their attacks in their articles and on social media. In his *Pugilist* column, Ren suggests that Simmons' column should be retitled 'The Ren Duka Digest' because she pays scant interest to any other topic (he also heavily implies that Simmons is sexually obsessed with him). His detractors' zeal only fuels admiration for Ren Duka among Sikhs, Middle England, and the disgruntled. In his column he calls for a reinstatement of old-fashioned values: manliness and femininity; the primacy of the family; temperance, honour and chastity. He champions militarism. He calls for a renewed colonising drive. He denounces atheism as 'the last refuge of moral scum', and suggests that the 'slobs' he sees plodding up and down English high streets can learn something from the country's Sikhs, Muslims and Hindus. He urges Great Britain to invade Ireland, and for the Irish to assist the invaders in a regressive 'war of dependence'. Ominously, he encourages a 'healthy suspicion towards the outlander, the foreigner', on the grounds that 'a civilisation that has lost its prejudice has lost its hard-on'.

To many, Ren Duka's fulminations lose their appeal over-night when a Sikh extremist hijacks a zeppelin and crashes it into Stonehenge, apparently incited by Duka's recent attack on 'the pagan fads seducing our credulous young' (fortunately, the monument is closed to the public at the time of the attack, and the would-be-martyr is arrested bearing minor injuries). In the aftermath of the incident, Duka's supporters on the right move quickly to distance themselves. Rumours circulate that Ren was brainwashed during his captivity in the Islamic State and is now operating as a *jihadist* fifth column. Some suggest he is an agent of Russia, disseminating cor-rosive ideas to demoralise the West. Panel-show invitations again dry up. Taking their cues from the conservative press, moderate Sikhs cool off in their admiration. Finally, *Pugilist* cancels his column. Suzanne Simmons writes one last, gleeful broadside against him (this time, Ren is not alone in noticing the strangely sexualised tone of her denunciation). Once more, Ren Duka finds himself cast to the margins, shunned by the crowd, facing an uncertain future.

Ren Duka is One With the People (June 2026)

As the novel begins, Ren Duka has partially re-emerged from banishment to grind his axe as a wilfully offensive stand-up comic. His 'Auto-da-fé Tour' is promoted with the tagline 'Jokes with nothing left to lose.' In small to mid-sized venues around England, Duka riffs on race, feminism, trans rights, and immigration to largely male audiences for whom his lack of natural comedic talent is compensated by his recklessness and nihilism. (Sample joke: 'How many feminists does it take to change a lightbulb? Two. One to change the lightbulb, the other to suck my dick.')

Soon, however, Ren grows weary of such tired provocations. Looking out each night across the dim, beery venues, he feels nothing but contempt for his audiences. The rancour and sadism that enlivened his opinion column have run dry, and with them his taste for confrontation. The esteem of swilled-up racists in forgotten satellite towns is not enough. It's cold outside – he wants back in, to the warmth and acceptance of the tribe. Two months after his stand-up tour ends, he writes an article for the *New Statesman* titled 'I'm Sorry'. In the article, he claims that his incitements were the regrettable acting out of an ugly, repressed political id, and that he is as weary of the populist right as he once was of the progressivist left. The times we live in require urgency and seriousness, he insists, not contrarian cheap thrills. He admits that he spent the final leg of his recent comedy tour in a fug of depression, no longer believing in the jokes he delivered mechanically, and that he is donating all the profits from the Auto-da-fé Tour to a charity for migrants. He intends to put the jaundiced provocateur behind him and, in all humility and eagerness to learn, align himself with the forces seeking a more just and equitable society. Striking in its apparent candour, the article is met with cautious approval, with only a few prominent voices (including Suzanne Simmons') warning that we shouldn't expect a neo-reactionary leopard to change its spots. At a book-signing event some weeks later, Ren requests that people of colour and trans people move to the front of the room so that they can be first to have their books signed. Although there turn out to be virtually no such persons in attendance (an embarrassed young woman of faintly Asian appearance shuffles forward), the gesture is widely commended on social media. The consensus forms that Ren Duka has returned to the fold.

Thereafter, Duka behaves like a man newly awakened to the activist's calling. When a black teenager is shot dead by police in Hackney Downs, Ren joins the masses in posting a pulsating psychedelic cube on his official social media accounts. Seemingly not content with a one-off digital protest, he posts another cube every day. A new edition of *Ren Duka's Seen a Few Things* appears whose cover depicts a giant, gold-plated Ren Duka taking the knee. Ren spends most of his waking hours on social media, leaving supportive comments under posts that vilify white men. Often these affirmations – 'So true!', 'You said it', 'Absolutely', '100%' – are accompanied by brown-skinned fist-bump emojis. After several weeks of this, he posts that, despite his possible African ancestry, he has no right to speak, having for so long benefited from systemic injustice and the exploitation of 'black babies' (he does not clarify what he means by this). Therefore, from now on he will use his platform exclusively to promote those less privileged, the one small exception being the opinions he will permit himself to express on the fortunes of his beloved Everton Football Club. His social media feeds become cascades of contradictory assertions from trans-rights campaigners, anti-racism activists and radical feminists, interspersed with real-time commentaries on Everton matches, transfer speculations, and screeds against the club's owners.

Some dismiss Ren Duka's 'ethical turn' as more trolling from a noted misanthrope, but for the most part he is taken at face value. The pulsating psychedelic cubes continue to appear daily on his accounts for over a year – well past the peak of the race protests. Just when it seems he has transitioned fully from right-wing bulldog to tireless social justice advocate, the rumours begin to circulate: Ren Duka was once a guest on Jeffrey Epstein's 'Lolita Express' private plane and luxury island. On the day he is due to appear on a major US chat show, an image goes viral of Duka sitting on a deckchair in a Hawaiian shirt with two very young girls on his lap, as Jeffrey Epstein stands by holding a pina colada. He immediately issues a statement insisting that the images are fake and that he never met Epstein, but it is too late – the mob has turned. The fury is overwhelming. By that evening, an unhinged Duka is threatening to release 'heavy Kompromat' on prominent anti-racist activists and on his literary rivals. The next day, the scandal has blown up into a worldwide frenzy of unbridled hate. Ren posts an unprecedentedly abject apology, grovelling to the camera while pulling out clumps of his hair – it only feeds the outrage. Overnight, his reputation as a champion of noble causes is destroyed. Former friends write articles condemning him. News outlets issue statements that they will never again carry his byline. Piles of his books are burned on every continent. The hashtag #youvilecunt trends, tagging images of Ren Duka with swastika eyes.

Accustomed to the public's fickleness, Ren is philosophical about his latest shaming. 'Easy come, easy go,' he tells his neighbour Mrs Desmond over the back garden wall of his Hackney home in *Ren Duka is One With the People*'s final scene. 'In a way it serves me right for stepping into a role that never suited me,' he says. 'I suppose I'll just get back to writing books. I think they'll let me do that.'

Mrs Desmond looks at him in silence, a far-off look in her eyes. Then she takes the remaining clothes down from the line, remarks that there's 'ah fine stretch inna evenings now', steps into her home and closes the door.

Ren Duka Takes a Break – US title: *Duka in Benidorm* (November 2026)

In this short and enjoyable novel, deciding that he needs to get away for a spell and reassess after his public mauling, Ren Duka books a three-week stay at a resort hotel in Benidorm. In the evenings he sits out on his fifteenth-floor balcony over the Mediterranean, drinking screwdrivers and strumming a nylon-stringed guitar he bought from a teenager outside a sports bar. By day he lounges by the pool or lies on the beach. A few days into his stay, he goes to a local English bar where they're showing an Everton match. Watching his team while drinking lager, he strikes up a conversation with a deeply tanned, silver-haired man from Greece named Stefanos Papatonis. After the match ends (a one-all draw with Aston Villa), the two men move on to another bar, discussing women, football, Spanish history, and the nature of time and chance. They take to drinking together each night on the strip of beachfront bars; soon they are also meeting up in the afternoons. They admire the women on holiday who laugh and roam in groups, but are too shy (or relaxed) to approach them. As the nights blur together under a flow of lager and screwdrivers, Ren learns Stefanos's story. He was happily married for eleven years, working as an electrician in the outskirts of Athens. Then he found out that his wife had been cheating on him for five of those years with their friend

Georgios, a software engineer and amateur actor. Compelled by ancient laws of the blood, Stefanos confronted his friend one evening after rehearsals for an upcoming play (in which, ironically, Georgios would play a cuckolded husband). 'Is it true?' he asked him. Georgios put up his hands and said his friend's name, buying time, his eyes darting left and right. Then Stefanos knocked his lights out. That would have been that – the score was settled, as far as Stefanos was concerned. But as he walked away, Georgios, having regained consciousness, launched himself at Stefanos and grappled him to the ground. Acting on instinct, Stefanos threw off Georgios, fell on top of him and landed a sequence of blows to his torso and head. When Georgios's skull hit the concrete after the final and hardest punch, Stefanos knew his friend would not be getting back up. He served five years of a nine-year sentence for manslaughter. 'I didn't get to see my little girl turn into a young woman,' he says, swirling the ice-cubes in his glass. 'My wife wanted her to come visit me, but I wasn't going to let her see her daddy in a convict's suit.' He forgave his wife, but they agreed that they'd reached the end of their road together. As soon as he was released from prison they finalised their divorce. 'She's shacked up now with an architect from Thessaloniki who looks like he ought to eat more red meat. I even hope she's happy… sometimes.' After prison, Stefanos worked at a friend's bar for a while. Then his parents died and with his inheritance he bought an apartment in Plata, which he leased out as he went on long, open-ended journeys and did all the travelling he'd have liked to do when he was young.

When Stefanos's story ends, Ren realises he has found in the Greek what has long been missing from his life: a kindred spirit. Drunk one night at a pub emblazoned with Saint George's Crosses, he tells Stefanos that although he has never killed a man, he has wanted to kill plenty – perhaps the only difference between them is Ren's timidity. 'No,' says Stefanos. 'It isn't timidity that makes you refrain from killing. It's faith, or lucidity.' He doesn't explain this remark, which soon gets forgotten amidst rounds of screwdrivers and the dirty jokes Ren reprises from his time as a stand-up comic. Ren goes to bed that night drunk and happy, deciding that fate has led him to Benidorm for a reason, namely to make the acquaintance of the remarkable Stefanos Papatonis, redeemed murderer and poetic soul. When he returns to their usual place the following day, Stefanos is not there. Ren waits over a couple of lagers, distractedly reading literary news on his phone (Kevin Mulvaney's second novel, *Wife Beater*, is on the shortlist for a major award; Ren calls for his first screwdriver of the day). Hours pass; Stefanos never shows. The two men have not exchanged contact details or bothered with social media. That night, and for those that follow, Ren gets drunk at the bars where he and Stefanos had drunk together. Eventually he accepts that their friendship was destined to be a brief one.

Comprised predominantly of Stefanos Papatonis's story and a celebration of his personality, *Ren Duka Takes a Break* is dedicated to the real-life figure who had inspired him. A modest commercial success, the novel's homage to friendship heralded the deeper explorations of selfhood, memory, belonging and the human condition that were to follow.

Excerpt from *A Cool, Dry Place*

After the first Ren Duka novels blew up, I went from being a writer who'd have a couple of dozen people turn up at his readings to someone as recognisable as a screen actor. Dublin is an overgrown village where each of us knows the others' business, but before the Ren Duka circus came to town I'd been able to go about with relative anonymity. Now and then a reader might recognise me, say something complimentary about my books and wish me well – but otherwise I was just another citizen. Then one day I woke up in a city where everybody was staring at me, nudging their friends as I passed, taking photos as I bought a coffee. Soon I began to have the impression that people were smirking at me, as if I were the butt of some inside joke. The smirk seemed to follow me around the city, hopping from face to face as new pairs of eyes recognised me on every street. If that ubiquitous smirk was all I'd had to endure I might have got used to it. But I began to feel exposed, even menaced. I'd long been aware that my books attracted a particular type of reader. I thought of them as the Travis Bickles: intense, solitary men (they were more often men) who turned up at my readings to listen with an unnerving stillness, eyes closed or else locked on mine with ambiguous fervour. They'd send me emails (or letters) that were either terse or very long, some assuming a ribald familiarity, others icily formal. Judging by their messages and the things they whispered to me as I signed their books at public events, the Travis Bickles perceived in me a cracked ally, a brother in rancour and desperation. I'd never regretted this core readership nor found it surprising that they were the type drawn to my work. I recognised myself in them as they did in me. But I also knew how volatile that inner fury could be, how quickly it could turn, and so I'd always maintained a certain wariness around my readers. I'd even say I was vaguely afraid of them. And then, suddenly, my readers were everywhere. The psychic weather was too close, too foreboding. I needed to get out of Ireland.

First we moved to Granada. I wrote two novels in a white house in the narrow, cobbled streets of the old town. My wife, Isabel, being Spanish, we both spoke the language and felt at ease there, eating tapas on cafe terraces above that sensual, Moorish city. But after half a year the old restlessness – and Isabel's rare but terrifying psychotic episodes, which soured things with the neighbours – moved us on. When our lease in Granada was up, we relocated to the Greek island of Paxos in the Ionian Sea. The nine months we spent there were in every sense idyllic, although at first I was so absorbed in my work I was scarcely aware of my surroundings. In the evenings we'd walk to a pretty village near the island's centre, or to a beachside bar run by a tiny old lady and her gruff, middle-aged son. It was there that we befriended the man I'll call Javier. In his late fifties and originally from Madrid, he'd lived on Paxos for seven years. He was charming, eloquent and courteous – Isabel quickly took a shine to him, saying he reminded her of her father (an Irishman). Javier accompanied us on walks around the island, speaking knowledgeably about its geological features, his conversation peppered with references to Greek myth, Herodotus, the Presocratics. Drinking with him a few nights, we learned that as a younger man he had published two books and had at one time been regarded as among Spain's most subversive writers. The second book, a novel set inside a prison cell, had been published when he was thirty-five. There'd been none since.

One night after Isabel had gone to bed, I stayed out drinking with Javier. On first meeting him I'd been surprised to learn that he didn't know who I was; now he explained that he'd been avoiding contemporary literature for a decade and a half. 'I've withdrawn into the classics,' he admitted in his sumptuously enunciated English. 'Anything later than Cervantes seems to me clamorously modern.' He didn't seem to hold my success against me, perhaps because on Paxos he'd made significant progress in cultivating the Olympian or Troglodytic detachment he aspired to. There were moments, however, when his serenity lapsed. After a few glasses of ouzo, I made the mistake of voicing my admiration for a Catalan novelist whose heyday had been the early 2000s. Javier winced as if I'd jabbed needles into his balls. He even seemed to shrivel, as if the life force had burst out of him and spilled in the sand by our table. Startled, I awkwardly changed the subject. He fell silent and for a time we nursed our glasses, watching the darker-than-wine sea from the bar where we were now the only drinkers. He proposed a final glass at his villa. His home was a short walk up a hill from the village, shyly backed off the main road. It was cheerful enough and bore signs of a feminine presence, though the companion from Valencia he'd mentioned wasn't around. I sat at a table in the living room as he went to fix us drinks. There was a deck of Tarot on the wooden surface with one card upturned – the Hanging Man. When Javier came back with a bottle and two glasses, he sat with me and we toasted. A little later he gestured towards a stack of printed typescripts half a metre high in a corner next to a bookshelf. 'You asked if I've been working on anything. Well, there it is – some of it.' He motioned for me to take a look through the pile: there were several novels, some loose short stories, what appeared to be a memoir, and a collection of essays or sketches. I remember some titles: 'El Padre', 'Los Sueños de Silvio', 'Calle Otoño', 'Maldiciónes y Oraciones'. 'There's another stack in the bedroom,' Javier said, 'and all manner of things in varying states of incompletion on my computer. You see, they've long stopped publishing me – or rather, I've long stopped asking them to with any great energy – but I can't seem to stop writing. However, I can't seem to finish anything either. I get excited by an idea and set out with great energy and confidence, but as the work unfolds a sense of impotence comes over me, a piercing futility. And so I fall dormant again until the next bright hope awakens me... and the cycle starts over. Sí, una enfermedad!' He rose from his chair and lifted a typescript from the top of the pile. 'This one I wrote last year. It's about an agent in Franco's secret police who was a closet homosexual and published poetry under a pseudonym. I took my inspiration from a real individual. The man in question killed himself when an enemy in the government tried to blackmail him.'

He refilled our glasses – we had moved on to a delicious Rioja. My vision began to swim as Javier spoke about the 'exquisite horror' of being a once-promising writer. He claimed that in such cases as his a 'bifurcation of destiny' takes place which summons into being a second self, a metaphysical double. This shadow self – 'el otro', he called it – ascends in the world and achieves a life that is more or less glorious... in fantasy. Meanwhile, the scrawny, all-too-actual self finds he is oppressed by the old dreams, victim of a promise that turned out to be not only empty but cruel. 'This is the marvellous torture of it,' he said. 'You are forced to watch him *outrace you and leave you in the dust... but nobody realises you are enduring this defeat which lasts the rest of your life, because he is invisible to everyone else.' Finishing his wine, he held the stem of the glass between thumb and forefinger, peering through it. 'It's easier to live with unrealised promise if you've never disclosed it. Once you* declare yourself, *you give him form – your disappointment is a golem born from your dreams.'*

I last saw Javier a few days before we moved on from Paxos – first to Seville to spend time with Isabel's family, then to London. I played ping-pong with him on the beach next to our regular bar. I've never known anyone to take the game of ping-pong so seriously. I can picture him now, old Javier, with the sun at his back and the Ionian waves roaring like an audience, and him full of ridiculous passion. We played for two hours that hot afternoon, game after game with Isabel looking on. And never – not even once – could he beat me.

Excerpt from *Night Taxi*

Henry K. Dillon awoke at noon and lay a while in the after-glow of dreams. Lately they'd come in torrents, his dreams, high-definition and drunk with colour – the fruits of with-drawal. For several weeks he'd taken to eating hash yoghurts after his shifts, cooking up the cannabis resin on a teaspoon with some olive oil, circling its underside with a lighter flame, then mixing it with the yoghurt. His friend Trisha, who bounced at a nightclub out in Swords, had recommended he try it after he'd complained about his sleeping. He hadn't smoked hash or weed in many years, but the yoghurt method was a revelation. There was no paranoia – and he slept like a Buddha. A few days ago he'd run out of hash. Ever since, his dreams had been feverish, enigmatic, otherworldly – and peppered with false awakenings.

Lying in the midday quiet, he contemplated the dream's dissolving impressions, its unique strangeness. He'd dreamed that he was himself, yet in another life. In the dream he was younger than he was now, with a different face. He wasn't living in Dublin, but in Germany, perhaps Dresden or Berlin. He was married to a short, blonde woman who, like him, was a writer. He and his wife lived in a small, bright flat with a balcony and plants and high ceilings, and together they got by and supported one another. In the dream they'd made love – the relaxed, forgettable sex of a married couple.

On a shelf in their living room were some of their books: he'd tried to read the titles though the letters were indistinct. One of them (hers?) seemed to be called *Planet Without End*; another was something like *Daybreak in a Machine City*. A slim, red-sleeved paperback about robot music that they'd seemingly co-authored was titled *Rogue Fractal Gardens*. His dream self was active across social media – something Henry hadn't bothered with in years – and called his online avatar tenseOgura.

When he woke up, Henry searched for the account online. He found that there was in fact one with that name belonging to an Irish artist in Germany. The profile photo was artfully blurred, a futurist glitch of a man hunched over a laptop. The account displayed images of sculptures, paintings, cities, land-scapes. A pinned photo showed the gangly artist in a bright flat with a balcony and plants, a blonde woman hovering by his chair, her hand resting on his shoulder...

When he woke up for real, Henry resisted going online till after he'd had his coffee. He drank it looking out the window at the drizzly street and the Dubliners going about their day. When he searched for the dream profile there was, of course, no such account.

It was his day off. He meditated for forty minutes, sent some messages, read a news site (militias now controlled Marseille, Lyon and the Paris *banlieues*; another prime minister was claiming to be in contact with a non-human civilisation). He had brunch at a nearby cafe, walked around town for a while, bought a book on millenarian sects in Tsarist Russia. Throughout the day the dream stayed with him – this tantalis-ing sense of a forked-off self who'd followed other desires, taken an alternate path. There was no great melancholy to it, more a sense of intrigue, wonder.

In the evening he drove to Alicia's flat in Ballsbridge, parked inside her gated block. She'd just flown back from Sardinia, where she'd spent two weeks in white, spacious houses by the sea, being photographed while tied up in ropes, in various erotic scenarios. She showed him the pictures, said the photographer was a genius. In other photos she was in a sea that sparkled brilliant turquoise, swimming like a dolphin, her black hair glinting in the Mediterranean sun.

She cooked an asparagus risotto. They ate it with a bottle of Sardinian red wine she'd brought back just for them. She always treated Henry nicely, and it was fine with her that he didn't want anything too serious.

'I had a strange dream last night,' he said, filling Alicia's glass. 'I was myself, but in another life. I still wrote books. I was living in Germany.'

She reflected on this, watching the play of light in her wineglass, as if seeing herself swimming through it.

'It sounds silly, or just obvious,' he went on, 'But I'm left with the timeless question of whether he was really my dream – or I'm his.'

'Maybe it's both?' She sipped her wine, looking into his eyes. She put her glass down, moved around the table and straddled him, her short black dress hitching up to her hips. He kissed the acidic taste of wine. There arose an impulse to tell her he loved her – just to see what happened. He let it dissolve.

They made love on the floor. She was greedy, her sex like laughter. He closed his eyes, kissing her neck and her silky black hair. She whispered words he couldn't make out, words not even meant for him. Her fingers pressed furrows into his bald head. When he opened his eyes she was blonde, her skin pale, her body slight and lovely. He held it there, watching her in the form of a different woman with a different face. Then he closed his eyes and when they opened again she was her dark-haired self, coming hard, sighing long and deep, a woman in the centre of her life.

Tommy Rhys Cunningham

I've known glory and I've known disgrace. One always comes wrapped inside the other, like a dick in a condom. Like *his* dick in my hand, or mine in his mouth. It's laughable, but in spite of everything that went down, just saying that makes me hard. The dick never learns. It follows its own agenda, its interests are distinct from and very often at odds with our own. My whole life is a testament to that.

I played Ren Duka in the first three films. The best three, in my opinion. You'll say I'm biased, but there isn't much I can do about that. After Helen Kormann replaced Amy Yoon as director, the series disappeared up its own arsehole, never to be seen again. People say those first three films – *my* Ren Duka films – were silly and camp, but that's really to miss the fucking point. The turn the series took later on, ramping up the moral darkness, the graphic sex, the sleaze and violence – all of that was a joke. The essence of the Ren Duka cycle is *panache*, if you're asking me. Hidden depths and an intangible poignancy. To me there was always a mysteriousness to the series, as if the harder we look at Duka, the further he recedes. At least, that's how I tried to play him. And I'm not the only one who says I did a good job. Go online. Look at Reddit. That's where the real Duka discourse happens, not on the other bullshit platforms where everyone is so tense with fashion that they just parrot the party line, which is that the first three films were an embarrassment. Fuck them. I was the best of the five Dukas. Why should I be modest or politic now that they've turned on me, or turned me in, or just turned me off like I'm some toy bunny you can play with whenever the mood takes you? But you can't turn me off. You can't suppress me for long. And so here I am, fit and working again, if only in the margins, out of the spotlight, banished from the court of the treacherous boy-king, Vinny fucking Levine.

I want to state what happened, for the record, even though I know they won't print the half of what I say. But I don't want to dwell too much on *him*, the golden faggot with the immaculate arsehole who led me to my ruin. The entire world already knows. That fucking memoir! I don't want to give him the satisfaction. And yet – and here, you see, here we get to the crux of my problem – I *do* want to give it to him. I want to give it to him very much. Him and only him. Vinny Levine, with his golden balls and his luminous arse. My co-star in the first and, in my opinion, the best of the Ren Duka films, even if I can't watch it for the hurt it brings.

Vinny was twenty-two when we shot the movie, I was forty-five. To think how different my life might be today if Amy Wong had cast somebody else as the narco-poet Paulie Sheehan. That kid played me like a fiddle. I know I should have seen it coming, but what can you do when you're forty-five and you feel like the ship has sailed, like you're standing on the harbour watching it race to the horizon and you wish more than anything that you were up there on deck, at the prow, with the sun and the ocean spray on your face? Didn't some old queen write a poem about that? Maybe I'm wrong. I don't read many poems. That cruel little faggot, he never read any fucking poetry, I'll tell you that for nothing. He never read a book in his life. Why would you, when you're that beautiful, that young? You're the book everyone is reading, and all you have to do is lie back and enjoy it. The ships all sail in your direction. You're the golden island everyone wants to get to. There was nothing in that boy's head but sex and ambition. The first time he sucked me off I cried. I mean I wept with abandon, just like that. I wept and sobbed while he was sucking me. I wept before I came and while I was coming and after I'd come. Maybe I wept because I foresaw all the harm he would do to me. My fate was sealed the moment he got on his knees and took me in his hands and clasped his pretty lips over my cock – which, by the way, and I'm not making this up, grew an extra half inch just for him. Take that how you will, but I'm telling you the truth. I have a nice cock. It's fat and thick but it isn't especially long – five and a half inches at full mast. I measured it years ago, when I was twenty-one and fucking everyone in London. But when I got hard for Vinny, it grew to six inches. I can't explain it, but it's a fact. I know because I measured it. At first I kept telling myself it was an illusion, that it just looked bigger because of how good he made me feel. But one night when we were back at my place after the day's shoot, I pulled it out of him and measured it. Six inches. Now that he's gone, it's five and a half inches again when erect. That first time, he sucked me like a god would suck you, and when I came he licked up every last droplet as I twitched and spasmed in his hands. He kept wanking me till it was good and sated. And he kept kissing the head as it slowly detumesced, I remember that.

After that I was lost. There was no coming back. I was at his mercy – and he has no fucking mercy. That first time, we were in my trailer, the night we'd shot the scene where Duka and Paulie meet on a Dublin rooftop while Paulie is on the run. The orgasm wiped me out and I fell asleep with him lying next to me, purring like a cat. I must have been asleep for at least an hour because I dreamed that I was transitioning – not from man to woman, but from mundane flesh to supernature, from a chrysalis to a butterfly made of diamonds and light, a butterfly that could flicker between worlds with a beat of its wings. After that, we fucked for weeks. It was an intensive shooting schedule, but every moment we weren't filming, my cock was in that boy's arsehole or his was in mine. The truth is, those were the greatest days of my life. It was bliss. Here's a detail for the ages: Vinny Levine is the only man who could ever make me come *without so much as touching me*. He could just look at me and I'd erupt, I'd jizz over my thighs or my belly or into the air. It didn't happen often, but it happened. Three, maybe four times. And every time he fucked me or I fucked him, it was the greatest fuck of my life. I mean that. Every time. He fucked me so that all the other fucks vanished, every cock or arsehole I'd ever known. Let me explain something to you. I'm someone who has had, by any metric whatsoever, a truly fucking inordinate amount of sex. I've fucked just about anyone who's ever looked at me. I've made a point of it. There isn't an arse in the London theatre world that I'm not acquainted with, or at least there wasn't when I was in my twenties and thirties, an arrogant Belfast faggot off the leash in the bottomless capital. And as soon as I got my first major film role, just two years before I landed the lead in the Ren Duka films, I cashed in my celebrity chips to *really* fuck anything that moved. Otherwise, what's the *point* of being famous? So I'd had a lot of cock before he and I met on the Ren Duka shoot. But when Vinny Levine fucked me or when I fucked him it was like I'd never fucked or been fucked before. I can't explain that, but it's the truth. I told him he was my *tabula rasa* because he wiped the slate clean. He didn't know what the fuck I was talking about but that was part of his charm – his pure ignorance, the ignorance of a newborn angel. Everything was part of his charm – even the filmy silver snot when he blew his nose and chucked the tissue in the bin in my trailer. That's how it is when you're a god.

Here's the laughable or the terrible truth: I regret nothing. Not one fuck. Not one shot at the title. Even after all that's happened, all he did to me, I don't regret one moment I spent feasting on his luscious, 22-year-old arse. That scrotum. How I licked it from behind, wide-eyed and gazing into his arsehole – literally praying. Praying into his arsehole because there was no other way to express the sense of completion I felt, in that instant when my tongue touched the soft silken contours of his perfect arsehole. I saw universes in there, the starry heavens and the moral law. I saw glacial immensities and the sky over mountain peaks. How can I even get across to you how sweet, how true, how *noble* that boy's arsehole really was? I'd have to say something like: it was autumn and spring at once. It was a white flower, the holy of holies, the call to prayer in the cool early morning. It tasted of nothing, but that nothingness was voluptuous, radical, terrifying. That arsehole changed me. It saved me and it destroyed me. It *gave birth* to me even as it sucked me in. I'm its slave, its eulogist, its shadow. It was my high-water mark – I knew it then and I know it now. The loss is irrevocable. And yet, to see it once – to know it and relish it and taste it even once (and I tasted it way more than once, believe me) – is to be justified. Merely to know it exists.

Then it all turned to shit. Vinny waited two years, till his once-promising career was starting to flag. He was good as Paulie Sheehan, no one would dispute that. Credit where it's due. He brought a sensitivity, a *danger* to the role – knacker poet, diamond in the muck, drug-dealing waif. He was good. But afterwards he appeared in a few romantic comedies that sank without a trace, and soon he no longer had the aura of one-to-watch. I was on the up and up, enjoying a great flowering in my forties. I was one of those actors, like Gene Hackman or Philip Seymour Hoffman, whose time is destined to come only when they reach middle-age. Whereas Vinny was starting to look like one of cinema's innumerable also-rans. That's when he rewrote history. He decided that all along he'd been my victim. That I'd taken advantage of him, stolen something precious from him that he could never get back. That I'd *groomed* him. Honestly, the levels of exquisite hypocrisy and self-deception required to tell a story like that and keep a straight face are beyond me. It's impressive, in its way. To be so certain of his own tragic victimhood and moral spotlessness – it boggles the fucking mind. He went about it like a pro because that's what he is, a pro. First, the weeping video on social media, seen by millions. Then the press, the talk shows, the documentary, the memoir. That fucking book! And it worked. In two weeks he went from early career decline to constant media presence, offers rolling in from all over, everybody's darling. Now he's lord of the fucking world. What was the last film he *wasn't* in? Buying mansions and Porsches for everyone in his family. Catwalking for YSL. He's even a superhero now – and it was all built on top of me. I'm the one buried under his throne and everybody knows it. I tried to defend myself, naturally, but you're dealing with a force beyond all reason. It's like trying to debate with a forest fire. Thousands of individual citizens on their phones cohere as a wrathful, unhinged baby-god who tears down skyscrapers and hurls them at the moon. I didn't stand a chance. They went on about power differentials, like I had some godlike authority over Vinny Levine by dint of my fame and money and advanced years. What they didn't say was that that twink had the power of life and death over *me*. The power of a Pharaoh over a slave. Absolute power – and absolute fucking corruption too. Have you read that memoir? My fucking word. *Like Lambs to the Slaughter*. Never did an honest word pass that kid's lips, and there wasn't a single honest word in his illiterate book either. He belongs to that rare category of those who've written more books than they've read. But then, he didn't really write the book, it was ghostwritten by that phantom-hack, Tina Tarantula or whatever the fuck she's called, who ought to be ashamed of herself. Vinny Levine, man of letters – *please*. All writers are snitches, memoirists especially. They snitch on anyone in sight, but in the end they really snitch on themselves. To this day, Vinny still believes himself to be my victim. I don't doubt that for a second. There's no reckoning with a capacity for self-delusion so magnificent, a narcissism so sublime. You'd try to pass it off as the folly of youth, but

I'm long enough in the tooth to recognise the type – he'll go to his grave in the serene certainty of his own innocence, confident that anything that went wrong in his life was the fault of someone else, and anyone he stepped on to get where he is now had it coming. He's up there on his boy-king's throne, everyone fawning over him – the way they fawned over me, brief though that was, when I was riding high as Ren Duka. The whole world kissing his ring, like I used to kiss it – like I still kiss it in my dreams. It doesn't matter that anyone with half a brain can see he has all the moral integrity of a tapeworm. The brain never was the organ he tickled in order to get what he wanted. He fucked *my* brains out, that's for sure. How else to explain it? Dicknotised, dick-drunk, dick-sick. Vinny Levine on his golden throne, lording it over the rest of us, and whenever his supremacy is threatened he wheels out another historic grievance or alleged victimhood and they all bend over backwards and do what he says. Like a mafia boss whose currency isn't violence but tears, histrionics, blame.

But look, I don't want to seem bitter. I decided some years back that succumbing to bitterness would only be to let that preening cocksucker win. Even if he *has* won. But life moves on. I'm still here. He took a lot from me but not everything, despite what I might have said earlier. The truth is, I can't even hate him. Not for very long. I can't help myself. He betrayed me and burned my palace to the fucking ground, but here's the glorious, preposterous truth of the matter: he's still the one I bash off to. He's still the one I see when I spurt. And when I pay for boys in LA or London – yeah, I've started paying for it, not all the time but whenever I feel like it, big fucking deal – I scroll through the photos and pick out the ones who look like him. Two or three at a time, if I feel like it. I've got Vinny clones I go back to in several major cities. They're not too hard to find. So many twinks wear their hair like his now, copy his style, ape his mannerisms and parrot the brainless bullshit he says on TikTok or in his interviews which all seem to go viral. Some even have the same tattoos. When he dyed his hair blond last year, overnight half the rent boys in the Western hemisphere went blond too. And when he dyed it back, they reverted as well. Now *that's* power. But he has even more power over me. I'm karmically bonded to that preening little fairy. Once, in the wilderness years when I was persona non grata and the phone wasn't ringing and I was horribly alone in the world, I did an ayahuasca ceremony. Someone had suggested I might benefit from it, and I was desperate because there's only so far that six therapy sessions a week and continuous self-medication with booze, Valium, cocaine, and Ecstasy will go in staving off the pain and fear. I did the ceremony in a forest in Devon. It was led by some Midlands shaman, an old dreadlocked crusty who I wouldn't look at twice if I saw him in the street. A bunch of vegans sitting on cushions in the half-lotus posture, with buckets beside them to puke into, and Enya or something playing on a Bluetooth speaker. I felt ridiculous – until the brew started kicking in. It was like living a whole lifetime in a few hours. Actually, it was like living several lifetimes, and in each one I saw *him*. The ayahuasca showed me that he and I have been bound together across many lifetimes, many worlds. In one vision, we were brothers, two little boys playing in a field on the windswept plains of what looked like the American Midwest. In one, he was my mother. He raised me in a high-rise in some crowded, steaming city. I cried for his tit and when he gave it to me I felt a fullness such as we never feel in adult life unless we shoot heroin. In another – this sounds like a joke, but it's what I saw – he was my dog. I was a woman living in a suburb of some Spanish or Portuguese city, and I took him for walks. In the saddest vision of all, we were at school together and I was the ringleader of the bullies who made his life hell, and finally he killed himself because he saw no way out. By the time the trip was over my lap was drenched with tears and I'd forgiven him everything. It didn't last for ever – within a few weeks the sight of him on a screen had me in paroxysms again – but even now, I can't hate him. Not really, not even when I want to.

So here I am. I had my years in the icy tundra, banished beyond the city walls like Coriolanus (who I played for a glorious run at the Apollo, back in the days of innocence, the prelapsarian days I thought would never end). That cold and that loneliness would have killed other men. It damn near killed me. If you ask me which of my achievements I'm proudest of, I'd have to say: my survival. Vinny Levine maimed me, he tortured me, he even ruined me, but he didn't kill me. My career will never again hit those heights. Certain doors are closed to me now, certain possibilities annulled. But that's the way it goes. The wheel of fate, the ineluctable laws of karma, whatever you want to call it. But I'm back. Not up there in the peaks where he is, but back. I starred in my first feature film as a director two years ago – *Hades for My Ladies*. Made for a tenth of the budget of a Ren Duka film, or a thousandth of the budget of the superhero bollocks Vinny stars in, but it did all right. Some nice reviews, attention at a few festivals, a couple of award nominations. A future cult classic, so they say. There were protests and snubs, the funda-mentalist contingent saying I'd lost the right to make films when I decided to take advantage of that blameless lamb to the slaughter, and anyone who bought a ticket was complicit in heinous crimes. But the culture had moved on and those voices were in the minority. In September I'll be in Sweden to play the lead in *Revenge of the Men*, a satirical queersploitation number about embittered Nazi fags who travel back in time to snuff out the feminist movement in its infancy. Low-budget, ultraviolent and a bit tawdry, but the script has something to it, a sparkle, a knowingness. As for Vinny Levine, he'll get what's coming, I'm convinced of that. Not from me, but from someone else he's thrown under the wheels. There are already stirrings online. Rumours. Scandal brewing. I keep an eye on it and try to keep my *Schadenfreude* under control, but it's hard. The truth is that, more than a settling of the scores or a rebalancing of the karmic scales, what I really dream of, what I long for even though I know I can't have it, is just one more taste, one more kiss, one more magical second with my tongue pushed deep inside that stupid boy's miraculous arsehole.

4. Origins

Ren Duka's Childhood (May 2027)

'Never repeat yourself,' the author once told a packed auditorium in Kristiansand, Norway, where he had been invited to give a talk about creating a vital body of work. 'Move on, don't become a bore who expects to be applauded for doing the same thing fifteen times.' In the talk, which is viewable on YouTube, he described the effort to stay creatively fresh as like being pursued through a jungle at night: 'You're fleeing the predator, which ultimately is your own shadow, in other words your will to inertia and collapse, to just lying down and letting the vines swallow you up.' The chief means of postponing the inevitable defeat, he insisted, was to 'always be mutating'.

True to his word, having said all he wanted to say about his era's moral confusion in what Lily Babenko has called his '*Auto-da-fé* novels', the author veered away from satire and looked instead to his own past. The novels he wrote next were fictional retellings of his pre-literary life and the experiences that had made him a writer.

Ren Duka's Childhood recounts Duka's earliest years in a tone pitched somewhere between blackly comic misery memoir and lurid Oedipal melodrama. The author seems to relish wheeling out every cliché he can muster of a 1980s, Irish Catholic childhood. There is an alcoholic and taciturn father named Donald who, after a long day working at the jam factory, retreats from his wife and children into a miasma of vodka, Thin Lizzy cassettes and television; a priest filled with shame and longing (one of the novel's more sympathetic characters); sexually repressed women; and an unchallenged patriarchy whose reign is evoked with ambivalence verging on nostalgia. The prepubescent Ren is terrified of girls and filled with an obsessive, confusing desire for his hated Irish-language teacher, Miss Ryan. The boy draws dozens of icon-like images of the young woman (always nude, always pregnant) which he pastes into a copybook he conceals in his mattress – a foreshadowing of the elaborate cut-and-paste erotic albums of his adolescence. The most uncomfortable passages in *Ren Duka's Childhood* involve detailed fantasies of perverse sexual encounters between the nine-year-old boy and this woman in her mid-thirties. Dramatic tension derives from near-misses when Ren's mother, sister or classmates come close to discovering his copybook shrine to Miss Ryan.

This teacher fixation is not the novel's only instance of troubling attitudes towards women. The relationship between the boy and his mother Sibéal borders on the gothic. He depicts her as a monster, revolting and vicious. In a special issue of the *Journal of Modern Literature* dedicated to the Ren Duka novels, Lily Babenko sought to redress what she felt were the wrongs done in the novel to Sibéal's real-life counterpart, by offering a sketch of the author's mother as seen through the eyes of friends, neighbours and family. To Babenko, the toxic depiction of Sibéal (which readers would doubtless assume was based on the author's mother) is symptomatic of a deeper streak of dishonesty and self-pity running through *Ren Duka's Childhood*. Babenko was not alone in her distaste for the novel. The critic Padma Panaev's takedown of *Ren Duka's Childhood* in her widely shared essay 'Long Dark

Stag-Night of the Soul: the Problem with Our New Male Writers' won her a place among the author's lifelong enemies. Her *ad hominem* broadside is worth quoting at length:

> Having come into his own as a novelist during the patriarchy's terminal phase, just as its once impregnable citadels were about to collapse, he is too miserly of spirit to cede the power to which he no longer has a legitimate claim, too wilful or obtuse to evolve with the times, and too ineffectual to launch a credible opposition. And so he retreats into vengeful, onanistic rancour, pettiness, camouflaged grievance, automatic contrarianism and – since he's so fond of alluding to Nietzsche – *ressentiment*. The 'Ren Duka' depicted here is interesting primarily as a reminder of how much vigilance is still required, and how much work still needs to be done. The most generous thing to be said (of both author and creation) is that, in spite of everything, it's for the best that 'Ren Duka' decided to become a writer. Otherwise, he would have made a dangerous Incel.

The novel's most successful (and least objectionable) element is an account of the rivalry among Ren and his peers as to who can draw the best MechWarrior. The craze begins when Ren shows his classmates a pencil drawing he has made in his copybook of a Mech – the colossal battle robots featured in video games and manga. The picture (which owes a clear stylistic debt to Katsuhiro Otomo) has the hoped-for effect: the other boys admire it and tell Ren how skilled he is at drawing. A red-haired boy named Mark Donovan takes to following Ren around, listening keenly to everything he says.

Two days later, another boy, Robbie Cleary, brings in his own MechWarrior drawing. The boys lean around the image, pointing out innovative features and stylistic flourishes. Ren hangs back, watching them fawn over Cleary's Mech. Guided by the opinions of a popular boy named Brian O'Brien, they form a consensus: Cleary's new image is a definite advancement on Ren's. There are more and better details, a sophistication to the weaponry, and a degree of ornamentation to the cockpit that makes Ren's drawing look under-imagined. Cleary's Mech has 'balance' and 'poise', they say, echoing O'Brien. One boy suggests that Ren's picture was never really that good to begin with – they were merely taken in by its novelty, but now they can see how it's really done. Ren goes home wounded by the crowd's inconstancy. During Geography class the following day he begins drawing a new MechWarrior, taking pains with even the minutest detail. He keeps working on it that evening in his bedroom. By 9 p.m. he is done. He takes the drawing to show his sister Nicole, who is finishing her homework in her bedroom. She says she likes it, it's a good picture, but he knows she can't appreciate it like they will in school. The following day, he waits till the morning break to show it around. The boys are unanimous in their admiration: once again he lords it over the classroom. By the following week, several more pupils have drawn MechWarriors, incorporating features it would have never occurred to Ren to draw. It seems to him that there are now more Mech artists than there are boys content to simply admire the drawings. It stings him to see how easily the boys' heads are turned by some newcomer whose Mech is weighed down with garish embellishments. He misses the brief period when he was the special one, alone in being adored. One day he comes into school to find that fickle dimwit, Mark Donavan, attaching himself to Robbie Cleary, who has bounced back with a much-hyped new Mech. Ren rips out a page from his copybook and lists the flaws in this picture that the boys are praising to the skies. He photocopies the document in the computer room and distributes it to his classmates. Brian O'Brien, who still has the power to sway classroom opinion, accuses him of sour grapes. The others turn on Ren and say he's just jealous that his MechWarriors aren't the freshest any more and his style is redundant. Humiliated and furious, he sits alone at the back of the class, speaking to no one. In his bedroom that night he sets to work on a new MechWarrior. This one will show them, this will be the ultimate Mech. What flows from his pencil is pristine, assured – and defiantly minimalist. His previous images, he believes, have taken the MechWarrior concept as far as it will go in terms of adornment and complexity. To add further gadgets and weaponry would only clutter and detract from the basic concept. Although he does not have the vocabulary to express it, what he has discerned in his peers' recent drawings is a decline into *vulgarity* and *mannerism*. His new drawing will get back to what counts, the essence of the Mech. Halfway through the sketch, he loses confidence. They won't appreciate where he is going with this. They will fail to see that by *taking away* elements he is attaining a new purity of vision. Their faculties of discernment have been dulled by superficial ornamentation. Nonetheless, he decides he will finish his new Mech, even if only for himself. He finishes the drawing in a state of serene satisfaction, then contemplates the image in silence.

Ren Duka Watches Football – US title: *Duka's Oedipus Complex* (August 2027)

A brief, passionate work connecting *Ren Duka's Childhood* and *Ren Duka's Adolescence*, *Ren Duka Watches Football* recounts twelve football matches viewed by Ren and his father Donald (and sometimes Ren's sister Nicole) over a single English Premier League season. Its chapters are named after the matches along with the scores: 'Everton 2 Middlesborough 0', 'Sheffield Wednesday 1 Everton 1', 'Everton 0 Arsenal 1' and so on. The complex emotional dynamic between Ren and his father is woven through vivid accounts of the on-field action. Donald is portrayed as a cold, repressed man whose emotions find expression through the sport he follows with a zeal typical of working-class Irish males. A prologue shows Ren as a young child attempting to win Donald's love by mimicking his support for Everton. He pins a large poster of Peter Beardsley to his bedroom wall and venerates it like a shrine, drawing tiny love hearts and roses in the corners. When Everton win, his father roars with delight and lifts his son in the air like a trophy. If the team is beaten, Donald curses at the telly, drinks heavily and slaps his kids around. By the end of the prologue – which includes a montage of goals, sendings-off and sliding tackles – Ren's devotion to Everton is no longer a question of mimicry.

The novel proper takes place when Ren is twelve. Donald

and his son begin the league season with high hopes. An early 3-0 win over Manchester United has the pair euphoric. But as the weeks pass it becomes clear that Everton are having their worst season in over a decade. At one stage, it looks as if they might be relegated. By mid-season, the atmosphere in the household hits a nadir. Ren hears his parents screaming at each other downstairs while he lies in bed. One night he hears a shriek followed by a dull thump, then nothing. The next day his mother sits in silence in the front room with the curtains drawn, pressing a pack of frozen peas to her cheek. At such times, Ren is frightened by the ferocity of his hatred for his father. As the season unfolds, football gains a tyrannical sway over his emotions. If Everton are beaten on a Saturday, he plunges into a desolation that does not relent for days; if they win, he becomes elated to the point of mania.

In the spring, when the danger of relegation has been averted, father and son travel to Liverpool on the ferry from Dublin to see their team play a home game at Goodison Park. Everton beat Nottingham Forest 3-0. Ren will thereafter recall this as the happiest day of his life. A euphoric passage describes each of the goals, along with the sights and sound in the crowded stadium on 'that eternal day'. Rather than end on this rapturous high, the final pages of *Ren Duka Watches Football* recount Everton's last game of the season, away to Manchester City. They are badly beaten – 5-1 – and finish the league in thirteenth place. Two Everton players are sent off and a sordid atmosphere falls over the players and fans. In the days that follow, Donald is morose and ill-tempered – it's as if the Goodison Park victory never happened. Ren compares his father to a dead sun, draining the light from anyone who draws near.

On the final page, looking back across decades, Ren Duka recognises that all of his life's seeking and questioning, his appetites and addictions, his opiates and alcohol, were expressions of a longing to experience again the sense of wholeness and bliss he felt one magical afternoon in Goodison Park, 'when Beardsley buried the ball in the top corner and the crowd – *we* – lost ourselves in a joy beyond language'.

Ren Duka's Adolescence – US Title: *Duka Hardcore*
(December 2027)

While some might have expected the accusations of misogyny
that followed the publication of *Ren Duka's Childhood* to
prompt a conciliatory turn, the author's novel of teenhood was
no less provocative. In many respects a barrage of tastelessness,
Ren Duka's Adolescence is shot through with inchoate yearning
and wide-eyed perplexity. While working at a series of menial
jobs throughout his adolescence in suburban south Dublin,
Ren Duka elaborates long, sadistic fantasies of revenge on
his bosses and boorish co-workers. As if trying to force his
readers to experience for themselves the tedium of these jobs,
he narrates his daily tasks in grinding and repetitive detail. The
flat, affectless prose is relieved only by teenage Ren's violent
and sexual reveries. The abjection of adolescent male sexuality
is hardly unbroken literary ground, yet few have written into
it with such kamikaze dedication. Of the novel's 137 pages, 61
have descriptions of masturbation, 77 show Ren lusting after
co-workers, teachers or random girls on the street, and zero
contain instances of actual sexual intercourse. Fleshing out
the scenes of jerking off and rejection are accounts of gigs
in grimy pubs by the numerous punk bands Ren plays in to
vent his aggression and thwarted libido (band names include
Acrobats of Vacuity, Little Hitler, Desolations, Miss Treblinka,
and Stab!).

'All teenage boys are fascists,' Ren Duka declares in a section devoted to the brief and tumultuous career of one of these bands, Effete Prognosis. Ren forms the group when he is seventeen with three similarly disgruntled school friends. He plays guitar, and his bookish friend Pete Hinley, with whom he spends many nights getting blackout drunk, is the vocalist. At first they rehearse at a studio in the suburbs, but their sessions soon migrate to the dank basement of a huge, dilapidated house in the middle of an industrial estate which an older friend is squatting. One Friday night, celebrating the band's formation with a bottle of vodka and a quarter of hash, the four members decide that Effete Prognosis's *raison d'être* will be to swim against the tide, do everything wrong, embrace the most reactionary and moronic attitudes. Following Pete's lead, they take inspiration from the Marquise de Sade, the IRA, Valerie Solanas, Lenin, Pol Pot, Al Qaida, Eminem, the Baader-Meinhof group, the film *Battle Royale*, Yukio Mishima, and the Italian Futurists. Where other bands celebrate freedom and hedonism, Effete Prognosis will stand for order, purity and dogmatism. They adopt certain postures from the Futurist Manifesto, such as contempt for women and reverence for war. The first rule Ren lays down for the band is that, while songwriting duties are to be shared, no band member is allowed to write songs if he is currently in a romantic relationship. This suits Ren, who does not have a girlfriend, and annoys Pete, who does (namely Martina, whose attractiveness wounds Ren). Ren argues that he has seen other bands crumble into laxness and mediocrity as soon as females come on the scene. Reluctantly, the others consent. The second rule Ren posits is that no one in the band can let their hair grow longer than two inches – long hair breeds slackness of thought and blocks out subtler frequencies, he insists. To assert himself and keep Ren's dictatorial tendencies in check, Pete agrees to these two rules on the condition that Ren accepts a third: the jersey or insignia of any football team may not be worn at gigs or during rehearsals. Ren accedes. Effete Prognosis practise for four hours every weekend, playing fast and bellicose punk songs (and some surprisingly quiet, gentle ones) before throwing the instruments aside to get blitzed on vodka, cans of Dutch Gold and hash. They devote a great deal of time to discussing the band's ideological underpinnings, collating quotes from philosophers, theocrats, revolutionaries and spree killers, and dreaming up insurrectionary stunts to further their agenda. They write a manifesto in which they call for a militant Christianity, mass executions, traditional gender roles, war for war's sake, a ban on contraceptives, 'purity of the will' and racial agitation. Although they have yet to record a note, they debate whether to title their first album 'War on Women', 'Cruel Youth', 'Sexual Terminator', 'Pity Makes Pain Contagious', 'Third World Problems', or 'Fate is Cruel and Men are Wretched'. One Friday night, as they're drinking cans in the drummer Steven Foley's cramped bedroom, Pete casually announces that he's going to bring Martina along to the following afternoon's rehearsal. Ren stares at him for an uncomfortably long time. No one speaks. Then Ren hurls his can of lager at the wall next to Pete's head. Steven Foley curses as foam sprays the room. 'No fucking way,' Ren snarls. Later he apologies to Steven for throwing the can. He spends the rest of the night in a dark mood, drinking steadily.

Pete doesn't bring Martina to rehearsals the following day,

but Ren senses his power recede and is desperate to cling on. During a cigarette break in the rehearsal space, he reads an eccentric list of new decrees. First of all, band members must only wear black (with an optional dash of red) during rehearsals and live performances – 'all these purples and blues are making us impotent'. Secondly, no more drinking cider or Jaegermeister: only lager and vodka, solid proletarian drinks. Thirdly, guitars should be slung as low as the adjustable straps allow. Fourthly, band members must refrain from masturbation for one night before rehearsals and four nights before playing live. Fifthly, band members with girlfriends must not see these girlfriends for two nights before rehearsals and three nights before live performances. On hearing this rule, Pete laughs in disbelief. Then he picks up one of Steven Foley's drumsticks and hurls it at the floor. It ricochets and bounces off Ren's head. When Pete walks out of the room, the band's mild and jocular bass player, Johnny Fitzmangan, makes to go after him. Ren raises a hand to still him. 'Let him go,' he says.

The band play their first ever live show one Saturday afternoon at a venue in Temple Bar. They've put up posters around the school and a surprising number of their classmates turn out. Both band and audience get drunk on concealed naggins of vodka. Effete Prognosis play a selection of their own songs – 'Reject Life', 'Carnal Dominion', 'Sickened Woman', 'Smack of Love', 'You're Very Intense', 'The Media Lies' and 'She's Coming to Molest You' – mixed with some covers (Throbbing Gristle, Suicide, Avril Lavigne). As they are about to close their set with their newest song, 'We Shit On Your Prophet', Ren steps up to the microphone and tells the sozzled crowd, who have been moshing since he struck the first powerchord, that the days of carnage are coming. He says it's a crying shame that his own band has a pussy-whipped yuppie for a frontman but he isn't concerned because 'the movement will overcome'. He begins a count-in, but as he reaches 'three', Pete slugs him in the side of the face. Ren reels as the audience goes into uproar. Immediately he reaches for the mike and bellows the count-in again. The band kicks into 'We Shit On Your Prophet', Pete grabbing the mike to snarl its rapid-fire verses.

As the last power chord resounds to a climactic cymbal crash, Pete hurls the mike-stand at Ren and strides off. Ren throws his guitar after him like a spear, but misses. The crowd storm the stage.

Following the gig, Pete and Ren no longer speak. With Effete Prognosis effectively defunct, Ren recruits Steven, Johnny and some friends to help him record a solo album on a second-hand, analogue four-track. The music is introspective and melancholy, the lyrics focusing on themes of betrayal, isolation, the primordial forests of Europe and the corrupting softness of women. He calls the album 'Peter's Tears'.

Although the author would later suggest that he wrote *Ren Duka's Adolescence* as a send-up of his troubled teenage self, it became a much-cited work among certain far-right and Incel online subcultures. A post-hardcore band in Nebraska recorded versions of Effete Prognosis songs using titles and lyrics included in the book. While not all of the novel's de-votees belong to politically questionable communities, its tone of sexual bitterness and apparent celebration of a warped, corrosive masculinity repelled many readers and critics. The author would later say of *Ren Duka's Adolescence*: 'It's ugly, but it was *meant* to be ugly. It could have been worse. There's stuff I didn't put in. Maybe I should have.'

Excerpt from *A Cool, Dry Place*

Much of the flak I took for Childhood *and* Adolescence *was a result of disingenuous or literal-minded critics choosing to take the novels as factual accounts. My real childhood differed in ways both gross and minor from the one I depicted. In certain regards, the reality was far more squalid. Like my creation, I attended an all-boys Christian Brothers School in south Dublin whose name has since become synonymous with abuse. If the hysterical headlines and breathless news reports were to be believed, my old school could have been the setting of a novel by the Marquis de Sade — which isn't to say there was no fire behind the blackly billowing smoke.*

I was never really abused, but a number of my classmates weren't so fortunate. In fifth year, we had a maths and geography teacher named Mr Manly. A lay teacher rather than a Christian Brother, he was a huge, walrus-like man, more horizontal than vertical, whose jowls rippled like slapped blubber. Jocular and seemingly benign, he was even popular, insofar as we were capable of regarding a teacher with anything other than automatic scorn. We'd all heard stories about him, but that wasn't uncommon with teachers at our school. We would joke that in his family life he was known as Manly Man, his children were called Manly Boy and Manly Girl, and his wife — we imagined her obese, tyrannical and flatulent — was Manly Woman. Later it would transpire that he wasn't married, but lived with his widowed mother in her house in Ballyfermot.

One morning we turned up at school and found even our most intimidating teachers in a state of blank shock. We soon learned that the previous night, two members of An Garda Síochána had paid a visit to Mr Manly's home and informed him that he was to be placed under investigation. A number of allegations had been made by current and former pupils, some of them going back many years. Mr Manly was instructed to appear at the Garda station two days later for formal questioning. After the Guards had left, he attached a note to his bedroom door warning his mother not to enter, then locked himself inside. On discovering the note before going to bed, Mrs. Manly began shrieking and pounding the door with her fists. A tiny woman of seventy-one, she found the strength to bust the lock – and discovered her son dangling on bent knees in the wardrobe, a leather belt around his neck.

We got a morning off classes to attend the funeral. Curiously, none of us joked about what had happened. We were, frankly, odious little creatures who respected nothing, but even we realised that something had taken place in a zone beyond mockery or cheap laughs. In the days that followed, I began to ruminate on the night of Mr Manly's death, imagining his last hours as a sequence of film scenes: the Guards informing him of his situation; his mother thumping on the bedroom door while he rotates in his makeshift noose; an ambulance pulling up as neighbours watch from their gardens. Each night in bed I visualised Mr Manly's final moments until they came to feel like my own memories. By now I'd moved on from the gory xenomorph fictions and was writing dark, un-redeemed short stories in imitation of Patricia Highsmith. I wrote a story from the perspective of Mr Manly: in a dungeon of hell, he recounts his last night on earth as a suburban echo of Christ's ordeal at Gethsemane. I kept quiet about all this at school, but a *strange tenderness, even a kind of love grew inside me for Mr Manly. In my final school year, under the influence of transgressive French literature, I developed a private mythology that venerated the paedophile as the last existential outlaw, thrown into a world where he is universally despised, an object of revulsion whom the community can hate without restraint. I imagined Mr Manly as an abject saint who dwelt in a zone of truth inaccessible to the human family from which he was a born pariah.*

There's another reason why Mr Manly's lonely life and sordid death have resurfaced in this autobiography. Any writer of fiction will tell you that when they invent a character, they will often borrow the appearance of some real-life person, who as they write they will see in their mind's eye. The physical resemblance – usually to someone the writer doesn't know well, for instance a stranger they notice in their daily routine or a face from the past – anchors the fictional creation, breathing substance into the cypher on the page. As I write the Ren Duka books, when I envision my narrator I never see myself, as I assume my readers do. Sometimes I see a lanky kid I used to notice on the estate when I visited my parents in Crumlin. Sometimes I see a shadowy middle-aged man with reptilian features who runs the stiles at a certain Dublin train station. Sometimes I see a youngish Philip Seymour Hoffman. But most often, I see Mr Manly.

Excerpt from *Night Taxi*

In a lay-by near Dublin airport, Henry K. Dillon killed the engine and waited. A plane angled in low, almost directly overhead, burying the car in its turbine roar. The blinking lights from departing planes trailed to the horizon. This night-circuitry of traffic lanes – its flow seemed mysterious to him, sublime. Each voyager a singularity in consciousness, lighting out for love or work, discovery or escape. A planet overdosing on experience.

Tillman Küblböck's plane from LA was late by forty minutes. Henry appreciated the chance to sit watching the air-traffic – and besides, Küblböck was paying him a generous flat rate to drive him wherever he needed for the next three days. Henry would make a fortnight's fares chauffeuring the great German composer. Küblböck had taken a liking to him after Henry had picked him up here at the airport three years ago. As they'd driven to what had turned out to be a mansion in Killiney, they'd talked about contemporary music, Prague and Lisbon, the life of a taxi-driver, *sean-nós* singers, science-fiction scores, the novels of Olaf Stapledon, native mythology, Küblböck's ex-wife Bridie Flynn from County Cork, and what were then only rumours of a European war. When Henry had given him his card, Tillman had declared – with the faintly alarming zeal that journalists habitually noted in him – that henceforth, anytime he was visiting Dublin he would rely exclusively on Henry K. Dillon's services, and he would of course remunerate him fittingly for the pleasure.

Still, it had come as a surprise when Henry received an email a week ago asking if he could pick up Küblböck at Terminal 2 from his transatlantic red-eye. Before their first encounter, Henry had been dimly aware of Tillman Küblböck's reputation. Since they'd met, he'd noticed Küblböck's name on the credits of films he'd gone to see, listened to his compositions in the car. He read profiles whenever they appeared – less frequently in the previous eighteen months or so, since Küblböck had announced he was taking an extended break from touring and composing while he dealt with unspecified personal issues. There were rumours he'd had some sort of breakdown, although he was still married to the cellist Marina Yudina, and there had been no great attack on his reputation (as some had speculated).

Watching what he surmised was Küblböck's plane angling in to land, Henry pulled out of the lay-by and cruised to Terminal 2. When the composer emerged from the Arrivals Hall twenty minutes later pulling a single black suitcase, his groomed, svelte appearance and beaming smile suggested that the media chatter had been overheated.

After a warm greeting, Küblböck fell quiet as they left the airport. Looking out the window from the back seat, he exuded what Henry assumed was pleasure at being in Ireland again, or perhaps at finally being off the plane. They were headed for an address far out along Dublin's southern coast, almost in Wicklow. They'd have time to chat.

When they were halfway to the city centre, Küblböck exhaled, turned from his reveries and said, 'So! My dear

Henry. We are meeting again. I thought of you sometimes, you know. Your funny stories, these warm memories you left me with. How goes the life of the nocturnal cab driver? I hope you haven't been shot at again. Oh, and I read your book, did I tell you this?'

Henry smiled, amused. Küblböck was an odd fish. The whole world at his fingertips, and he'd bothered to seek out and read the forgotten novel of a once-published Dublin taxi-driver.

'I found it impressive, but then I wondered, as no doubt many others have, why is this man no longer writing? Why is there just this one book? Is he *blocked*? Did his creative psyche burn itself out? But my intuition is pretty good, and I don't believe this to be the case. No. I feel it's something more than that, something subtler and more interesting.'

Henry glanced at Küblböck, smiled, put his eyes back on the road.

'Philip Glass used to drive a taxi too, you know this? Until his forties. I used to think he was an asshole and totally over-rated, but then I became successful and I realised that this was only jealousy. A marvellous man, though between ourselves I wonder if his real work wasn't completed by 1985.'

They conversed in a general way as the taxi cut through the city, tracing the DART line along the southside coast. Küblböck would stay in Dublin for three days, at the home of a conductor friend. Then he would spend several weeks on an island off the Donegal coast, borrowing another friend's cottage. 'Quite remote, very picturesque. I'll be alone out there. Like some Romantic, in his torment!' He was vague about what he would be doing on the island, but Henry inferred it was a mixture of rest, research into native music and folklore, and generally getting his head together.

When it seemed a natural moment, Henry asked Küblböck how he'd been since they'd last met. 'It's hard to know what to make of the stories they write about you,' he added.

Küblböck sighed. 'Yes. The journalists are creating mountains from molehills. That is their job. Discretion or reserve inevitably becomes mystery. The world assumes that something scandalous or dreadful has happened, or that I have become crazy, when in fact this is not the case.'

He admitted to Henry that he had indeed suffered a sort of breakdown – 'though even using that word seems to me histrionic, excessive'. He outlined the context, familiar from the press's regurgitations. For a decade Tillman Küblböck's career had been soaring. His score for the *Genesis Blue* trilogy had lifted what was already a garlanded reputation into the stratosphere. There was a Pulitzer Prize, offers to work with the greatest filmmakers alive, Küblböck's face on the cover of *Time* and *The New Yorker*. By his early fifties he could say without hesitation that he was one of the very best-known composers on the planet.

'I found I was living beyond my wildest dreams,' he said. 'The people and the places I saw, the splendours I witnessed, the social strata I now had access to – they amounted to a world exceeding anything I had imagined even as a fantastical child or a dreamy adolescent. Los Angeles is one of those cities, like Tokyo or Berlin, where one can become mad from sheer possibility. Desire is limitless – it feeds on itself. I relished this life of renown and access. I don't mean mere hedonism or sensuality. I mean extreme beauty, the highest subtleties, a state of perpetual elation. But this was when the worm began to turn. The maddening questions. The doubts. Not about myself, but about all this splendour. What precipitated the crisis, strangely enough, was a news story I read. An appalling story about a little girl. She had been abducted at the age of six. A madman with metaphysical delusions had imprisoned her in a cage underneath his floor... It is too horrific to recount. Who knows why, but this one story, more than all the other horrors on this planet, broke something in me. The doubts metastasised. My own compositions became abhorrent to me, because they could not approach the loneliness of this little girl. My thinking was skewed and extreme. I know this. But something opened up in me, there was an important message in this experience.'

'Come on, Tillman,' Henry said, turning to glance at his passenger. 'With all respect, how could that be the right attitude? You can't really believe that music shouldn't flourish just because there's suffering in the world. That's rubbish.'

Küblböck said nothing for a time. Henry heard him sigh. Had he been too blunt?

'Henry,' Küblböck finally said, 'what unravelled me was not, in truth, this dreadful story about the little girl. This was the catalyst, not the cause. Forgive me for even mentioning her. What was really driving me mad was a broader question, namely the question of beauty. What do we do with it? What is its *weight*? One can feel betrayed by beauty, abandoned by it. It promises the world, but the promise had come to seem to me empty. Just as there are slaves to money or sex, power or drugs, so too are there slaves to beauty. It's when you begin to apprehend it in its fullest magnificence that you discover:

all beauty falls on deaf ears. Silver rain on an endless desert. You want to reach out and touch it, become one with it. But you cannot. It evaporates. None of it *adheres*. Even performing in New York City to the most rapturous crowd of your life, this knowledge will pierce you. Anything that happens only once may as well never have happened at all – and everything happens only once. I found I was living in a cathedral of light, a dazzle of forms that continually astounds the mind, but I was completely alone in there. Art had become a ruined paradise, a forgotten temple. What the philosophers of the East have long told us became brutally clear: all things are penetrated by emptiness. Art, music, the play of forms – all lead to the deserted palace of the lonely god. I came close to believing that beauty itself is evil, the great deceiver. This was incorrect, yet there is something to it. I became unable to compose or perform, stricken as I was by an unendurable sense of imposture. All of this splendour amounted to less than nothing insofar as it distracted me from the face of the other, the cry of the other. The fragility of a child or a woman as she is sleeping. A small animal you could crush in your fist. I decided I needed to leave the cathedral and descend into tears and grief. To be with the others in hell.'

The lights of the city were far behind them. Henry flicked on the classical music channel. The car was filled with a blizzard of frantically mutating voices, or perhaps just one voice careening between styles and registers, accents and languages, melody and rhythm – as if an entire century's music had been poured into some supercollider.

'Most intriguing,' said Küblböck.

'It's an Irish composer,' said Henry. 'I recognise this. They've played her work before. She's our resident genius, you might say. I can't remember her name.'

'Oh, I know exactly who this is,' said Küblböck, and named the composer.

Henry laughed. 'You had me thinking you'd given up on music. The last thing the world needs is another guilt-ridden social worker. Play the hits.'

Küblböck let roar an extravagant laugh, drowning the alien music. 'Indeed, indeed!' When his hilarity had resolved, he said, 'But yes, yes, you are right of course. All of this is transitional. I know my role in this world. So many do not. I would not want to abuse my privilege through neglect or perversity, nor even through perverse compassion. It's more a question of processing experience, finding a way to earth myself so that the lightning can flow through me again. That's why I've flown here to Ireland, Henry.'

'We're almost there. I think it's that house over the cliff road. Great views.'

'Yes, that is the one. I recognise it from the photographs.'

The taxi rolled over the iron grill leading into the driveway and crossed the gravel.

'As I mentioned, they have a guest room ready for you,' Küblböck said as Henry secured the handbrake and cut the engine. 'No one will bother you, but if you need anything, let somebody know. They are very accommodating. I will see you first thing in the morning. But before we say goodnight, I really must ask, this time in earnest: Henry, tell me, why did you never write another book?'

5. Alienation

Ren Duka Leaves Home (March 2028)

The author considered the three novels that comprised the 'origins' sub-sequence a rounded success: they sold consistently well and, after the accusations of misogyny had died down, extricated him from the culture-political skirmishes he had come to find tiresome. Deciding he was not yet through with fictionalising the period of his life prior to his emergence as a writer, he now turned to the turbulent years when his literary ambitions began to gather momentum.

Ren Duka Leaves Home narrates the phase of drift that follows the end of Ren Duka's formal education. After enduring a period of severe depression and internal disintegration, Duka spends his rattled early twenties wandering in Algeria and the Maghreb, living cheaply, in flight from the capitalist grind. He works as a part-time tour guide in Algiers, Oran and Constantine, peddling a hyperreal vision of Algeria's past to willing tourists. He reads Albert Camus's Algerian essays and laments that Camus's land of sensual, tragic existentialism has been overlaid by a harsh Islamism. During his time in north Africa, Duka writes two novels, both of which will remain unpublished. The first is a sub-Kerouacian effusion titled *Music of the Sad Sahara*, which fictionalises Ren's travels and emotional upheavals. The second, *Legends of Bab El Oued*, is a thriller in which the shisha cafes, brothels and bazaars of Algiers are the setting for a conventional murder mystery.

Ren Duka Leaves Home takes a somber turn when Duka, deciding that his two novels are worthless and he has nothing to show for his years in north Africa, withdraws the funds he has managed to save while working as a tour guide, and boards a one-way flight to Istanbul. He rents a tiny studio apartment in the Kadıköy neighbourhood, separated from the European side of the city by the mouth of the Bosphorus. There, having disengaged from online life without telling anybody where he is, Duka burns the printed typescripts of his two aborted novels, and begins drinking to excess. By night he wanders among the bars along the waterfront, or crosses the strait to drink in the backstreets of Galata. Turkey's is not a culture of heavy drinking: he stands out as a morose and solitary drunk. From slurred dialogues with random figures, we learn that Duka feels like a failure, that he dreads returning to Ireland, that the working life that's in store for him if he can't get his writing published is his idea of hell. Late each night, when he gets back to his tiny room and falls into bed, through the wafer-thin walls he can hear the grunts and shrieks of a couple having sex. While the woman's voice is always the same, it sounds to Duka like a different man is with her every night.

Each day, arising no earlier than noon, Duka winces through his hangover as he swallows a handful of Ibuprofen and a steadying measure of gin. Then he goes out pacing the streets till the sun goes down. Most days he rides the commuter ferry across the Bosphorus. Watching the Turkish families on deck, the laughing little girls and the boys with inquisitive, innocent faces, he is filled with a terrible sense of loss. How has his life spun so badly out of joint? Why does everybody on the planet seem to have their shit together more than he does? He recalls the idealism and camaraderie he shared with his friends when they played in the band together years earlier. None of them are on speaking terms any more, their brief solidarity burned up in a firestorm of betrayal and accusation. Pete Hinley, he heard, moved to London and became a junkie after learning that his beloved Martina had been fucking her boss for years. Johnny Fitzmangan spent stints in the psychiatric hospital after too much acid and weed triggered his latent schizophrenia. Steven Foley was accused of rape in a viral post by the guitarist in a feminist hardcore band – the last anyone heard he was in Australia. So much for Effete Prognosis.

Carrying a hipflask at all times, Duka takes to visiting Istanbul's mosques. During his time in north Africa, he rarely set foot in one, but now he feels drawn to the Muslim places of worship, strangely comforted by the call to prayer that drifts over the city's rooftops. Istanbul's mosques seem to him inviting structures, where men stand or kneel in prayer as children run about at their feet, the women segregated in a screened-off area to the side. At the scheduled times of prayer, the men gather in rows at the front of the mosque, bowing and rising in unison. Ren admires their near-fascistic display of masculine strength. Islam, he thinks, is as much army as faith. At the Kılıç Ali Pasha Mosque, sitting with his back against a pillar, he peers at the intricacies of Arabic calligraphy ornamenting the interior dome. Stirred by intimations of an alien, geometric divinity, he tells himself that self-pity and the ready acceptance of defeat are nothing but weakness, unworthy of men. What's needed is order, purity, severity of will. The defiance and rage of his days with the band surge through him once again. Maybe he'll reach out to Pete Hinley, put the past behind them, form a new united front.

Walking home late that night, a little less drunk than usual, Ren hears a cry and a scuffle from a dark alley near his studio rental. Glancing into the shadows, he sees a group of young men surrounding a skinny boy whose back is against the wall. The skinny one is pleading with them: Ren can see he's shaking, his voice high and desperate. The others slap him several times in quick succession. Then the tallest of the gang steps forward and drives a fist into the boy's face, cracking his head against the concrete. Before cowardice can hold him back, Ren rushes at the crowd, shouting. As they turn towards him without flinching, he realises he has no plan. When he reaches them, he shoves the tallest one. As the kid they were attacking runs off, the first blow hits Ren in the side, doubling him over. Kicks and fists fly at him from all angles. He is lucid enough to notice that one of his attackers is a young woman, dressed like the others in a black hoodie. An acute pain floods his side: he looks down and sees blood soaking through his shirt. As he slumps to the concrete, his assailants shout in fright and run off in various directions. His vision fills with red light. The novel ends with Ren Duka lying in his pooling blood in the dark alley, circled by a trio of mewling cats.

Ren Duka in London – US Title: *This Is Ren Duka* (July 2028)

Middling sales and mixed reviews had some commentators wondering if *Ren Duka Leaves Home* marked the beginning of the end for the Duka series. The author found himself under unexpected pressure with the next instalment.

Ren Duka in London begins in a vivid, heightened realm that, we soon understand, is neither the familiar world of the senses, nor the afterlife, but a liminal zone the author terms 'the interworld'. Duka wanders through a radiant city that is at once intensely foreign and strangely familiar: a composite city, or perhaps the pure, perfect form of the city, of which all others are emanations. Duka walks its infinite streets in search of a woman – the lover – who remains perpetually out of reach. The pursuit leads him deeper through mysterious backstreets, shadowy courtyards, teeming markets, and towering structures of concrete and glass. The lover, Duka understands, is in the city and of the city, but she is also the city itself.

The vision unfurls in the theatre of Ren Duka's morphine-dosed psyche as he lies in an intensive-care unit in Istanbul. When he comes to, a nurse tells him that he's lucky to have survived, that he lost a considerable volume of blood after being stabbed in the abdomen, and that he must contact his loved ones so that they will care for him. 'I don't know anybody here,' he says, drowsy with opiates. 'They're all far away. No one knows where I am.' Two policemen visit him in the hospital and take a statement. He never hears from them again.

As soon as he is sufficiently recovered, Duka notifies his landlord that he'll be moving out, and books a one-way flight to London. For his first weeks in the city, he sleeps on the couch of a Palestinian he met in Oran, who has agreed to put him up until he finds a place of his own. Shortly after his arrival, Ren reconnects with Pete Hinley. Outside of social media posts, they have not seen one another in years. Now in their mid-twenties, the two young men are initially cagey. But as they drink in pubs and concert venues around Brixton (where Pete is living), their friendship is soon re-established. Ren thrills at finding Pete holding forth as vehemently as ever about books, bands, radical philosophers, Japanese films. His monologues joust furiously between scorching passion and withering disdain. It strikes Ren that he has laughed more in a few evenings with Pete than he has in his years of solitude and drift.

For his part, Pete is excited to learn of Ren's determination to become a writer. Together they visit South London's radical and second-hand bookshops. Pete, who works as a philosophy tutor to the children of the rich, relentlessly pulls from the shelves books Ren absolutely must read on accelerationism, film theory, rogue metaphysics. He loans Ren underground novels, cult comics, terrorist manifestos. Ren thinks: he's read everything. And: he remembers everything. Pete finds Ren a job checking tickets at a concert venue off Brixton high street. One night, after seeing a synth-band called Black Santi, the two friends drink in a pub near Pete's flat. Ren tells him what he's heard: that Pete turned to heroin after things ended badly with Martina. 'Although, you don't seem like the strung-out mess I was expecting,' he adds.

Pete makes a dismissive gesture. 'Typical Dublin. The exaggeration. People are so bored that they tell each other stories with only the flimsiest connection to the facts. I smoke a bit of gear. Not all the time. Now and then. It's not like back home, where heroin is the ultimate stigma and only the lumpenproletariat go near it. Half the artists in South London use the stuff. Especially the rich ones. And most of them are rich, though they're good at hiding it. The first time I smoked it was with this cokey rich girl whose friends were all models and influencers. It was fashionable in their scene. You want to try it? All the shit they say is true. It's like this one drug that contains all the others. The meta-high. Just don't do it too often and you'll be grand.'

'Ok,' says Ren.

The following weekend, they go to a house party in Streatham. Around 1 a.m., Pete says to Ren, 'It's boring here. Will we go and try the pure stuff?'

They take a night bus to Brixton, walk down a backstreet, and stop outside a building next to a food and wine shop. Pete rings the bell and a rasping voice greets him, then buzzes them in. Locking each of three doors behind them, they climb two flights of stairs and enter a cluttered flat with posters and art photographs covering the walls. Dub music rumbles from a stereo hidden somewhere in the detritus. A white-haired, bearded man who might be sixty waves for them to sit down. He's measuring out powders with a digi-scale.

'Hiya Jeffrey. We're after a bit of brown,' says Pete. 'We were hoping we could smoke some here.'

'Not a problem, Peter, not a problem,' says Jeffrey. He looks to Ren like a roadie for some long-forgotten hard-rock band.

Pete performs the ritual Ren has seen in films and read about in William Burroughs novels: lighter, silver foil. Pete goes first. Following his lead, Ren fills his lungs with smoke and holds it in for as long as he can. Then he groans from the depths of him and sinks back into the couch.

'Now you'll discover the secret of heroin,' says Pete, some time later. 'Until you try it, you can't understand what it means to be without pain. To be truly without pain. But you never *knew* you didn't understand it. Then you try it, and then you know.'

Ren laughs. He's having an orgasm with his entire being. Jeffrey potters about, making calls, drinking tea, measuring out his product and muttering to himself as if Ren and Pete aren't there.

'Next time, we can smoke some crack,' says Pete.

Ren laughs again. 'You smoke crack now?'

'It's normal,' says Pete. 'But I only smoke it when I'm on the brown. Otherwise it's horrible. But fuck crack. Heroin is the one, man. Heroin is the one.'

A few days later, when the drug has left his system, Ren understands with absolute clarity: he can never touch that stuff again. Not so much as a single pull, no matter how late into the night or how much of an edge he's got on. It's too good. If you're free of trauma, he thinks, you can enjoy a high like that semi-casually, like Pete and this middle-class art set he's in with. But he, Ren, is all trauma, all wounds and shame.

Instead of exploring heroin, he begins writing a novel. It's a novel about Effete Prognosis, about Pete and Steve and Johnny and Ren, but the names are all changed – and when he changes the names, everything else changes too. The novel's magnetic, self-destructive protagonist is modelled on Pete. But he's not only Pete, he's several other people Ren has known, and Ren himself. At key narrative junctures there appears a spectral, middle-aged taxi-driver who seems to inhabit a borderland between life and death, reality and dream, and who communicates with the young friends in gnomic utterances (this figure will come to play a key role in Duka's imaginative life, and will inspire thousands of pages of writing). When he's not writing or working, Ren spends most of his time with Pete. Pete knows he's writing a novel, but he's shrewd enough not to ask too many questions. Meanwhile, their lives in London unfold in a happy dream of alcohol, speed, gigs, raves and parties in warehouses or in the last of the city's squats.

One night, they meet a girl at a party in Dalston. She's from Argentina, though her skin is pale and freckled and she's a redhead. She's in the city for a few nights before moving to Edinburgh to start a new job. They drink vodka. They dance. Over the blaring music, Pete tells them that once, as an experiment, he lived on nothing but ice-cold vodka and celery for a week, and on the sixth day he saw God. The girl laughs. She invites them back to her hotel. On the way they buy two bottles of wine. In the hotel room, Pete pours the wine into cups. The light is fluorescent cool, the walls and fittings blue. Afterwards, Ren cannot remember which of them suggests they have a threesome. They all agree. But instead of beginning immediately, they talk. Pete sits cross-legged on the floor, Ren sits on a chair by a small desk, and the girl sits on the bed.

'This is kind of weird,' she says, laughing.

'Have you ever . . . done it before?' asks Pete.

She says she hasn't, but the idea has been in her mind since her ex cheated on her with her best friend and a girl they met a party while she was out of town. Pete then tells her about how he was in love with Martina, until one day he discovered she'd been having an affair with her boss at the NGO. He talks about the shame he felt, the hatred. He says he eventually forgave her – he had to, otherwise his whole life would be poisoned – but he's not looking for a new relationship anytime soon.

Ren thinks: he's so candid. He thinks: people will always like Pete, they'll always forgive him, because of his candour. They drink more wine. Pete asks the girl if he can change the music on her laptop. He puts on what sounds to Ren like Middle Eastern dub. Ren thinks it's strange music to play in this charged situation, but then Pete sits on the bed next to the girl, puts a hand to her face, and kisses her. Ren watches them. The girl draws back from Pete and turns to Ren. 'Come over,' she says. He gets up from the chair and joins them on the bed, the girl between him and Pete. They take turns kissing her – more gently, Ren thinks, than if only one of them were with her. Then they carefully undress her, one piece of clothing at a time. They lie back in the bed. Ren kisses her neck as she helps Pete unbuckle his jeans. Then Ren puts his hands on her breasts as his friend penetrates her. She gasps softly, as if surprised, and lets out a deep sigh. As Pete moves in her, she turns rapidly from kissing one friend to the other. Soon, she comes. As she does, it seems to Ren as if her cheekbones and jawline are lit up from within by white, electric light. Moments later, Pete comes too. Afterwards, he starts laughing. The others laugh too. Then they put back on their clothes (in fact, Ren never took his off).

After she moves to Edinburgh, Ren stays in contact with the girl, whose name is Molly. They text every day. Ren tells her about the novel he's writing. She asks him what it's about. He says it's about a nihilistic punk band who descend into hell, only to learn that hell and paradise are one and the same. Six weeks after the night at the hotel, Molly flies back to London to visit Ren. They spend the weekend exclusively in one another's company. The second time she visits, a few weeks later, Ren and Molly go to a Moist Consequence concert with Pete, and afterwards they hang out with him at a party in Elephant and Castle. Ren had wondered if it would be awkward, but it isn't.

But something has shifted in their friendship. Often Ren doesn't hear from Pete for weeks (they used to see each other every day). Ren's texts go unanswered, until Pete eventually calls him and they go to see a band or hear a famous writer discuss their work. Whenever they meet, Pete talks up his plan to go back to college, do a PhD and eventually lecture in philosophy.

Ren finally finishes his novel. It's the first piece of work he's produced that he's convinced is good. By this time, he has been in London three and a half years. A year later, the novel is published. His face is on websites and magazines. Molly is now living with him in London: they sublet a flat near Hampstead Heath that belongs to a much older friend of Ren's who writes graphic novels. By now, Ren hardly sees Pete. On the very rare occasions when they meet for a drink, Pete is subdued, gaunt, abstracted. It's obvious to Ren that his heroin use has intensified. Pete has quit tutoring in philosophy: now he's on the dole. He talks monotonously about a film he's editing on his laptop, which is composed of found footage, and video Pete shoots on his phone at overpasses, bridges, train stations, nightclubs. Pete says it's a film about the horror of modernity, the silence of time, the emptiness of cities. He no longer talks about going back to college.

'I read your book,' Pete says, on what will be the last time they ever meet. They're drinking at the Windmill, though Pete seems to have lost interest in alcohol (his half pint and glass of rum sit barely sipped on the table). Ren waits. Eventually, Pete says, 'It's clever how it all plays out in the underworld, the land of the dead, but you never state this directly, you leave it to the reader to figure out. A novel set in Hades.'

Ren doesn't respond. He considers asking Pete what he thinks of the character Alex Savage. He had assumed that Pete would recognise Alex as a version of himself, but now it strikes him that this might not be the case. Interrupting his thoughts, Pete asks about Molly.

'I think it's ending between us,' Ren replies. 'I think she's going to move back to Argentina. Things have been bad. She's crying half the time. And we're fighting the rest of the time. She's self-harming again.'

'I still think of that night in the hotel,' says Pete, staring vaguely into the gloom of the pub. Ren feels uneasy, without quite knowing why. 'I see it like it's a film, like a flashback someone has while they're dying. I see us from above, the three of us, as if I'm hovering over the bed. But the image keeps changing. Sometimes you're the one having sex with her, and I'm at her side, gazing at her face. Sometimes it's just you and her, I'm not there at all. And sometimes I'm fucking her and you're not there, you're nowhere.'

Ren flinches at the word 'fucking'.

Pete continues: 'Sometimes we're three skeletons just lying on the sheets together, and the hotel is a tomb in some endless graveyard.' He laughs in a way that Ren finds both repulsive and sinister. 'Anyway, whatever. The experiments of youth, all that shit. I haven't had sex since that night.'

The final forty pages of *Ren Duka in London* comprise a mystical evocation of the metropolis after dark, dense with the names of pubs, cinemas, graveyards, parks. The lone figure of Pete Hinley drifts through the streets and the wastelands, an addict or a ghost.

After the muted reception that had greeted *Ren Duka Leaves Home*, the sombre *Ren Duka in London* would become one of the most widely discussed and admired of the Duka novels. It marked the end of the *Künstlerroman* cycle that had begun with accounts of Ren Duka's childhood and adolescence. What came next was a pair of provocative novels that explored the life of a celebrated author at the apex of his success... as new demons emerged in place of the old.

Excerpt from *A Cool, Dry Place*

I probably enjoyed myself most in the year I spent writing the novels about Duka's youthful wanderings. By that point, I'd finally learned to take pleasure in life and realised I didn't need to be constantly at war, provoking or assaulting my rivals. Looking back, I'd never made things easy on myself. By the time a book bearing my name first saw print, there was hardly a contemporary or an elder I hadn't offended. Caustic reviews, online taunts, sweeping disparagements – the manoeuvres of a young man who feels he is nothing and should be everything. It wasn't even personal: I'd only ever known how to define, how to perceive *myself, by lashing out at whoever was around. A damaged and shady character, no doubt. Still, fame is an election of the tribe – the nod of approval must be given in back rooms, by secret committee – and even now mine seems an unlikely election; one that took place, in a sense, in* spite *of me. I kept waiting for it all to be pulled abruptly away, for a notification to arrive declaring there'd been an administrative error. But it never did arrive, and by the time I wrote the* Künstlerromane *in which I reimagined my artistic genesis, I'd begun to feel I was now part of the furniture. It wasn't so unpleasant: after years on a war footing, I could finally put my feet up and enjoy the view. But soon I found myself thinking about those musical acts I'd listened to twenty years earlier who were still around, and how they were granted publicity out of nostalgia and habit but no one really expected the music to be any good: it* was understood that such acts had outlived the moment of their relevance, that they were no longer dangerous. *Such ruminations made me mistrust myself. Had I been co-opted? Was I now just one of culture's dancing monkeys, a heritage act? Was the largeness of my success really indicative of my* failure *(of nerve, mettle, severity)? And had I not been at my best when I still craved retribution on the world for all the unpaid attention I felt it owed me?*

A person can live happily for years with a cancer growing inside them, ignorant of the tiny black seed until it announces itself in a bloom of pain. Later, when things began to go wrong and I found myself unravelling in the manner in which Hemingway claimed we go bankrupt – first gradually, then suddenly – I looked back on that outwardly peaceful period and realised that the internal saboteur had been tirelessly at work: putting plans in motion, issuing orders to sleeper cells, orchestrating a massive uprising. Meanwhile, I wrote books, travelled the world, revelled in the acclaim, and enjoyed the steady serotonin flow of the high-status individual – in short, I went about like a sleepwalker.

Excerpt from *Night Taxi*

Torrid dreams, delirious dreams. Dreams within dreams, but awakenings within dreams too, and dreams of falling through the other side of sleep. Henry K. Dillon dreamed he was buried alive in ancient Mexico. Then he dreamed that he was watching his own cremation. The urn was placed inside a slot in the wall of a crypt, everything went dark.

He dreamed he watched all of creation unfold on a screen made from the consciousness of everyone who ever lived. But there was no terminus for all this consciousness, nowhere to log the input and make it weigh, make it matter. And so it was kept in circulation, its significance endlessly deferred, like a skimmed stone that never sinks, just bounces perpetually across infinite waves. He perceived Los Angeles through Tillman Küblböck's sensorium, his newest concerto a squall of blind, meaningless will, the howl of a million mad ghosts. And now he was in the bright, small room in Berlin, with its balcony and plants. He was a prolific writer who'd just woken from an afternoon dream in which he was Henry K. Dillon, taxi driver and one-time novelist. As the dream dissolved, the writer turned towards the balcony. Sunlight streamed in as his wife, blonde and petite, entered the room. 'Oh you're awake,' she said, and poured a glass of sparkling water. He turned back to his work, writing a new chapter in the life of the impassioned Rita Doloroso.

When Henry woke up in his Dublin flat, for a long moment he could not believe in this seeming identity, these memories and this *name* coming over him. He was being fobbed off with an obvious forgery created from nothing an instant ago. He went into the bathroom and faced the mirror. Same bald head, incipient jowls. Same tired, intelligent eyes; same weight in the features. He peered into these eyes he knew were not his own. He was not who he was. He clung to this knowledge, determined to absorb it. He would not believe that *this* was really him. And then – irresistibly, dismayingly – he could conceive of no other possibility.

Henry ran the hot tap, pushed in the stopper plug and filled the sink with steaming water for his morning shave.

Akira Nishikido

I was born in the Osaka Prefecture. I grew up there in an apartment next to a large park, with my parents and my sister Ayumi. I began drawing as soon as I could hold a pencil, and from the age of six, comics were my life. Like so many of the mangaka I've known down the years, as a schoolboy I used to draw continuously. It's not that I would draw because I didn't want to listen – I drew because that was the only way I *could* listen. Still today I draw when I need to concentrate. As a child I used to draw while watching television, and in fact I still do. The fact that mangaka habitually draw while engaged in other activities suggests to me that images come not from the rational mind – not as a product of will or effort – but from elsewhere. I think of the imagination as a lake underneath the ground, vast and deep: when we draw, we are drawing from the lake the way you draw water from a well. When you see it this way, you realise you need never run out of images. But to be honest, I don't think very much about such questions. My thoughts on the matter have never progressed very far beyond what I've just suggested.

I printed my first comic at age nine and gave copies to my friends at school. It was a story called *Majestic Feline*, about a black cat with serious, furtive eyes like yellow moons who travels between worlds in search of his soulmate, a tabby who is on the run from a shadowy organisation. Just as I knew from an early age exactly what I wanted to do with my life, I knew too where I would live. When we were still children, my grandparents brought me and Ayumi to Tokyo to visit the shrine to Senju Kannon, the thousand-armed deity of compassion, to whom they were devoted. I still have the drawings I did of Senju during that trip, which was full of wonders. I remember my excitement at being taken to Akihabara Electric Town – where I still like to go to wander amidst the endless gadgets and machines. My grandmother bought me a robotic cat, which I later put into my stories. Everything about Tokyo delighted me. I remember first seeing the Tokyo Skytree, the huge television tower that dominates the skyline. Years later, when I visited Berlin to discuss my work at a manga festival, I saw the giant spike of the TV tower that looms over Alexanderplatz and it seemed to me that Tokyo and Berlin are sibling cities, or mirror cities that fold into one another across time and space, whose inhabitants are each the dreams of the other. That was when I conceived the idea for *Bushido Reich*.

I moved to Tokyo when I was eighteen, to study art and design at Tokyo University of the Arts. Living there as a young man was a dream – a dream I have never woken from. To me it was always Neo Tokyo – like the anthology anime film from the 1980s to which the master, Katsuhiro Otomo, contributed a wonderful story. Living there as a student, I felt as if I was dwelling inside the thousands of manga and anime I'd been devouring since before I could even read.

At twenty-one I published my first manga, *Tokyo Soul Detective*, in *Bessatsu Shōnen Magazine*. It ran for only five issues before being cancelled, but I was undeterred. Somehow, I never doubted that I would find success as a mangaka. When you think of all the manga that is produced in Japan – the endless shelves of titles presented each year at Comiket; the enormous shops teeming with stories – it can seem insane to try to make a name for oneself as a manga artist. It often seems to me that there are now more comic series being produced in Japan than there are readers. I ask myself how a new manga can hope to attract anyone's attention amidst such clamour. It all starts to seem futile, and I begin to despair for the new artists coming up. But then I tell myself to stop worrying about such things and get back to my stories, my drawings, my characters. In many ways I am not a confident person. I am timid, hesitant, easily embarrassed. I don't look people in the eye, and even now my voice shakes when I talk to a woman I find attractive. I prefer others to lead, to make decisions for me. But when it comes to my profession, I have always believed in myself.

Real success came to me in my late twenties, when I began creating the *Kazuko X Glittergnosis* comics. That series ran for forty-four issues and sold very well. I followed it with *Bushido Reich*, then *Gunfather* (a collaboration with Shogo Tabe, a great talent and at one time a good friend, though we have since fallen out), then *Teknocity Sisterhood*, which was not as successful as my previous mangas but which I consider my favourite among my own works. Amidst this rich creative period, I met and married my wife, Satomi, and we had a child – my daughter Reiko, who would later become so difficult. The truth is, before marrying Satomi, I did not have a great deal of sexual experience. Nor was sex an especially prominent aspect of our marriage, even when we were happiest together. I don't mean to suggest that we never made love – of course we did, and sometimes it was even very enjoyable, although I always imagined I was disappointing to her, unable to satisfy her desire. In truth, I have never had a strong sexual appetite. People may be surprised to hear this, because sex – graphic sex, perverse sex – has always been a strident element in my work. It fascinates me to draw people having sex – with animals or demons, machines or alien entities.

For several years, life proceeded along calm and rewarding lines, or so I believed. Then, when I was thirty-seven years old, within three days of each other two significant things happened to me. First, my editor, Hiro Matsumoto, suggested that I adapt for manga the *Night Taxi* series of cult novels. Then, later that same week, Satomi told me she was leaving me. I was utterly shocked. Satomi's sudden announcement pulled the ground out from under me and sent me plunging into what was to be a severe, agonising depression. In one sense, I can truthfully say I didn't see it coming. Undoubtedly, there were difficulties in our marriage. We had not been truly happy for some time, and after Satomi had endured a series of personal blows – the deaths of her mother and a beloved mentor within a couple of months; an incident at her workplace that she regarded as a deep humiliation – she'd begun to incessantly find fault with me, as if I were to blame for her misfortunes. Because my response to criticism has always been to assume that my disparager is correct, I'd come to believe that I was in truth an appalling person, a monster. But it had never occurred to me that Satomi might leave me. She simply did not seem like the type, if indeed there is a type of woman who suddenly leaves her child and husband. And yet, I wonder now if I did sense, unconsciously, that something dreadful was approaching. In the year or so preceding Satomi's announcement that she wanted a divorce, my work had become unremittingly bleak and apocalyptic. The violence that had always been a feature in my work had become ever more extreme – men, women, children, and animals were subjected to hideous mutilations, blunt force trauma, gruesome tortures. I was at this time still working on *Teknocity Sisterhood*. The narrative arc was nearing its natural end, and many readers have remarked on how what had begun as an exuberant, manically colourful series terminated in dystopia and darkness. It is not difficult to conclude that the inchoate sense that something was terribly wrong in my private life was forcing itself to the surface in my work.

Three days before Satomi's announcement, I'd sat in Hiro Matsumoto's office, across his broad and lightly cluttered desk, as he pitched me his idea of turning the *Night Taxi* books into a manga. Hiro Matsumoto is like a father to me. He is among the most admired editors in the industry, universally respected for his record in discovering and nurturing new talent, his superior taste, and his shrewd business sense. Moreover, he is a man of impeccable moral character. Hiro has always been not just my editor but my guardian, protecting me from the perils of the industry, steering me on the right course and keeping an eye out for me generally. He spoke to me that day with characteristically infectious passion about the *Night Taxi* books (I knew nothing about them), articulating why he believed they would make excellent source material for a mangaka of my range and sensibility. He assured me I would have a wide margin for creative reinterpretation: as long as I adhered to the series' broad narrative arc, stayed faithful to its tone, I could be as imaginative as I wanted with the stories – or indeed think up new stories to set within the *Night Taxi* world. It is uncommon for a manga artist to adapt novels – especially *gaijin* novels – but Hiro spoke about the stories in a way that intrigued me. As I listened to him I could feel my imagination firing up, that glimpse of new expressive horizons which is the true joy of the creative life. Hiro told me to go home and think about the offer; I told him I didn't need to. I agreed then and there to adapt the *Night Taxi* novels, even though until an hour ago I'd never so much as heard of them. (We would work out the contractual details later – I have always trusted completely in Hiro Matsumoto's good faith, always believed he wanted only what is best for me.) Delighted that I had agreed to undertake the project, Hiro gave me a stack of the books in Japanese translation and told me to start thinking about how I would make them come alive on the page. I was to begin working on *Night Taxi* as soon as *Teknocity Sisterhood* reached the end of its run.

Two weeks later, Satomi moved out – first to her father's house, and then into an apartment in Nakano, near her place of work. The arrangement we agreed upon was that, for the time being, Reiko would continue to live with me. She was twelve years old and had become a taciturn, sullen child. In truth, I was out of my depth, completely clueless as to how to navigate this perilous realm my life had become. I began to have terrible dreams: scenes of war in which I was forced to execute prisoners, or forced to watch as they were tortured to death. And yet, for all my inner turmoil, the work came along beautifully. I attacked my new project with a fervour that was intensified by my difficult personal circumstances.

Frequently I was flooded with gratitude to Hiro Matsumoto for having gifted it to me, as if he had sensed that my survival depended on a new and consuming task. In truth, work has always been faithful to me in this way. Somehow, no matter how much pain or confusion I may be in, my ability to create stories has never been impaired. And so it was with *Night Taxi*. While I was drawing, the fear and suffering receded. As soon as I stopped – I work from 9 a.m. to 3 p.m. Monday to Saturday, and, on Tuesdays and Thursdays, also from 5 to 7:30 p.m. – the pain would rush back in.

After I'd read the *Night Taxi* novels, three things immediately became clear. First, I would set my comics not in Dublin – a city I have never visited – but in Tokyo … in Neo Tokyo. Second, rather than retain the character of Henry K. Dillon and put him to work as a *gaijin* taxi-driver in Neo Tokyo, I would render him as a Japanese – Takashi Endo is the name I gave him – and I would colour him in with the longings and preoccupations of the contemporary Japanese male, such as I understand them. Third, Takashi Endo would have a young, female friend – a girl he is fond of and protective towards, but not sexually attracted to. This third decision led me to invent the character of Yukie Fukada, who soon emerged as a fan favourite and went on to feature in her own spin-off manga, *Coven of the Blade*, drawn by the excellent mangaka (and a cherished friend of mine), Mirei Toda.

For the first six or seven issues, I stuck more or less closely to the original storylines. My *Night Taxi* was significantly more violent and sexually explicit than the source material. Takashi Endo frequents strip clubs and brothels, keeps low company, becomes embroiled with criminals and hoodlums.

However, my aesthetic strategy was not one of mere sensationalism. The passage in the original books that had impressed me most was an internal monologue in which, while cruising the moody streets of Dublin by night, Henry K. Dillon reflects on the condition of life in the twenty-first century, and in particular the mutating relationship between art and reality. He elaborates his conviction that *reality is coming apart*, and that a disintegrating cosmos is no longer the preserve of psychotics and visionaries, but is now a widespread intuition whose societal symptoms include depression, addiction, mistrust of authority, and the awakening of dangerous, atavistic political forces. The night-driver believes that a new mode of fiction is called for that can mirror this widespread sense that reality is dissolving before our eyes. The passage spoke to me in an electrifying way. I believed that by transposing the night-driver's narrative from books (prose) to comics (images), I could honour and fulfil his aesthetic call to arms.

Meanwhile, Satomi proceeded with our divorce (I saw no other option than to comply with all of her demands). Communicating mainly through lawyers, we agreed that she would take Reiko for three nights out of every week. Each time that Reiko came back from staying at her mother's apartment in Nakano, she seemed to have become more withdrawn, darker, less spontaneous. At first, she told me of Satomi's erratic behaviour: how she would scream out in the night; how some days she would start drinking wine or saki as soon as she got home from work, and continue drinking till she passed out on the couch with the TV on. This was all the more disquieting because Satomi hardly ever drank while we were living together. Other times, Reiko said, Satomi would work herself into a panic over some minor setback or inconvenience – spilled coffee, a bad telephone connection – and then she would hyperventilate, rant incoherently about sinister powers and vague threats, and require a benzodiazepine to sedate her. From what Reiko told me, Satomi acted as if she had already forgotten me. In truth, *I* have few clear memories of that period. What I do remember is that, after a certain point, whenever she came home from her mother's apartment, Reiko stopped talking to me at all. I couldn't tell if she hated and blamed me, or if she was simply depressed and retreating ever further into a shell of silence. Like I said, I was out of my depth. I didn't know what to do. I kept cooking for Reiko and me: simple meals of noodles, fish, vegetables, chicken. Increasingly, I ordered in instead of cooking in the evenings. We both liked sushi, though we ate it so often that we eventually tired of it. One night I dreamed I was in bed again with Satomi. I turned to her for comfort but when I tried to put my arm around her, it fell through empty space.

When Reiko began cutting herself, she did so not in the precise, neat way that is said to be typical of female self-harmers. Rather, she took a razorblade and hacked ferociously at her forearms. Although I never actually witnessed her cutting herself, each time she did so the cuts were messy and violent, leaving a churned-up wake of slippery, crimson flesh. It was as if my daughter was determined to show the world (or me? her mother? herself?) that she was nothing but meat, rough carrion that didn't merit being treated with the slightest finesse. I tried to talk to her but there seemed to be no way I could get through. Her head teacher, Erizawa San, was a decent and sympathetic woman, but in the one meeting I had with her about my daughter's problems, she told me that self-harm was increasingly common among Japanese schoolgirls ('an epidemic', she called it), and that in many instances it was no more than a phase they passed through, an expression of confusion and distress at the onset of puberty, the difficulties of coming of age in an often lonely, alienating society. In such cases, she said, the self-harming ended after a few months and the girl learned to enjoy life again. But sometimes, she went on, self-harm was a symptom of problems that ran deeper and were chronic, in which case it might be a question of medication, therapy, even time spent on a psychiatric ward. We would simply have to wait and see.

By this point, receiving almost nothing by way of support from Satomi (who contacted me only with regard to our ongoing divorce proceedings), I saw no choice but to continue as best I could with my work, meanwhile being there as a father for Reiko in the hope that things would somehow work out for the better. I was by now several issues into the *Night Taxi* comics. I took some comfort in how well the series was turning out. The imagery, dialogue and storylines came effortlessly. Mood – atmosphere – was the series' bedrock. Whenever I had to decide what to do next, I simply attuned myself to the source novels' peculiar mood in the way you might listen to a piece of music to savour and intensify a particular emotion. And then, without fail, the next image or incident would present itself to me. I'd enjoyed similar experiences of flow while working on my previous series. However, something uncanny and perturbing began happening that I did *not* recognise from prior endeavours. Put bluntly, I began to believe that my drawings and storylines for *Night Taxi* were somehow influencing, or perhaps predicting, events in my actual life. Put another way, it seemed to me as if the images I drew were echoes, ripples, or *memories* of the imminent future. I would draw a strip on a certain day, and later that week, something eerily similar would occur. For example, one Monday I worked on a strip in which Takashi Endo picks up a woman at a bar in Harajuku. She has blue hair and pale skin, and in the frame in which we see her naked and straddling Endo after they've gone back to her apartment, I drew a small, black tattoo of a coiled serpent above her pelvis on the left side. That Saturday night, with Reiko staying at her mother's, I met my old friend Natsume at a bar in Shinjuku that had been there since our student days. I got drunker than I had been in years. The night led us to a dancefloor, and in the blur of flashing lights, thumping music and raucous laughter, I went home with a pale-skinned woman whose hair was not blue but black. When I clumsily pulled off her clothes and she drew me onto my bed, I was only faintly surprised to see that she too had a coiled serpent tattoo, above her pelvis on the left side.

Other 'resonances', as I came to think of them, were so minor I could more readily explain them away as mere coincidence. I would write a line of dialogue and then, during a conversation a day or two later, someone would repeat it back to me, verbatim. Or I would introduce a new minor character with an uncommon first name, and later that week I'd receive an email from someone with the same name. But certain incidents I could only regard as sinister. One afternoon I worked on a strip in which a man is killed in a very particular way: as a transport lorry swerves to avoid a collision, a plane of glass flies loose from the back of the vehicle, decapitating a passerby. The next morning, while seeing Reiko off to school, I happened to turn on the local TV news – and I learned that a woman had died in precisely the same manner the previous evening, just a few streets from where we live in Shibuya.

At this time I was sleeping badly, tossing and writhing amidst a helpless montage of every embarrassing, shameful, or immoral thing I'd ever said or done. And when I wasn't writhing in shame, I was clenched in fear, beset with brutal night-thoughts of a future that seemed to be closing in around me, covering me like cold, damp earth shovelled over a grave. Perhaps because my defences were weakened, I had little will to resist the irrationalism I could feel eating into the tissue of my thoughts and perceptions. In short, I surrendered to magical thinking. I began to firmly believe that I was able to guide the course of external reality through my work on the *Night Taxi* comics. More specifically, I became convinced that Yukie Fukada, Takashi Endo's enigmatic young friend, was in some mysterious way an avatar for my troubled daughter, Reiko. And I believed too that I – through Takashi Endo – needed to protect her, to lead her out of danger. By saving Yukie Fukada, I told myself, I could save Reiko. By this point in the series, I had already written Yukie Fukada into a criminal conspiracy that linked Neo Tokyo's police commissioner to the city's most feared crime family. Multiple hostile parties were pursuing Yukie, and they were closing in by the hour. When I'd begun writing this storyline, it seemed probable that the narrative train I had set in motion could only end, irrespective of my preferences, with Yukie Fukada coming to terrible harm. I concluded that I had little choice but to draw the story without allowing myself to consciously plot anything out, utter a prayer to Senju Kannon and hope it turned out for the best. I devoted three whole issues to following Yukie's narrative to its conclusion. In fear for her life, she turns for help to her tough but kindly friend, Takashi Endo. After a series of car chases and a desperate pursuit through underground trains and rain-lashed rooftops, I – or Takashi Endo – eventually extricated her from danger. Yukie had survived her ordeal, and as I finished drawing the final frame I was flooded with relief.

When I emerged from my home studio late that evening, having uncharacteristically continued working for an hour and a half beyond my scheduled 'shift', I found that Reiko had cut herself especially violently. She was naked on the floor of her bedroom. Her arms and inner thighs were a mess of latticed, gushing wounds, and she had lost consciousness. No father should have to see such a thing. In the minutes before an ambulance arrived to take her to the Metropolitan Hiroo Hospital, I wept and held my daughter in my arms, filled with shame, despair and self-disgust for having believed I could somehow save her by drawing a stupid comic strip. In that moment, my entire profession seemed to me absurd, contemptible, an industry that kept men like me lost in opiated dream-worlds.

And yet, after that night, things *did* begin to change. Reiko was kept in the hospital for three days, then allowed to return home. I continued working on *Night Taxi*, no longer expecting anything from the work beyond the pleasure it afforded me, nor caring to notice any further 'resonances' between my manga and the real world. *Night Taxi* was just a comic, just a story – finally, like all fictions, just a dream. But Reiko did begin to get better. After that awful attack, she ceased cutting herself, and gradually, over a period of several months, the darkness that had enveloped my daughter lifted. She started talking to me again. She laughed at the TV, showed me videos on her phone that she found funny. She began writing poems and doodling in her diary, like she had done since she was five. She made models of jellyfish and octopuses from wire and papier mâché, and hung them up in her bedroom. Satomi and I were finally divorced, and she began seeing another man. Reiko continued to stay with her three nights a week, but she no longer returned with tales of problem drinking or ominous monologues. The *Night Taxi* comics are still running – Hiro Matsumoto recently gave the green light for a further twenty-four issues. There are certain storylines I am eager to develop, ideas or inklings I want to explore in the shimmering nightworld of Neo Tokyo, with Takashi Endo behind the wheel of his black taxi that glides like a bird of prey through the radiant arteries of a city without end.

6. Defection

Ren Duka in the Orient – US title: *Duka: Ad Lib on Nippon* (December 2028)

When news leaked that the *Künstlerroman* sub-sequence would be followed by a novel in which Ren Duka journeys to Asia, some, noting the author's recent advocacy of an 'evil' literature, predicted an acerbic riff on Western jadedness and Third World sex tourism. While its opening sections do depict sexual exploitation, *Ren Duka in the Orient* is for the most part a somewhat derivative romance novel. Having gorged on hookers and ladyboys in Thailand, Ren Duka flies to Tokyo to perform in an advertisement for the Japanese whiskey brand Shinsho. Keen to synergise their product with a cultural luminary, Shinsho's marketing department have come up with a slogan: 'Ren Duka's Had a Few Drinks'. A company fixer explains to Ren that whereas Western liquor brands downplay drunkenness, preferring to project an image of elegance and sophistication, Japanese consumers equate frank inebriation with quality of beverage. During the shoot at a series of locations around Tokyo, Ren is encouraged to drink freely. He obeys with gusto, slurring his lines and stumbling around like a clown. During a shoot in a glamorous hotel bar in Harajuku, he loses his footing and crashes to the floor, pulling a table of glasses on top of him. A clip from the incident makes the final cut.

In between shoots, Ren explores the karaoke joints,

nightclubs and gaming arcades of Shinjuku and Roppongi. Topping up his whiskey buzz with a steady flow of beer and saki, he is constantly drunk. In such a sloshed condition he meets Yua, a Shinsho executive who attends a dinner given in Ren's honour at a rooftop restaurant in Asakusa. Quaffing saki throughout the meal, Ren orders eel but takes only two bites. Frequently repeating himself, he regales his hosts with anecdotes about his life as a celebrity novelist while they listen politely, bowing their heads.

Romance blossoms between Ren and Yua. After finishing the shoot, he stays on in Tokyo to be with her. The Shinsho ad is rolled out across Japan. Billboards, TVs and phones beam the line 'Ren Duka's Had a Few Drinks' over footage of him staggering about in a suit. Meanwhile, Ren's offscreen drinking escalates as he whirls through Tokyo's neon wonderland with the submissive Yua at his side. Never once does she complain about Ren's drinking; rather, she fills his glass without needing to be told, then carefully lights his cigarette. Louchely dishevelled with several buttons on his shirt undone, he alternates between lecherous wisecracks and drunken moroseness. One night, sitting in his penthouse with Yua and a tumbler of whiskey, he buries his face in her breasts and sobs. When Yua tries to comfort him, he shrugs her off and calls her a slut, accusing her of taking part in gang bangs. 'You Nips are all the same,' he slurs. 'You act all obsequious to the white man, but deep down what you really want is to be bound up in chains by some Yakuza.' Yua takes this in, startled and aghast. Then she slaps him.

The rest of the novel is a rambling, melodramatic love note that reads like a fairground-ride through hyperreal Tokyo.

When Shinsho publicly announce that they have signed a contract with a Canadian novelist who will be paid twice Ren Duka's fee to star in the next campaign, his relationship with Yua deteriorates. After she spends a night in the company of the new Shinsho star, Yua leaves Ren. He passes his evenings sprawled on a sofa in his penthouse, tumbler of whiskey in hand, looking blankly across the Tokyo skyline. The novel's final pages comprise a wistful ode to Japan's young people, whom Ren Duka regards as the most stylish, graceful and 'disciplined' in all of Asia.

Ren Duka in China – US title: *Duka: Sino the Times* (February 2029)

Towards the end of the 2020s, the author made his one and only detour into non-fiction since beginning the Ren Duka novels to write a memoir titled *A Cool, Dry Place*. Amid gossipy tidbits on the literary scene, avuncular writing tips, and a brutally frank account of his emergence as a writer, the book includes a provocative chapter titled 'Vying for Supremacy' in which the author confesses his anxiety about 'younger writers coming up on my flanks'. It disturbs him to imagine that these newcomers look on him as he had upon the majority of his literary elders: with contempt or indifference. Riffing on the theme, he claims to abhor and fear not only these up-and-comers, but *all* writers, each of whom represents a 'threat' to his 'dominion'. He insists that he is not alone in this 'fundamental despotism': 'Basically, every writer wants to be the *only one* being read. Perhaps a handful of the writer's heroes get a pass – the select elders and the safely dead – but that's it.' Every time the reading public 'goes with someone else', he insists, all other writers experience it as a wounding infidelity and a mark of bad taste. 'Essentially, you want your peers to die. To fail and then die.'

While the introspective, tentative and melancholy novels that followed were arguably of greater substance, *Ren Duka in China* marks the summit of the author's commercial power.

Across all translations, it sold more copies than any Ren Duka novel before or after, and sales of the English edition stand almost level with the wildly successful *Ren Duka's Seen a Few Things.*

It is also the author's lone dalliance with the spy novel. Typical of his incursions into popular genres, *Ren Duka in China* splices conventional plotting with literary intrigue and reflections on the nature of writing. Invited to travel to Beijing on a 'junket' in the company of two fellow writers, Ren Duka mischievously puts it about that he is planning to defect to China. The prank serves to vent his alienation from a Western artistic culture in which he feels perennially misunderstood and – ironically – under-appreciated. 'I'm done with the West,' he tells his friend Fran during a night of heavy drinking in a pub off the River Liffey, neither entirely serious nor in jest. A few days before flying to China, he posts on social media some images and texts of what might be regarded as a pro-CCP bent. These are met with hostile comments from his more earnest followers, including the journalist Selina Gilligan.

'What, you mean to suggest you admire contempt for individual liberty, the lack of any semblance of a free press, totalitarian control of every aspect of life, and the ongoing liquidation of the Uyghurs among other minorities?' Gilligan demands. Ren doesn't respond.

The truth is, he is happy to be going to China, all expenses paid. Whereas a number of Ren Duka books have been translated into Mandarin, the Duka phenomenon hasn't fully caught on the way it has in, say, Japan or Korea. Two days before his flight, Ren meets his agent Laura del Valle for afternoon drinks at a bar near Leicester Square. 'All it might take is one high-buzz visit,' she tells him. 'A few readings in Beijing to get the hipsters talking, some articles in the *People's Daily* and the *Beijing News* – who, by the way, want to profile you.'

'Has Kevin Mulvaney been published out there?' asks Ren.

'There are posters of you around Tiananmen Square,' she goes on excitedly, raising her Martini for emphasis. 'A booklet is circulating in the universities – a sort of hagiography. They do things differently over there. Here's how it is: China owns the future and the CCP knows it, but they have a lot of catching up to do when it comes to state-of-the-art cultural production. They want to know what we're about – the West, I mean – so that they can mimic or appropriate the best of us. As it stands, they make the phones and the dildos, we give them the avant-garde literature and the tech innovations. They're *waiting* to be seduced. This could be big for us.'

On his first, jet-lagged day in Beijing, Ren explores the city with the writer Mariya Marinello, whose first book, a collection of surrealistic fictions, has garnered much acclaim. The following morning, he is driven with Mariya and the heavily tattooed poet and essayist Tamlin Berkowitz to one of the city's major universities. Before a large hall full of students, they discuss the state of contemporary Irish literature – 'On its last legs,' quips Duka – the possibility of Sino-European literary intercourse, and the role of fiction in contemporary society. Mariya Marinello talks about how the literary imagination is inherently disruptive to ideology and power-structures. A ripple of unease spreads through the lecture hall as she goes on (glibly, Ren thinks) about artistic subversion and the power of 'counter-hegemonic perspectives'. Ren notices three suited men in the corner of the hall, sitting slightly apart from the student body. As the crowd applauds, the men exchange glances and confer briefly. Prompted by the host, Marinello launches into a dismayingly long reading.

That evening, the three writers attend a dinner given in their honour by the publishing house that has translated Marinello's stories (Ren's publisher, Zhonghua, has similar events lined up for subsequent evenings). The vibe is relaxed and irreverent – Ren is surprised to hear anti-government sentiments casually voiced over the rotating dining wheel. After the meal, the group moves on to a bar deep in a *hutong* – the long, narrow alleys that interlace Beijing. They drink glasses of Baiju, beer and rice wine. As the empty bottles accumulate, Ren becomes enchanted by Li, a tall and graceful woman from the publishing house. They measure hands across the bar, pressing their palms together. His dwarf hers. She laughs and someone takes a photograph. By the time they move on to a nightclub in another part of town, Ren is very drunk. While slumped at the edge of the dancefloor on which Beijingers slam and writhe to frenetic electro-punk, he notices three men watching him from across the room. All three are slim, dark-haired, in their late twenties or early thirties – and incongruously dressed in suits. It takes a moment before Ren realises they are the same men he noticed at the university. One of them detaches from the group and manoeuvres to his side. He seems friendly. He tells Ren he enjoyed hearing him read, as did his 'associates', and offers to buy him a drink. As the pair stand by the bar, the Chinese man leans in to make himself heard over the music. He tells Ren that he and his colleagues have taken note of some of the things he's been saying on social media and in press interviews, and that they admire his non-conformist opinions on international relations. Ren's views on China's social and political arrangements have been particularly appreciated in 'certain ministries, certain corridors', he adds.

'I didn't get your name,' Ren shouts over the music.

'Ah, forgive me, I am Xu Chen.' Two glasses of expensive Baiju arrive. By now Ren's head is spinning like it did when he got drunk as a teenager. He looks over his shoulder, sees Li laughing with Mariya Marinello and a colleague from the publishing house. Li glances up and meets his eye, smiling at him. Xu Chen seems to notice Ren's distractedness – he finishes his drink, wishes him a good night, and leaves with his two associates.

The following day, Xu Chen is again present when the three writers read from their work at a chic bookshop in central Beijing, an interpreter relaying their words into Mandarin. Before the event, Ren drinks two shots of whiskey at a nearby bar to steady his nerves. His eyes are red and bleary, his grinding headache suppressed by four Ibuprofen. To his relief, Li is again in the crowd. She smiles and waves when he meekly takes to the low stage. Watching her as a prominent Beijing literary critic introduces the three writers, Ren indulges a fantasy of ditching his life in the West, moving to Beijing and marrying this sartorially impeccable woman. The writers are to read for twelve minutes each. First, Tamlin Berkowitz reads two poems – one about glaciers and buried deities in a Himalayan landscape, the other a meditation on time and destiny. Next, Mariya reads a story about three young women sharing a house on the coast at Puget Sound in Washington, each of them recovering from some trauma or sadness. The women swim in the sea together each morning. An unspoken erotic energy swirls among them as they turn away from the world of men and refashion themselves as 'exiles from the city of cruelty, the city of violence'. In the heightened receptivity of his hangover, Ren can almost feel the renewing spray of the Pacific waves, hear the song of seals and seabirds. When it is his turn to read, he is still discombobulated by the power of Marinello's performance, but he manages to give a passable reading from a scene in *Ren Duka's Childhood* that evokes the Poolbeg towers looming over Dublin Bay. The readings are followed by a question-and-answer session with the audience. A young man asks the writers if it's true that in his books James Joyce summoned the ancestors, literally giving voice to the dead. Silence follows. Marinello glances to either side, hoping one of her companions will speak. Berkowitz looks at the floor while Ren gazes blankly into the middle distance. After exhaling irritably, Marinello extemporises about Joyce as a 'cosmic radio', not so much a writer as an alien technology attuned to the subtlest frequencies of life and death, past and future, the here and the hereafter. The young man looks profoundly moved. He thanks her with a slight bow.

After the event, the three writers mingle with booksellers, editors and cultural journalists, drinking champagne amid the bookshelves. Xu Chen detaches from the two women he was talking to and greets Ren. 'A fine reading,' he says. 'Your evocation of Dublin was exquisite. I hope to visit your country one day.'

'I'm not sure how much you'd enjoy it,' Ren replies. 'It's a bit … sloppy.' Xu Chen laughs politely. When the writers are taken to yet another restaurant, Xu Chen sits opposite Ren at the rotating tray. With charm and erudition he converses with the group about books, films, philosophy and world affairs. Ren finds he is impressed by him. At a certain point in the evening, Xu Chen peels Ren and Li off from the group.

'Come, let me show you some of the more appealing places to drink,' he says. 'We can catch up with the others later.' A taxi carries them deep into the warren of *hutong*. 'I grew up in this part of Beijing,' Xu Chen tells them, looking out the window at open doorways into living rooms with sleeping mats on the floor. They drink in a bar with violently coloured abstract paintings on the walls. The barman operates a record player on which he spins jazz, punk, and some kind of native choral music. Xu Chen matches Ren drink for drink yet never seems to lose his composure. It's as if drinking makes him *more* alert, thinks Ren, whose night has taken on an agreeable blur. Li, who has drunk only a fraction of the men's intake, excuses herself to make a phone call and steps outside. Ren feels it coming – and sure enough, Xu Chen now makes his pitch.

'We admire you, as you know,' he begins. 'But that is not all of it. I believe you and I can help each other.'

'What do you want from me?' asks Ren. 'I'm just a writer.'

Xu Chen laughs. 'Just a writer. Indeed – how modest you are. Let me clarify. Your position, your status, the circles you move in – all of this puts you in close proximity to certain … conversations, ideas, energies which are of considerable inter-est to us, and to which we as yet have little access.'

'What do you mean?' asks Ren, looking towards the door, where he can see Li talking into her phone.

'What I mean is . . .' Xu Chen pauses, gazing at Ren as if to take the measure of him. Then he speaks with great conviction. 'China, the People's Republic, is pre-eminent in so many regards now. This is no secret. My nation has become the primary global superpower without needing to wage a single war. We have risen to dominance not through military aggression or the destruction of the weak, but through force of will and discipline. I *know* you admire this as much as I do. Yet in some ways we here are still quite . . . underdeveloped.' Swirling his Baiju glass in his palm, Xu Chen holds Ren's gaze. 'Next generation fiction, my friend. Non-linear novels. Fractal autobiography. Quantum realism. The kind of work that disregards obsolete formal conventions and exhausted modes of expression. The literary meta-modernism of the twenty-first century. The – how does one say – *bleeding edge* of writing. This is among the areas where we are sadly lacking. Individualism is the poisonous fruit of your civilisation. The West has proven it possesses neither the mettle nor the discipline to withstand its climactic innovation. It has bitten deep of the fruit, and now it has fallen ill. What a pity that is. Yet we, here, the Chinese – we can *absorb* this innovation, configure it according to *our* code, our system, our values. The fruit can nourish us even as we reject the poison. Individualism need not be a hostile body in the organism of China, but an element in its unfolding dialectic. Confucianism meets the infinite exploration of selfhood. Order and discipline animated by free expression of the spirit – the world has not yet seen such a thing. When it is in place, there will be nothing to impede us from becoming the greatest civilisation the earth has ever known.'

Ren takes this in, looking past Xu Chen's shoulder. He can no longer see Li. 'But isn't that why you invite us here to talk about our books?' he asks. 'So you can learn our moves, glean some ideas from us?'

'True, my dear Mr Duka. But it is not enough. We must accelerate the process of evolution, take *great* strides, not over decades, but in the next five years. In our ministry we have been planning this with great focus.'

'I'm still confused, Xu,' says Ren. 'I don't get what you need from *me*. My novels are already being published here.'

Xu Chen throws up his hands in an amiable gesture. 'We require very little, I assure you. All I'm asking is that you contact me every so often, using channels I will make open to you. I want only for you to report to me little things you hear, what's being said at the parties and launches in Dublin, in London, in Berlin. Literary gossip, in essence. Who is *hot* and who is *passé*. What is worth reading. Scandals, disputes, controversies. Secrets. Think of me as your curious, bookish friend in Beijing. That is the substance of it. Perhaps I will very occasionally ask you to influence literary tastes in one direction or another – for instance, to favourably or unfavourably review a particular novelist...'

Ren drains his Baiju just as Li comes back in from the street. He looks at Xu Chen and says, 'Come on, Xu. You're not seriously trying to tell me you believe innovative prose fiction is the missing upgrade that will allow China to complete its hegemony.'

'Of course not. But it is *one* of the assets. Perhaps among the most crucial, in that it is where the West's individualism attains its true efflorescence. There are many others. Your musicians, your game developers, your influencers – we are working on all these fronts, and we have had considerable success attracting exceptionally fine minds to our cause. There are many more Westerners than you might think who are only too willing to share their knowledge and their networks with us. Some of them you already count among your friends. Just like you, they realise they were born on the deck of a leaky ship that is already going under, and the best they can do with their gifts is deliver them for safekeeping to a power that still has a great destiny in its future.' Xu Chen falls silent, assessing Ren's reaction. With a raised arm he gestures at the bar and the city beyond. 'Imagine it, Mr. Duka. Wouldn't you like to relocate here? Four or five years down the line, you could begin a wonderful new life in China. Believe me, we are very generous to those who choose to help us. As for the West, what is it you think you owe them? You've given them so much, yet all they do is spit at you and call you Nazi.' Xu Chen glances at Li, who has sat down at the table. Quietly he repeats, 'You could be very happy here. You could have anything you want.'

Ren peers into the dregs of his glass. The Baiju has tipped him over – he wants to tell Li that he's in love with her. He turns to Xu Chen and says, 'I don't know, Xu. Let me think about it.'

Xu Chen smiles. 'That is all I ask. Now please, let us talk no more of this tonight. There are some superb bars and a peerless nightclub I wish to show you. Let us finish our drinks and move on.'

Late the following morning, Ren awakes with a satanic hangover. He recalls that Xu Chen had left some time after midnight, so it was just him and Li. He blurrily remembers taking a taxi home with her, and reaching out to take Li's hand in his own – or had she taken *his* hand? Anxiety roils his guts. He seems to recall that she got out first, glancing back at him as the taxi pulled away, her face pale and inscrutable. He has a sense that something terrible has happened. Disturbed by how wretched he feels and how little he can remember, he wonders if his drink was spiked. Standing under the shower he feels slightly better. Having showered, he sits naked at the desk and opens his laptop. On his desktop screen he finds a series of unfamiliar files, already opened. Photographs – some in colour, some in black and white – show Ren at various bars, receptions and book events. A number of photos show him and Li in a nightclub. The photographer seems to have been close at hand, although Ren noticed nothing. More unnerving still is a video that shows him and Li in the back of a taxi. They are viewed from the front, both looking forward, neither of them smiling or saying much. Thirty seconds into the video, Ren places his hand over Li's. The camera zooms in on their linked hands, freezing on the image.

The harsh ring tone of his hotel phone startles him. He rises from his desk to pick up the bedside receiver. 'Hello?' he says. The line is silent. 'Is someone there?' He hears a click and the call ends. When he returns to his laptop, the desktop has been remotely wiped – only his familiar files remain.

At the hotel reception he is informed that Tamlin Berkowitz, Mariya Marinello and their institutional minder have all left Beijing early, taking a morning flight home after deciding that the air pollution had become intolerable. They apologised for having left without him, but had been unable to get through to his room. Just then, his mobile phone buzzes in his pocket. It's a local number. Already knowing who is on the other end, he picks up. Xu Chen's voice is measured and polite as ever. 'I must apologise for the heavy-handed and vulgar methods of my associates, these foolish habits of theirs. They are still living in Mao's times. They lack subtlety. Please do not feel offended.'

'They took *videos* of me, Xu,' Ren says. 'They secretly photographed me and Li. This is some Putin shit. What kind of way is that to treat somebody?'

Xu Chen's tone is conciliatory: 'I know. I truly do. Again, I apologise deeply for this foolishness. You may trust it will not happen again. Everything we discussed still stands. Please trust me. On your return to Dublin I will make known to you the channels by which you can contact me, any time. I am confident that we will work well together. Not only are our interests aligned, but the basis of our collaboration will be... our friendship.'

Ren ends the call. He steps out of the foyer into the city. Although Mariya and Tamlin have fled the pollution, the morning is clear and bright. The smog that hung over Beijing since their arrival has dispersed overnight. In spite of everything – the hacking of his laptop, his sense that his fate is henceforth bound up with the Chinese Communist Party – a wave of euphoria courses through Ren Duka. He is an insignificant speck on a civilisation that will remain forever inscrutable to him – but perhaps he can *serve* it, in some tiny way. On impulse he takes a taxi to Tiananmen Square. In the bright morning sun the space is immense and majestic. The portraits of Xi Jinping and Chairman Mao stir something deep in Ren – he finds his cheeks are moist with tears. Chinese tourists mill about in streams directed by men in grey uniforms while taxis soar across the square's vast surface in all directions, seemingly chaotic yet immaculate in their synchronicity. As Ren crosses between two pedestrian islands, a troop of soldiers in green uniforms and berets marches towards him in lockstep. None of the soldiers so much as glances up at him as they file past, the metronomic clomp of their boots reverberating in the morning air. He has never seen anything so magnificent. The sky over Tiananmen Square is bright, blue, and open, filled with risk and promise, the canvas of tomorrow.

Excerpt from *A Cool, Dry Place*

After Isabel and I divorced, I took the radical and not very wise step of moving away from everything familiar in order to isolate myself completely. I paid a year's lease on a house on the coast of Norway owned by a black metal musician who also composed film scores. As well as wanting to remove myself from the raw site of a collapsed marriage, I craved distance from the literary world, from the press, from my readers who had grown so wearyingly intrusive, and frankly from human society.

We nurture a fantasy of solitude whereby, having removed ourselves from proximity to others, we will be free of them and serenity will fill the space they vacated. But what I ought to have known by my mid-forties is that there is nothing as crowded, as clamorous, as isolation. In a white-painted wooden house a few kilometres from the coastal village of Stongfjorden, I did what I've always done in periods of distress: I flung myself into my work, going hard for twelve- or fourteen-hour days – producing, revising, fine-tuning. But there are limits to the therapeutic efficacy of strenuous work. The voices start whispering: in the dead hours between 3 a.m. and dawn; in the cold white light of afternoon. Soon they sneer and taunt and hiss all at once. Thoughts stab – the prospect of enduring the rest of the day or even the next ten minutes seems incredible.

Yet you do get through the day. I lived out there for thirteen months, breaking the monotony with rare visits by train to Oslo.

In hindsight, I'm impressed I lasted so long. Perhaps it helped that the depression I'd fallen into was so total and enveloping as to seem almost comfortable, like the dense white sky outside my house. If your body is covered with sores, it's bearable as long as you don't move a muscle. It's the same with a lacerated mind: if you stay very still, even immersed in horror there's only so much harm your thoughts can inflict. Amid unendurable memories and unspeakable fears, the flow of work and my lack of contact with the world lent me resilience, or at least distracted me enough not to hang myself. My unconscious was in tumult out there. I had chaotic and magnificent dreams, which I recorded in a green notebook I kept by my bed. I dreamed that a critic called my work a veiled confession to the atrocity of being born. I dreamed of flocks of flaming seagulls over the fjords. I dreamed of dead gods who lived in a cave waiting out the collapse of civilisation. I dreamed of underground rivers of shit. I dreamed of hearts skewered like kebab on black dildos and tossed in a landfill. I dreamed of mutant children raping animals in a radiated city. I dreamed of Isabel giving birth to a skull. The turmoil of my dream life gave me hope that my psyche was attempting to repair itself. But whenever I wasn't at my desk, I fixated on the book that Isabel, in one of the screaming fits that punctuated our marital endgame, had vowed she was going to write. 'The world deserves to know the truth about you,' she'd screamed, her face streaked with tears and eye-liner. She never did write the book, but in icy, remote Vestland I took sick pleasure in doing it for her in my mind, paragraph by paragraph, honing each sentence in the crucible of lucidity as if the book was my black and culminating masterpiece. While walking by the fjords, or to the village several kilometres away where I bought groceries, I meticulously crafted scenes from our marriage that ought never to be witnessed by anyone. With nihilistic relish I portrayed myself at my most cruel, abusive, jealous, bullying, damaged, needy, vindictive and toxic – an ogre who manipulated Isabel's latent mental illness with satanic cunning, driving her mad by resurrecting the spectre of girlhood traumas, directing her psychotic episodes like a sadistic puppeteer. Soon I couldn't tell if I was recalling incidents that had actually happened, or inventing extreme moral failings and unforgivable transgressions in a voluptuous masochism.

I wrote three Duka novels during my time by the Norwegian Sea, but I never committed to the page a single sentence of the diseased, perhaps more necessary book I ghostwrote with my ex-wife, entirely within my skull. At the time, the process felt purgatorial, but today I can't shake the feeling that the invisible book in some manner now exists, that it's at least as real as the others, that it's the one I'll be remembered for.

Excerpt from *Night Taxi*

Henry K. Dillon dreamed a pregnant woman was visiting his grave. As she stood over the headstone, her round belly burst open: a pack of squealing rats scurried away.

He dreamed he was drinking whiskey in a dark, smoky bar with the lord of death. Henry confided his woes, his regrets. The lord of death peered into his glass, rolling the ice-cubes. 'Yeah well, you know what they say. You get too involved with a sexy woman, you ruin your fucking life.'

He dreamed he found an old, red notebook that had lain under his pillow for centuries. He opened it at the first blank page and wrote down four words. Then he drew arrows between them:

He tore out the figure and set it on fire, watched the ink markings being eaten by flame.

He dreamed he was in a nightclub deep under the earth. Techno boomed like artillery fire. A girl from Leipzig, dressed in black, beckoned for him to follow her down a long, narrow passage. On the walls, electric bulbs illumined alien hieroglyphics. He knew the passage led to the centre of the world, the room wherein all mysteries lay. He expected the inner chamber to be black, but as they approached the threshold, he saw that everything beyond it was red.

He dreamed that he and Alicia were eating sushi at her place, with a bottle of heavy Tuscan wine. Alicia said, 'Maybe your shadow is the one casting you.' Each piece of sushi contained a vagina. Some contained penises. When they had eaten all the sushi, they both licked their plates.

He dreamed he was on the birthing table, flailing in a mess of gore and shit. He'd been birthed from a womb-guillotine.

And then he dreamed he dreamed he was standing by a woman's grave on a silent afternoon. He lay flowers, made the sign of the cross. He ran a fingertip across her engraved name. He said, 'Cosmic wife.'

Rob Doyle

One of my problems – my talents – is that I've never been able to separate myself from the books I read. For instance, I recently read an extremely long novel narrated by a Nazi holocaust perpetrator. For the duration it took me to read it, I *was* a National Socialist, fervent and incontrite. The moral coordinates I live by grew indistinct as in a fog, then vanished. Human life seemed to me irredeemably wretched – I craved to hang myself. Immediately after finishing the Nazi novel, I reread *The Bhagavad Gita* (the same battered paperback I'd read while wandering in India, many years earlier). While immersed in that luminous text, I believed wholeheartedly in the Hindu conception of divinity: 'beginningless, unborn, the Lord of all worlds, the silence of hidden mysteries'. For as long as I was reading *The Bhagavad Gita*, I was saved – just as, while I was reading the Nazi novel, I and everything else was utterly damned.

Shortly before I began writing the novel that would push me to the brink of my sanity, I'd given up drinking alcohol. My fascination with the stuff, a constant since my first, revelatory taste of drunkenness at age fifteen, had escalated into an out-of-control problem (the planet was locked down; I was alone and idle in a house on the Wexford coast). Addictions, rather than simply cease, tend to shift object. Having accepted that the drinking phase of my life was over, I immediately commenced a period, lasting several months and alarming only in hindsight, in which my consumption of psychoactive drugs – psychedelics in particular – skyrocketed. That phase came to an end at the beginning of 2022, when I moved for half a year to Singapore. Any narcotic highs I might have chased out there would have put me at risk of the death penalty. There are worse ways to get clean.

In the summer of that year, I moved to Berlin to be with my girlfriend Roisin. Having made good use of the solitude and boredom of my spell in Singapore, I was by now a considerable way into writing my novel. It was during this period that something strange, subtle and difficult to describe began to happen to my psyche. The simplest way to put it is to say that a transformation occurred in my patterns of noticing. I began to have – to notice – certain experiences that were at once mysterious and disquieting. For example, coincidences abounded which, each taken on its own, might have been written off as merely that, but in their accumulation became unignorably eerie. Or I would have telepathic flashes, suddenly certain that a particular person was about to call or email me – and instantly they would. More troublingly, my memories no longer always pertained to a shared reality. For instance, at a party in Kreuzberg I talked at length about a 1990s dystopian science-fiction film starring Demi Moore that turned out never to have existed. Another evening, I reminisced in detail about the dramas, victories and final league placings of a particular football season – only to learn that the season in question hadn't played out anything like I'd remembered it.

Weird phenomena also began to manifest in my dream life. Most remarkably, I began to have what I thought of as serialised dreams. As in a recurring dream, the same setting and cast of characters returned night after night – but the narrative progressed. In these dreams I was older, with a tougher, heavyset face that I glimpsed in rear-view mirrors or in the grimy bathroom where I shaved. This dream-self was a taxi-driver in Dublin – my real-life native city, where I haven't in fact lived for many years. Just as the 'I' in the dream was at once me and yet not, this dream Dublin was both familiar and alien, and seemed to exist in a near-future Europe troubled by war, rogue AI and religious extremism. I felt as if I was living two lives: by daylight, I was an Irish writer in Berlin; by night, I was a bald, middle-aged taxi-driver in a *noir* cyberpunk Dublin, who listened to his passengers' confessions as silent and inscrutable as a priest, his thoughts flowing towards some vast revelation.

Naturally, I allowed these dreams to bleed into the fiction I was in the process of composing – a novel which had started out as a light-hearted, metafictional construct, but soon mutated into something more elaborate and uncanny. As the work gathered pace, I realised that the next phase in a lifelong project of mapping out the Self would require me to chart the inner being not only in its linear and vertical, but in its lateral and indeed cosmic dimensions. Now that I was deep into the labour of actually writing the novel, the serialised dreams seemed to me a gift from on high.

Each time I dreamed I was the nocturnal taxi driver, I was aware of having a past as a writer. Specifically, I had written just one book, a novel, quite a few years earlier – but across the dreams, the title of this novel kept changing. In one, it was *Against the Gnostics*; in another, *The Undefiled*; in another, *Red*

Meat for My Blue Eyes, and so on. I always woke up tantalised by the certainty that in the novel, he – the figure who, in my work-in-progress, I named Henry K. Dillon – had written the story of my life from beginning to end. If only I could read his book, I believed, I would learn when and how I was fated to die. The problem was, in the dreams in which I was the night-driver, I almost never thought about the book. It was part of my past, the dead skin I had long since shed. My daytime sense of being locked out of the night-driver's mysterious creation maddened me ... until I began to believe that by writing *my* novel, I could unearth this dream-text, and thus go towards my death joyfully, without terror.

Writing a novel, however, is a notoriously difficult under-taking. Readers who enjoy these long and complex stories have little idea of the moral agonies, satanic depressions and periods spent languishing in the doldrums that the writer has gone through in order to turn out the product that appears on bookshop shelves, all shiny and innocent. During the phase in which I was having these eerie dreams and weird experiences, I went through what in hindsight I can only call a minor nervous breakdown. Forced to acknowledge that working so feverishly on my novel was doing me psychic harm, I decided to put it away for a few months and work on shorter, less demanding pieces till I was in a more robust state of mind.

Meanwhile, my domestic life had become strained. The breakdown or whatever I was going through was making me difficult to be around – to put it mildly. And so, when Roisin flew to Dublin in July to talk at a book festival, she decided to stay back there for a month or so in the hope that some time and space would allow me to straighten myself out – and make me, as she put it, 'less of a prick'.

The space did in fact do me good – for a while. I worked each morning into the early afternoon. In the evenings, I read books on mysticism, the occult and the Western esoteric tradition which, for much of my life, I'd dismissed as nonsense, but now called to me more powerfully than the volumes by Adorno or Nietzsche that lined the shelves of our rented apartment in Schöneberg. At night I screened films on my digital projector, losing myself in images that flickered like cave art on the walls till I felt I was living yet another parallel life, this one as a shapeshifter whose identity merged with the faces and forms onscreen. If it sounds as if I wasn't in a normal state of mind while watching these films, that's because I usually wasn't. By this point, my usage of ketamine – the synthetic dissociative easily acquired on Berlin's app-facilitated drugs market – had passed from being casual and hedonic, to something like a private metaphysical investigation: purposeful, solitary, obsessional. I'd begun using the stuff to conduct what I thought of as seances, inducing visionary, out-of-body states from which I would return awed, mystified and sometimes deeply disquieted.

Addiction is a fetishism, an idolatry. The drive is towards a primal oneness that is deathly and amniotic, annihilatory and ecstatic. In other words, all addicts are slaves to the absolute. There was devotion, zeal, and a hushed, ceremonial wonderment to my nocturnal ketamine seances. The dealer would deliver the stuff to the front door of my apartment block half an hour after I'd texted him (in drug-dealing as in much else, the Germans have got it nailed). Up in my third-floor flat, which was spacious, comfortable and soulless, I'd go about pouring little heaps of the needle-like crystals onto a silver plate or the glossy cover of a black book. These I'd crush into lines under a flattened-out banknote using a plastic card. The crackling of the ketamine as it broke down into fine white powder (less hard on the bladder and kidneys) pleased me, just as the clunk and tumble of large, cuboid ice-cubes in a whiskey glass had delighted me throughout my years of drinking. Next I would kill the lights, inhale a line or two through a rolled-up banknote, and sit back on the chaise longue to watch whatever avant-garde film I'd lined up that evening – the more incoherent, surreal or experimental the better. In these seances the boundary collapsed between the viewer and the viewed (just as, if I was listening to music, I *became* the singer's voice, the scrape of callused fingers over guitar strings, the midnight moan of a lonely sax). The films and music lifted me out of myself, transporting me to a realm beyond language or reason wherein there *was* no self, only a molten, apocalyptic flow of images and perceptions which, I somehow understood, were hieroglyphs of a divine order, a luminous stratum beyond ordinary knowing. These seances, which I conducted perhaps twice a week, didn't so much put me in contact with the dead as allow me to experience *what it is to be dead.*

Near the end of August, aware that I hadn't had a real conversation in weeks, I called my sister, Carol, in London. She and I had never been close: we saw each other two or three times a year, at family events and Christmas. She had her south London flat, her job at a law firm, her investment-banker husband. Distance and politesse had long been the status quo between us – until, several years before the period recounted here, she'd combusted over what she saw as a heartless portrayal of her in one of my fictions. Her fury had stunned me: I'd written the story in question completely oblivious to any similarities between my character (one of the few female protagonists I've managed) and my sister. But once Carol had pointed those similarities out, they were indisputable. As far as she was concerned, I'd betrayed her by cruelly exploiting her private shame for the sake of a salacious fiction. Realising I couldn't expect to be believed, I'd apologised and tried to make amends. Curiously, after Carol's outrage had died down, the incident effected a slight but positive shift in our relationship. An opening was created whereby Carol and I would call one another up every so often to chat – previously unheard of – and even consult one another regarding our private predicaments.

'I worry I've fallen out of the universal,' I began, after a brief exchange of pleasantries, on the phone to her from Berlin. 'My estrangement is all but total. The process has been underway since I was born, and now it's reached its full fruition. First I estranged myself from you and our parents, then I estranged myself from my peers at school, and later at college and the workplace. Later still I estranged myself from other writers, from the literary scene. And now I'm estranged from society as a whole. I've fallen out of the grooves of tradition, shared narratives, common concerns. No kids or house, no stake in the mainstream. How can I write about human beings if I'm no longer part of their species? Roisin's flown back to Ireland to get away from me. Figures come to me in dreams and beckon me away to another world.'

The line was silent for so long that I thought we'd been cut off. When Carol finally responded, her voice was tense, like she was straining to control violent emotion. 'Why are you calling me like this? I haven't heard from you in months, and then suddenly it's *this*. Am I expected to feel sorry for you?'

'No! I—'

'Last year when I miscarried I had to wait three weeks before I heard from you, even just a text message. I doubt I'd have heard from you at all if Mam didn't pressure you. And now you call me up and just come out with this stuff. I don't think I've ever met anyone so self-involved. I'm sorry to be blunt, but it's the truth. And now Roisin's flown away because you're impossible to be around – am I meant to be surprised? I can't blame her. You've always been cruel to women. None of them are ever good enough. It's something I struggle to understand – where it came from. Was it something I did? You acknowledge it in your books, as if naming a grievous personal failing excuses it. But it doesn't. Something went badly wrong with you, something's been broken ever since you were what, fourteen, thirteen. And now your writing has given you what you've always wanted, which is to have an audience and yet to be left all alone, cut off from everyone so that nothing can hurt you or force you to look too hard at yourself, because for all the ruthlessly forensic self-analysis you put into your books, you're the one in control and you can turn it off whenever the heat gets too much. But if you really had to live around people, then you'd see reflections of yourself that you couldn't *bear*. That's why you need to be alone – you can't *stand* yourself. I liked you more when you were a teacher, in your twenties. Your *students* liked you. You were charming back then, shy and goofy and kind, with your ridiculous military coats and your Russian poetry. Now you're like some monster who lives underground and emerges only to drag straying children into the depths. That's a horrible thing to say about my own brother, but just look at how you live. It's sickening. What have you ever done for anyone else? It's no surprise you like drugs so much. In that artificial paradise you're completely sovereign. It's just you in there. Nothing can hurt you, no one can get to you. But one day the drugs will wear off and then you'll find you're a man out of time. Life will have moved on and everyone around you will have changed, but you'll have been suspended in amber. You'll emerge exactly as you were before you sank down into that narcotic sublime where your perceptions are no doubt so subtle, so exquisite, so ineffable.'

'I'm not some fucking heroin addict,' I finally got in, outraged at what I was hearing. 'I'm just asking you for advice, Carol, a bit of fucking support. But clearly I shouldn't have bothered. You never cared. Never. I should have learned that lesson long ago.'

'There are many lessons you should have learned by now. But you've learned nothing. Your books don't deepen your self-knowledge, they deepen your self-delusion. They're a magical castle you've built for yourself so you can flee reality and hide away in dreams.'

'I can't believe this. You talk like I live in a fucking crack den. I'm an *important writer*. Don't you dare fucking cross me. I have the forces of hell behind me and I'll bring this world to its knees.'

I ended the call, certain I was finished with my sister. Later, I would learn from my mother that on the day I'd phoned her, Carol had discovered that her husband's affair with a much younger colleague was not as completely over as he'd promised her it was. My mother urged me to make allowances for Carol's distress. But the damage was done and if there's one thing I'm good at, it's withholding forgiveness.

It was shortly after that painful phone call that I started to see the demons. I wasn't deranged: I knew that nobody else could see them. And yet there they were, as actual as the sky over Schöneberg or the summer rain. Like the tinnitus that had begun buzzing in my left ear shortly after I turned forty – a low, constant din that told me I would never again know true silence – the demons were private, unignorable, and pursued me wherever I went.

The first demon I saw was in a nightclub. I'd gone there on my own, as was my habit. Throughout the summer, I'd been putting myself into trance states in front of Berlin's towering sound systems through which flowed techno so subtle, urgent and sinuous it seemed to me like sorcery. It's a cliche of music writers to describe nightclubs as modern-day temples, but now I grasped that this was in no sense a metaphor. When you stepped past the guardians at the threshold – huge, burly men with face tattoos who looked you up and down and nodded you on your way – you were entering the futurist underworld, a realm of shades wherein the laws of daylight no longer held, and where you might experience things beyond reason. It was a Friday night. I was in one of the newer clubs, a sprawling complex on the edge of the city, secreted amidst warehouses and disused factories. Streams of faces flowed around me – young people out on their night-quests. I'd been listening to the set of a Bavarian DJ when I saw the demon. It was standing very still amidst strobe lights and frenzied bodies on the far side of the dancefloor: a long, black, featureless figure, several heads taller than the people around it. Its face was an indistinct darkness, yet I had the vivid sense that it was watching me. As I gazed at the looming black figure, I was overcome by a feeling of utter desolation, as if I'd plunged into the icy waters of a remote lake.

Although I had plenty of friends in Berlin, as the shifting light announced the coming of autumn, I drifted deeper into solitude. Carol's brutal appraisal still stung, but I converted her disdain into a prideful separateness, ignoring invitations to parties, deleting my social media accounts and seeing no one except the dealer who pulled up once a week outside my apartment block. By day I wandered the city, my thoughts clear, sharp and blown wide open. Everywhere I went I saw the demons. Sometimes there was just one; sometimes there were more. They were on the U-Bahn that clattered over elevated tracks between Kottbusser Tor and Kurfürstenstraße, and in the empty underground stations. They were in cinemas, lurking in the shadows to the side of the screen. They were on the streets, the squares, the weekend markets that already felt sparser at summer's end. They were in Gleisdreieck Park where I idled on Saturdays in the weak sun – always the same, tall figures off in the distance, watching me as families and young people laughed in the waning light. Each time I saw the demons I had the impression that they were drawing nearer.

In the nightclubs too they were always there, looming amidst the dry ice, the corridors, the bodies of the young. On entering a club, I'd wander around for a while, taking it all in. Then I'd step inside a toilet cubicle, fighting off shame at still doing this at forty, although in Berlin clubbing into your forties and beyond was as normal as going for a family picnic. In the cubicle I'd take out my phone and pour some ket onto the black screen, balancing the device on my knee or on top of the metal toilet-roll holder. Carol's voice echoed in my head – *The way you live is sickening* – but here I could raise the volume and drown her out. As girls and boys chattered in adjacent cubicles, I'd crush the needles and sniff up the ket. Then I'd put my gear away and walk back out to the dancefloor as the drug came on. The music would pour inside me then, filling me up, unhooking psyche from body and transporting me to realms of beauty so intense they threatened to annihilate the mind. What I was doing out there in the nightclubs, I told myself, wasn't really about drugs or techno. Or it *was* about all that, but only insofar as it facilitated these glimpses of a sanctuary, a homeland beyond the suffering and horror. How could my sister ever understand what I was gaining from all this?

And then I'd gradually float back down from these rapturous heights, and in my bliss I'd look across the dancing bodies and the strobe lights – and I'd see the demons. They were unmistakably closer now: circling in, drawing nearer all the time. I knew they'd get me in the end. I knew it was going to be bad. But as the drug wore off and I was swept up in the music – peaking now, ecstatic and marvellous – I'd let out a spontaneous cry of joy as the DJ lifted the whole thing off, bringing the room and the crowd and the dance and the demons into another world.

7. Crisis

Ren Duka Does Time – US Title: *Duka in the Slammer* (June 2029)

In the inaugural episode of the *Loose Lips* podcast that began broadcasting two years after the author's death and examined a different Ren Duka book each week, hosts Casper Tully and Amy Clovis discussed what they call 'late period Ren Duka' – the novels published in the final four years of the author's life. They begin by considering the theory that throughout this period, Ren Duka – and by extension, his author – was operating as an instrument of Chinese power, though mentions of the CCP or China in the late novels are in fact rare. Clovis argues that if pro-Chinese propaganda was somehow part of the author's mission, he would surely have worked to maintain the 'bestseller' qualities of the earlier work – 'But in the late books, it's as if he was *trying* to shed readers.' The episode is mainly devoted to appraising *All Against All: the Duka Notebooks* – a 700-page hotchpotch of jottings, fragments, quotations and sometimes uncomfortably personal reflections that had just been posthumously published. Agreeing with Clovis's remark, Tully reads a quote from the poet and aphorist Don Paterson that the author had entered in his journal on 30th November 2028:

Failures all dream of success; but what's less appreciated is that the successful often dream of failure, whose romance they have been denied. Not for them the nobility of going towards the grave, invisible, misjudged and misunderstood.

In turn, Clovis matches the quote with another included in *All Against All*, dated 1st April 2029, from E.M. Cioran:

This is how we recognise the man who has tendencies toward an inner quest: he will set failure above any success, he will even seek it out, unconsciously of course. This is because failure, always *essential*, reveals us to ourselves, permits us to see ourselves as God sees us, whereas success distances us from what is most inward in ourselves and indeed in everything.

Anticipating the question of why, if the author was so bent on casting off fame and glory, he didn't simply stop writing, Tully describes the late novels as the 'passive-aggressive' fruit of an inner conflict between the will to silence and cessation, and the desire to continue enjoying the fruits of artistic renown.

Ren Duka Does Time betrays only flashes of the forbidding anti-populist streak that would characterise the late work. The novel's biographical and literary origins are not difficult to locate. 'There's a short story by Don DeLillo that, when I read it years ago, really spoke to me,' the author told an interviewer for the *Financial Times* over a fry-up at a greasy spoon in Dublin's Liberties area. 'It's set in a minimum-security prison populated by white-collar criminals. And one of them, he's gone down for not paying his taxes. It wasn't that he didn't *want* to pay them, he just didn't. After what happened later on, I wondered if that story had hit me so hard as a sort of premonition, like I knew on some level that one day it would happen to me.'

The author admitted he had struggled to keep track of his finances once the Ren Duka books made him rich. 'I never had any objection to paying my taxes,' he told the interviewer. 'I just wished it would happen automatically, that someone would go ahead and deduct whatever was owed. Even with the help of an accountant there were too many forms to fill out, links to click, pages to read.'

The author had narrowly avoided a prison sentence for tax-related infractions, the judge letting him off with a hefty fine. Though stressful, the episode gifted the author with the inspiration for the first and only Ren Duka prison novel, published mere weeks after his trial concluded – the media interest in the case doubled as its publicity campaign.

Ren Duka Does Time recounts Duka's incarceration at Shelton Abbey minimal security prison on the banks of the Avoca in County Wicklow, where he is serving a one-year sentence for tax evasion. The Ren Duka we encounter in Cell 109 is stoical and contemplative. He shares his cell with Timothy Pink, a former banker who was caught passing share indexes to his wife using a series of codes involving references to the TV show *Fair City*. The men play countless games of backgammon while trading stories from their past. Although no great reader, Pink has read two Ren Duka books: *Ren Duka's Seen a Few Things* and *Ren Duka in China*. He compliments the author on the tales, adding that he would have done certain things differently. To relieve the boredom of prison life and maximise his chances of early release, Ren signs up for classes in home economics, French, and tai chi.

Three months into his sentence, he approaches the prison governor, Frank Morton, with the idea of teaching creative writing classes. Morton and the prison authorities accede. Ren begins teaching three lessons a week at beginner, intermediate and advanced levels. Prisoners read and discuss passages from writers including Dostoevsky, Akhmatova, Mandelstam, Koestler, Alexievich, Conrad, Limonov and Gogol. 'A preponderance of Russians,' Duka notes, 'because no other nation knows more about confinement, despair, and the holiness of the prison cell.' Occasionally he invites the groups to discuss extracts from his own novels. With the readings as stimulation, the inmates are guided through writing exercises which Ren specially devises to suit their unusual circumstances. For instance, in one exercise each prisoner must write three pages from the point of view first of their victim, then of a witness or accomplice, and finally of the police officer who apprehended them. Another exercise involves writing to a series of prompts which Ren lists on the whiteboard ('Who must pay', 'My blackest deed', 'The lie I told', 'Faces of evil', 'Regret, defiance, remorse', 'Juries and whores', 'The rapture of vengeance', 'Streets of fury'). He encourages the inmates to write without inhibition and say on the page the things they would never admit to a judge. The results range from the comical and fatuous to the lurid and disturbing. Ren's most gifted student is a quiet, slight, middle-aged man from County Mayo who is serving a twenty-year sentence for murdering his mother – the sole crime in an otherwise blameless small-town life. Neil Dolan owned a shop on Achill Sound, which he ran with his wife until the day he blasted his 74-year-old mother with a shotgun at her cottage home, taking off most of her head. The force and subtlety of Dolan's imagination impresses Ren. Each time Dolan reads aloud one of his stories during a writing class, the other inmates listen with keen attention – he has the gift.

When he is six months into his sentence, Ren requests permission from Governor Morton to put together an anthology of the inmates' writings. Permission is granted. Ren solicits the help of his cellmate Timothy Pink and the murderer Neil Dolan, and together the three men go about compiling the best of the prisoners' stories, poems and memoirs. One afternoon during the lunch hour, the three editors hold a meeting. They decide that a simple policy will steer their choices about what to include: *No redemption for redemption's sake.* 'That's what too many of them are after,' says Timothy. 'Easy answers to soothe their consciences. The usual narrative of sin and improvement, like we all come in here to repent and walk out the gates better men. Fuck that.'

Neil Dolan nods his head. 'No redemption for redemption's sake,' he repeats quietly.

After a vetting by the prison authorities and a representative from the Department of Justice, the anthology is published by Thwarted Despot Press under the title *Hard Time: an Anthology of Writings by Prisoners*. Ren provides an introductory essay that owes a flagrant debt to Jean Genet, in which he valorises the harsh regimen of prison life and his fellow inmates' refusal of self-pity. He comes close to calling for tougher conditions – including caning – to be imposed so that the inmates 'can know the full bliss of abjection, the bitter and sublime endpoint of sin'. The afterword is provided by Governor Morton, who insists that prison is above all a place of reform through self-reflection occasioned by lost freedom, and that we ought not to lose sight of even the gravest transgressor's essential humanity. The three editors loathe the afterword but are obliged to include it. A review in the *Irish Times* by one Patricia Keating remarks on the anthology's 'at times distressing tone of harshness and pessimism' and its 'downright weirdness', while cautiously praising its uncompromising quality. Special mention is made of Neil Dolan's short story 'Blind City', in which six teenagers tell each other fantastical stories as they march through an endless night. The reviewer admits to feeling discomfited on relishing a story penned by a man who committed so appalling a crime (the Achill Sound matricide had shocked Ireland a decade earlier), but adds that the author of so haunting and beautiful a work is surely not beyond salvation. She expresses distaste for the artlessly depraved contributions from certain inmates, denouncing one story in particular (by an inmate named Frankie James Boland) as irredeemably base. The story's narrator, a prisoner serving time for sex crimes, celebrates his release by having an orgy with his three teenage daughters. (The scene is described with a queasy pornographic relish that had in fact prompted heated editorial debate. Neil Dolan finally persuaded the others that the story, 'Daddy's Coming Home', merited inclusion by virtue of the author's sinuous prose and his ability to convey in a few phrases the distinct personalities of the three teenage girls.)

As the anthology makes its way in the world, Ren focuses on keeping his head down and serving the remainder of his time without incident. This becomes difficult when a hardened repeat offender in his fifties named Jimmy Johnson, serving eight years for grievous bodily harm after maiming a man with a pool queue at his local pub, lets it be known that he harbours a grievance. Johnson's autobiographical story, 'Ten Tonnes of Steel and a Hebridean Heart', was not included in the anthology, and he's unwilling to let the matter slide. The truth is that Duka, Dolan and Pink would have liked to include the story, but at forty-three pages it was simply too long. Moreover, favour had to be shown to inmates who regularly attended the writing classes – Jimmy Johnson had turned up only twice. The editors had given Jimmy the option of submitting a shorter piece, or else cutting 'Ten Tonnes of Steel and a Hebridean Heart' by half, but he declined on both counts. As word of the anthology's solid critical reception spreads through the prison, Johnson gives Ren a series of menacing signs: a pointed stare from across the mess hall; a finger drawn across his throat in the exercise yard. Ren considers reporting the threatening behaviour to Governor Morton, but knows there is nothing lower in the prison hier-archy than a snitch. He decides to confront Jimmy Johnson. He does this in the showers – either a brave or a foolhardy choice. Both men stand naked and face to face as the other inmates make themselves scarce. Jimmy Johnson is a beast of a man, his trunk-like arms swarmed with tattoos.

'Look, I know you wanted to be in the anthology,' Ren tells him.

'Aye, too right I did, lad, too right I did,' replies Jimmy Johnson as he inches nearer, sledgehammer fists bunched at his sides as steam billows around him.

Ren raises his hands in a conciliatory gesture and makes an offer: together, he and Jimmy will edit 'Ten Tonnes of Steel and a Hebridean Heart'. When they hone the piece to its most succinct and potent form, Ren will do what he can on his upcoming release from Shelton Abbey to get it published. 'Feedback is crucial, Jimmy, it's how we evolve as writers,' he says.

The big man's eyes narrow. 'What makes you think I'd let you mutilate my work?' he asks.

'Because you've got no better option,' Ren replies. He pauses, then adds, 'And because I know you're hungry.' For a moment, neither man speaks. 'There's no shame in the editing process, Jimmy,' Ren goes on. 'Only mediocre writers refuse to let anyone edit their work.' Jimmy looks unconvinced, still primed for an assault. 'Look Jimmy, your story is too long!' Ren pleads. 'Help me help you, for Christ's sake. I've been in this racket for years.'

Suddenly, Jimmy's demeanour softens. 'All right lad,' he says. 'All right.'

True to his word, on his release after ten months served, Ren submits Jimmy Johnson's edited story to a number of publications. It is rejected by two and then accepted by the magazine *Atoll*. The published version is twelve pages – a quarter its original length. 'And all the better for it,' admits Jimmy Johnson in the first and last letter he ever writes to Ren Duka, thanking him. 'You're not the daft wee nonce I had you down for,' he concludes.

Seventeen Suicides (November 2029)

Suspicions that the author's fiscal ordeal wreaked worse damage on his psyche than he made out during 'Lunch with the *FT*' were reinforced by the peculiar and discomfiting novel that came next. Beginning with its atypical title, *Seventeen Suicides* veers so violently from the established formula that some felt it ought not to be considered a Ren Duka novel at all.

Seventeen Suicides takes up Duka's story as he leaves prison and stares down the barrel of midlife despair. Incarceration has broken something inside him. He has lost his lust for life – for books and films, food and women, art and travel. Meanwhile, his rival Kevin Mulvaney has followed up his novels *Sex Tape* and *Wife Beater* with what many are calling his masterpiece, *Troll Farm*. Ren can't look at a screen without seeing Mulvaney's gloating and malevolent face leering back. He tries to write but is paralysed by the thought that he will never top the success of his China novel and from here on in there will only be a long and painful decline. Why bother going through the cruel indignities he can see looming in his future? Why not go out while he's still on top?

The novel now splices into seventeen parallel strands. In each we see Duka struggling to put his life back together and master the demons that have followed him out of the prison cell. In one strand he manages an under-elevens football team;

in another he works with a well-known director to turn the Ren Duka novels into a TV series; in another he packs in his literary endeavours and buys a pub in Primrose Hill, London. And so on. In each case, despite an initial surge of euphoria and determination, the black dog takes up residence in Ren Duka's brain till eventually he decides there's only one way out. For each of the excruciatingly described suicide scenes, the narration switches to the third person. Seventeen versions of Ren Duka kill themselves, each in a different way. In order, these are: 1 hanging; 2 overdosing on diazepam, Seroquel, Xanax and sleeping pills washed down with half a bottle of Tullamore Dew; 3 throwing himself from a bridge across the River Liffey; 4 cutting his wrists with a razorblade in the bath as Marlene Dietrich sings from his Bluetooth speaker; 5 shooting himself with a shotgun he obtains from a country farmer (this goes horrifically wrong and Ren bleeds out on the kitchen floor); 6 letting go of the steering wheel while driving at full speed on a coastal road in Killiney, crashing over a barrier and plummeting into the Irish Sea; 7 jumping from the roof of a high-rise where, as teenagers, he and his friends used to smoke joints; 8 walking into the sea at Sandymount with his pockets full of stones; 9 provoking the Garda Armed Support Unit into a high-speed pursuit around south Dublin and finally, on being forced off the road in Kilnamanagh, rushing at them while waving a hunting knife so that they shoot him dead; 10 asphyxiation with a 'suicide bag' purchased on the dark web from a vendor in Belgium; 11 lying on the railway track at the mouth of a tunnel in Greystones, so that when the DART train hurtles out he is decapitated; 12 putting his head in the gas oven, like Sylvia Plath; 13 locking himself in the garage and revving the engine of his car so that he is poisoned by carbon monoxide, like Anne Sexton; 14 intentionally drinking himself to death (this takes several months and comprises the novel's most gruellingly unpleasant section); 15 dousing a woodshed with petrol and igniting it while he is inside (he deliberately inhales the fumes so as not to die by burning); 16 electrocuting himself by dropping his grandmother's old toaster into the bath; 17 starving himself to death over a period of five weeks alone in a flat in London's Elephant and Castle, with the television on the whole time.

The author began to distance himself from *Seventeen Suicides* almost immediately after its publication. 'Believe it or not, that one began as a kind of joke,' he later said on the *Bookfight* podcast, 'but soon I found I wasn't laughing much.' In the same interview he admitted, 'I wouldn't read it again. I don't recommend that one.' The author's disclaimer aside, *Seventeen Suicides* is redeemed by its unusual structure and moments of tenderness, such as the eight occasions when the narrator takes leave of his mother, and the eleven when he bids farewell to his dog Mayakovsky. Although it has since achieved cult status, on publication it was widely regarded as a further indicator of its author's troubled state of mind and drift towards nihilism.

From this point on, the author declined almost all press interviews and public appearances. He fell out of the public eye to such an extent that, as the 2030s commenced, the words 'reclusive author' began to attach to his name. The novels did not cease their prolific flow. But now there was no longer a public author to represent them – there was only Ren Duka.

Excerpt from *A Cool, Dry Place*

I've read quite a few memoirs such as this one – the venerable artist, actor or statesman lays it bare, talks you through the struggles and triumphs, the agonies and the ecstasies. Typically, there'll be some gentle regrets to backlight the glories. But what's often lacking in such accounts is an acknowledgement of that tincture of malice, of spite, of vengefulness *which, unless I'm more of an aberration than I like to imagine, is absolutely indivisible from the drive to succeed.*

On the other hand, age and experience have taught me that revenge isn't something we need actively seek out. Time itself is a revenger's paradise, a sadist's utopia, the Coliseum and the ringside seat. With Chronos on your side, all you really have to do is stick around. The grudges, the wounds, the festering resentments you've nurtured over a lifetime will be avenged all by themselves – it's just a matter of kicking up your feet. I don't mean to say that time heals all wounds. *It doesn't. What I mean is that, one by one, all those who trespassed against you will be forced to their knees and kicked without ceremony into the pit of fire. Catastrophe, horrors – the world will do for each bastard eventually. Their screams will come together in a great choral symphony, sublime to the ear. Only, you won't be sitting snug in the audience, safe with your* schadenfreude. *You too will be there in the choir, singing your lungs out for the others whose screams drown out your own.*

So much for generalities and philosophising. I'd rather confess a particular vengeance, a specimen of cruel and unusual punishment that predates these mellow realisations.

When I was starting out, before anyone could have known what I would become, a certain aspiring writer – young, ambitious, a drinking buddy from the literary scene – crossed me. He'd cultivated my friendship and got from me everything he could. Then, calculating greater advantage in courting certain enemies of mine, he scorned me. So far, so generic: the ambitious get ahead by such methods all the time. Those who've been made fools of just have to suck it up, and life moves on. Only, in this instance, my one-time friend badly misfired. The grand success for whose sake he'd betrayed not just me but seemingly everyone around him never materialised. Perhaps he'd crossed too many people, made too many enemies. His literary career, which he had expected to rapidly overtake mine, never took off. Meanwhile, mine rose higher and faster than either of us could have foreseen. As I ascended, I did not forget about him. Pettiness, it transpires, doesn't melt away as we reach escape velocity. It intoxicated me to know that while he was failing, he was forced to witness my glory, my supremacy. The success I enjoyed was so outsized, so ludicrously vast that there was nowhere he could hide from it. The whole world became a hall of mirrors in which each way he turned he saw my face. With the Duka novels flying off shelves from Dublin to Dubai, there was nothing I relished more than imagining his horror at the totality of his defeat, the scale of his humiliation. I knew he knew I knew he was crushed. And I knew he knew I was relishing it. My fame had become his iron maiden. The pleasure was extreme.

I set up a Google alert for his name. Every now and then he would write an article for some website or magazine, and these I read very closely, alert to each indication of his moral suffering, his smashed dreams, his life gone wrong. As I did so, I felt close *to him – a strange and transgressive intimacy. Hurting him from a distance – torturing him by simply continuing to* be *– became my secret addiction. I hated him with an intensity that today seems to me unhinged, pathological... and curiously akin to love. It dawned on me that I was writing for him now, that he was my ideal reader. Several books into the Ren Duka series, I began to nurture the fantasy that my success would drive him to suicide.*

And then he fell silent. Searching his name turned up only old results. No one seemed to know what had become of him. It occurred to me that he really was in danger of taking his own life – if he hadn't done so already. All of a sudden I understood that if he was no longer around, there would be nobody out there to witness me in the uniquely intimate way that he did. There would be no one to hate me so impotently, no one against whom I could define myself so vividly, so violently. I needed him to keep living on in the shadow of my achievement. I needed his failure to give my success its meaning, its density. Without his obscurity, my fame was a vacuum.

Then one day Google alerts announced, out of the blue, that he would be publishing a new book the following spring. In the accompanying photo he looked purposeful, collected, energised. His novel had received advance endorsements from a cohort of writers I hated or despised.

Sales of the Duka novels had been declining for some time, and the bad reviews now outnumbered the favourable ones. The moment of my fashionability had passed. Moreover, the wreckage of my marriage to Isabel had left me feeling like an echo, a ghost, a parody of my higher self. And yet I was still unquestionably an influential figure, a man whose power was his persuasion. I had many connections, was owed many favours. I could make and I could break.

I contemplated the situation for a while. Then I began to make some phone calls.

8. Reprieve

Ren Duka's Violation – US Title: *Duka's Vision* (July 2030)

After enduring the prison ordeal recounted in *Ren Duka Does Time* and the bleakness in *Seventeen Suicides*, Ren Duka finds himself at an impasse. Unanswerable questions, haunting regrets, loneliness and a dread of the future assail him all at once. His literary status no longer steels him as it did through dark phases in the past. Even his reliable pleasures – reading philosophy and military history, playing online poker, walking his dog Mayakovsky – no longer mask the emptiness and torment that shadow his days.

When relief comes, it issues from an unexpected source: the Catholic religion in which Ren had been raised. The process begins with a dream: he dreams he is having sex with the Blessed Virgin Mary. She is at once a living woman and a larger-than-life statue, the Madonna. The union happens against his will – he is drawn to her as if by magnetic pull, and although he tries in panic and revulsion to resist, before he can help it, they are coupling. The dream confounds him – almost parodic in its symbolism of a tortured Catholic psyche (even if he has not practised any form of religion in decades, meanwhile keeping an open mind regarding metaphysical questions). Processing the complex feelings of excitement, terror, disgust, shame and mystery that the dream leaves in its wake, Ren wonders if, as well as laying bare something bizarre in his sexuality, it indicates a submerged longing to embrace the holy – and if this might be the same as embracing the forbidden.

Which is not to suggest that any sudden, Damascene transformation takes place – at least, not yet. Ren distracts himself with nights out in Berlin clubs (he has been living in the city since getting out of prison), becomes romantically involved with a singer and edits the proofs of his latest novel. However, the licentiousness and hedonism of Berlin seem to him increasingly distasteful, as if the entire city is a party that has dragged on past its best. And so, when the singer breaks up with him in a cafe in Friedrichshain, Ren decides it's time to move on. He returns with Mayakovsky to Ireland, where he rents a house in the midlands. There, haunted by his dream of sex with the Madonna, which he recurrently writes about in his notebook, he reads Saint Augustine, the New Testament, Joseph de Maistre, José García Villa, Simone Weil, Léon Bloy, Saint Aquinas (whom he finds impenetrable) and, above all, the writers of the Christian monastic period. Delving into the complexities and treasures of a faith which, he realises, he has only ever encountered in its crudest form, a gradual inner change comes over him. At first his religious intimations are accompanied by a piercing self-consciousness. He tells himself that his newfound interest in Christian theology is primarily intellectual, that he is conducting *research*. But while taking long, contemplative walks in the countryside, he begins to repent of his past. On one especially long and fraught trek (the sky darkens, thunder rumbles in the distance), he feels he is on the brink of an immense and fatal depression. All the sin and hurt and sordidness of his life rises up around him like black, drowning sludge. There is too much filth on him, too much misery has radiated out from him into others, to be passed on again in expanding rings of hatred and cruelty and abuse. It seems to him that he is damned – that there *is* a moral architecture to the universe and he has defiled it. But then a new and quieter note – of fragile hope – sounds amid the inner cacophony. Out on the hillside, he realises that his entire life has led him to this moment and now he is faced with a choice: to continue on a trajectory of heedless egoism, or turn towards the light. The light, he is astonished to hear himself affirm, is that of Christ.

In the grip of an out-and-out religious conversion, Ren secludes himself in his country house. He spends his evenings sitting on the step of the back doorway, gazing at the moon and stars, lost in thought. The vastness of space, which once seemed like the purest mirror of humankind's loneliness, now appears to him as the magnificent abyss of God's infinitude and mystery. God, he thinks, is the force beyond force, the law beyond law, the morality beyond morality. His dreams become resplendent with strange symbols – tongues of black fire; children of light ascending through the clouds; serene and regal beings walking through ancient hallways. By day he wanders through forests and fields, along the river, sometimes stopping to sit by a tree and lose himself for hours in reverie. By night he reads the scriptures, the writings of the saints and the great theologians. Memories flood him of scenes he hasn't recalled in years. He remembers his devout childhood of praying to God and the angels; going to confession on Saturday mornings; kneeling with his mother at a shrine to Saint Catherine of Siena, whom she adored. He recalls how, in the confessional, he and his sister Nicole sometimes couldn't think of any sins and would exaggerate what few they had. Once he confessed that he got pleasure from thoughts of Nicole dying; on another occasion that he spat in his father's tea. One Saturday morning he told the priest – whose face was veiled in shadow on the other side of the metal grill – that he couldn't think of anything to confess. The priest angrily sent him away.

While reading Saint Augustine's *Confessions* in the evenings, it occurs to Ren that he should embark on a period of celibacy. This will not be so difficult out here in the countryside. In fact, over the last couple of years, he has been aware of an unmistakeable waning in his libido even when he is in the city, which he had long come to regard as a machine for the agitation of desire in general and sexual craving in particular. In one sense, he knows he should welcome this calming of libido as a liberation and a convenience. He can relate more fully and compassionately to women, no longer seeing them solely through the stark filter of lust. It simplifies life not to be pulled apart by crude, imperious urges that override morality, reason, dignity and self-preservation. And yet, for the most part, his declining sexual greed has made him melancholy. In a life traditionally lived – the kind promoted by the religious system he was born into and is now rediscovering – the midlife waning of masculine sexual desire coheres neatly with the transition to a less selfish way of being whose primary focus is the protection of a family. For Ren Duka, who has no children and no great desire for them, the receding of lust signifies only loss, without compensatory reward. When sexual desire had run through him like a fire, life was chaotic, beset with delicious frustration, and punctuated by moments of violent relief that were blissful while they were happening and memorable thereafter – the peaks of experience. The problem with Augustine's book, he reflects, and with all such confessions by men who ran wild in their youth and now preach continence, is that he wrote it at the stage in life when such ostensibly moral choices make themselves – when the apparent sacrifice is hardly a sacrifice at all. It occurs to Ren that Augustine's secret motive in writing his *Confessions* was to promote celibacy among the young so as to lessen the goading evidence that others were getting what he no longer could. *Confessions* might have been a better book, Ren decides, if Augustine found no respite in God but meditated ruthlessly on erotic regret, on being banished from the garden of earthly bliss as his biological organism underwent the cruel process of dissolution – in short, *Confessions* would have worked better as a Ren Duka novel.

Ren begins attending Sunday mass in the church at the village nearest his house. At first he feels self-conscious sitting or kneeling in the church, like an imposter about to be unmasked. However, the congregation is meagre and his fascination with its meagreness overrides the awkwardness. Kneeling in the pew as the priest drones out the liturgy, he peers around the dim church and counts five other people: two men and three women, all of them elderly. The scene is frankly pitiable, and he begins to wonder if whatever newfound spirituality he has unlocked might better be cultivated in private. However, he sticks it out and rises when the others rise, sits when they sit, kneels when they kneel. He answers the priest's blessings and prayers with the requisite incantations. All of this happens automatically and without effort – he did it so often as a child that the rhythms are still part of him. He recalls enduring heavy boredom at mass throughout child-hood, but now he finds he can appreciate the strangeness in renewing these tepid rituals so many years later. Catholic mass now seems to him *exotic*, a cult of mystery and weirdness that has survived into rationalist modernity. He attends 10 o'clock mass each Sunday morning. At first, it's always the same priest delivering the sermon – a quiet, methodical man in his fifties – but then a younger priest begins to substitute for him. Ren observes him with interest: this younger priest seems to be animated by restlessness and even anger. There is an urgency to his oration, bursts of impassioned eloquence that seem to evaporate on the barren soil of his wizened flock. When mass is over, Ren usually walks home without speaking to anyone. One Sunday morning, after being told to go in peace to love and serve the Lord, he approaches the young priest who is standing by the steps at the front of the church exchanging words with parishioners. The priest greets him. 'You're new in town, aren't you?' he asks. He tells Ren that even when he was a child, a couple of decades ago, the churches of this county were still almost full each Sunday – not quite the hubs of the community, but not far off it. 'The decline had already begun, but it was nothing like it is now.' Gazing at his sparse, dispersing congregation, he admits to Ren that it will not be that way again, in his lifetime at least. 'Not unless the world goes to war,' he says, 'or there is some other great cataclysm and the illusion falls away.'

'What illusion do you mean?' Ren asks.

'The illusion of security,' the priest says. 'Of stability. Of an order than can be maintained by man alone, without the Almighty. The illusion of progress and comfort, of stillness. The illusion of a peace that is not the peace of God, of Christ, of the Church.' The two men watch an elderly, hunchbacked woman shuffling away. Ren turns to the priest and tells him he often finds himself thinking these days about the nature of evil, troubled by notions of damnation and despair. The priest watches him carefully. After a long pause, he says, 'Few people talk about evil nowadays. But you don't have to look far to see it. In most public venues in this country I'd be laughed out the door for what I'm about to say, but I'll say it. The dark one is growing in force, gaining ground. Take that how you will – as metaphor, as literal truth ... it doesn't really matter. This country has fallen into darkness, as have many others. There's something horrific coming down the tracks. I'm certain of this. I see it in my dreams, and I'm not the only one.' Ren stares at him in frank astonishment. The priest notices but continues. 'I believe it will be something like a catastrophe such as we've never seen before. I don't mean a war of armies and nations or even another nuclear conflict, though all of that may well be part of it,' he says. 'I mean a spiritual ordeal, a conflict within the cosmos itself for the soul not only of humankind, but of all Creation.' Ren lets out a nervous laugh – the edge of fanaticism in the priest's tone at once unnerves and impresses him. The priest smiles and a bland expression steals over his face. 'Laughter is a common response. I understand that. It's a defence. And yet, you strike me as a serious man. I don't believe your laughter runs very deep in this instance. I know who you are, by the way.' Ren does not react to this. The priest goes on: 'Did you know that

Saint Catherine of Siena, who I saw you lighting candles to some time ago, is the patron saint of those who are ridiculed for their faith?'

'I didn't know that, Father,' says Ren, faintly embarrassed to hear himself use the term for a younger man.

'She was a warrior of faith, and a politician of faith too,' says the priest. 'I knew something interesting was going on when I saw you making offerings to her. I got hold of your books and read them. Not all of them, but enough. I think I know why you're here. We've been discussing you. Listen to me, something immense is coming, and very soon. There are many of us who believe this, and we are preparing for it. Nothing in all of this is pre-ordained. To believe otherwise is to succumb to the Tempter, who relishes our complacency. You need to consider the possibility that you have a mission and a purpose in all of this, that it was not accident or happenstance that led you to where you are right at this moment, talking to me.'

The heavy church door bangs shut behind them, startling both men. Seizing the moment, Ren thanks the priest for the conversation and walks away. He can feel the priest watching him as he quickens his pace but he does not glance back. He knows he will not be returning to the church.

The final third of *Ren Duka's Violation* is devoted to arcane theological conjectures. Between describing, in sedate and hypnotic prose, the routine of his days – early morning rises; weekly trips to town for groceries; the preparation of meals; systematic reading – Ren Duka expounds on the meaning of the Kingdom of God and the nature of what he calls 'Christness'. His theological reflections are shot through with expressions of distaste, verging on revulsion, at the image of the zealous young priest who he sees as embodying everything that has grown sinister and destructive in 'Christendom'. On certain pages, Duka comes close to suggesting that the priest is an earthly manifestation of the Satanic empire, and that the true 'Christ-destiny' for the Church is to fall into decline and ruin, scorned and derided and then simply forgotten, all but vanishing from the face of the earth. He returns frequently to the image of a decrepit rural church with a scattering of wizened parishioners: he calls this 'the face of God'. He refers to the Church's final humiliation and defeat sometimes as 'the second Crucifixion', and elsewhere as 'the prelude to Resurrection'.

Ren Duka's Honeymoon – US Title: *Duka Does Paris* (December 2030)

'Happiness writes in white ink on a white page,' quotes Ren Duka in the opening pages of the novel that recounts the beginning of his marriage to a woman named Melodie Armanet, who he had first met four years earlier when she read a paper titled 'Futility and Fervour: Modes of Masculinity in the Early Ren Duka Novels' at a conference in Barcelona devoted to his work. By quoting the well-known adage, Duka invokes its implicit formal challenge: how to engagingly narrativise an idyll in which conflict and sorrow dissolve amid fulfilling love, sensual delight and newfound faith.

Opinions on the degree to which the novel succeeded fell in a roughly even split. One reviewer indelicately described *Ren Duka's Honeymoon* as 'even more masturbatory than *Ren Duka's Adolescence* – and that was a novel entirely about wanking'. The same reviewer suggested that *Honeymoon* is best read as the author's 'revenge novel', for how his alter ego 'parades his sexual and personal fulfilment and his newfound zest in life before the beady eyes of his haters'.

After first meeting in Barcelona, Ren Duka and Melodie Armanet had spent only a handful of nights together, then remained intermittently in touch on a basis of charged friendship. They rekindle their relationship at the exhibition opening of a mutual friend in Brixton, and seven months later the couple are married in a low-key civil ceremony in London, where Melodie has lived since she was eighteen. After spending the afternoon drinking wine with friends and then watching an Alejandro Jodorowsky film projected in a Notting Hill flat, they awaken on their first morning as a married couple and fly from Heathrow to Paris Charles de Gaulle. They rent a fifth-floor apartment in the eighteenth arrondissement for four weeks – a period Ren and Melodie will spend visiting galleries, seeing films in the cinema, walking for hours through the city and watching more films at night on the home projector (the couple have become interested in Westerns, and share a profound admiration for *The Wizard of Oz*). For two hours each morning, Ren adds a few pages to the pseudonymous erotic novel he is writing for pleasure, and as a break from his autobiographical fiction. The novel involves a classic *ménage à trois* and, judging by the passages included in *Ren Duka's Honeymoon*, wears its dated gender politics if not proudly then at least recklessly. This novel within a novel concerns the fortunes of a rakish Pigalle *chanteur* and occasional Montmartre tour guide named Dirty Philippe. He spends his days hanging out with internet rappers in the tower blocks of Seine Saint-Denis, or drinking glasses of beer at bookies around the city where he gambles on a variety of sports events (boxing, football, horse-racing, baseball). His nights are spent pursuing two equally passionate and deceit-ridden affairs. On a Monday he will meet Valeria, a busty, chic professor of nineteenth-century French literature at the Sorbonne. Fresh from her bed on a Tuesday morning, he will make plans to meet later that evening with the troubled, nymphomaniacal and remarkably beautiful Celine Le Lay, a student of film (also at the Sorbonne) who practises black magic, attends private fetish parties at the homes of wealthy Parisians and screams when she comes, which she does easily and often. While Dirty Philippe suspects (or assumes) that both of the women have other lovers, what he does not suspect is that they are also involved in a passionate affair... with each other. The energetically written scenes of straight and sapphic sex, voyeurism, male and female masturbation, and orgies are interpolated with ribald episodes of slapstick, bedroom farce and low comedy.

A week into Ren and Melodie's Parisian honeymoon, their friend Alissa arrives from Milan. The three of them toast their reunion with a glass of champagne. Then Melodie puts a disc on the vinyl-record player and all three spend the afternoon making love on white sheets in the bright bedroom as sunlight pours through the high windows. The threesome is described in no less lascivious detail than the erotic scenes in Ren Duka's pseudonymous novel: a languid pornographic dream of limbs, tongues and lips, the taste of salty sweat and sweet red wine. The women gently kiss one another's clits and lick each other's labia while male fingers churn inside them both at once. After both women have come, Alissa licks Ren's balls and the shaft of his cock while Melodie deftly flicks her tongue over the glans and frenulum. The two women's tongues dart and lap around the pulsing shaft, finding each other. Ren ejaculates abruptly, a long shuddering sequence of spurts. As goblets of pearly semen splash over his lovers' lips, tongues and smiling mouths, he screams.

That evening, the trio dine on the terrace of a bistro on Rue Marcadet. Ren orders onion soup, then the *filet de boeuf*, which he declares the most tender, juicy, pink and succulent he has ever enjoyed. Melodie orders avocado and prawns, then the *confit de canard*. Alissa orders cream of vegetable soup, then the ratatouille. They drink a bottle of Brouilly 'as clear and crystalline as the blood of angels' with the meal, then order a second bottle with dessert (*crème brûlée* for Ren and Alissa, strawberry meringue for Melodie), before finishing it all off with Armagnac and espressi. After they return to their apartment, they put on another record, then disrobe each other and sink again into a blur of limbs, cunts, cock and tongues. Afterwards, Ren falls asleep with his condom-sheathed cock still inside Alissa and a hand clasping Melodie's, whose head nestles in Alissa's neck. On briefly waking in the dark some time later, Ren's cock has slid out of Alissa and he finds that the condom is torn open at the tip. He unsheathes it, wraps it inside a tissue and places it on the bedside dresser to dispose of in the morning. Then he falls back asleep in the warmth between the two women.

Over the days that follow, while Alissa and Melodie explore the city together, Ren adds pages to his erotic novel, inserting surreal and fantastical flourishes amidst the bed-hopping. After realising that his feelings for the young and gorgeous Celine amount to more than simple lust, Dirty Philippe proposes to her. Following a period of vacillation (these passages read like the kind of nineteenth-century novel that Valeria teaches at the Sorbonne), Celine accepts. It is shortly after the engagement that the penny drops for Dirty Philippe regarding the curious triangle that has formed between him and his two lovers. At first, even as evidence mounts, he wonders if his suspicions are mere paranoia, the bitter fruits of a blooming jealousy towards his highly attractive fiancée. He needs to confirm his suspicions with his own eyes. One afternoon he sits on a bench in a small park opposite Valeria's sixteenth arrondissement apartment and observes as Celine arrives for what can only be an afternoon tryst. After she has been shown inside, he waits for fifteen minutes, then lets himself in through the building's main door as another inhabitant is leaving. He stands in the stairwell outside Valeria's apartment, from where he can hear the older woman grunt and moan as Celine's screams of pleasure resound through the landing. Dirty Philippe presses his ear to the door, his face contorted in what might be anguish or ecstasy.

At this point, Ren Duka's erotic novel breaks off into an extended essay which, we are told, takes up the entire middle section of the book within a book. Dropping the fictive charade and acknowledging his characters (Dirty Philippe, Celine, Valeria) *as* characters, Duka meditates on the meaning of sex and marriage at the close of the 2020s. Since the sexual revolution of the 1960s, he writes, marriage in the West has effectively become a failed institution. The deadly contradiction in the core of modern marriage, he goes on, is that while feminist ideology has made unacceptable the link between romantic love and *possession*, in the atavistic masculine psyche there has not been, and probably never will be, any corresponding evolution. Whenever a man marries a woman in the contemporary world, writes Duka, he does so in the awareness of buying *shopworn goods* – his new possession has already been passed around, enjoyed and cast off in bored satiation by other men. These men, writes Duka, have *left their stamp* on the bride-to-be, just as the groom-to-be has left his stamp on other women – as many and as trenchantly as possible. The groom's awareness of the bride's *shopworn* quality, he writes – his feeling of having purchased second-hand goods – survives the married couple's initial flush of optimism, and in many cases is the seed that eventually undermines the union. *Ultimately*, Duka asks, *what is it that men want?* His answer is blunt: they want a harem of virgins – or of sluts. In truly patriarchal societies where male desire has *laid itself bare*, he writes, that is precisely what men of high status have consistently gone about acquiring. Duka enjoins us to consider contemporary rap music, whose megastar elite enjoy power and glory comparable to that of the pharaohs. The male rapper, he writes, is a sexual despot who relishes humiliating other men through carnal ownership of their women, and millions of fans lap this up because the rapper thereby lives out *their* fantasy. The essay digresses to consider the moral panic around sex that had swept through the West on social media waves in the late 2010s. Duka tentatively welcomes the upheaval as an overdue phase of sexual *counter*-revolution – the punitive reining in of a wildly destructive instinct that, left unchecked, would prove fatal to the social order. Duka concludes his essay-within-a-novel by affirming the value of marriage even in a degraded socio-sexual landscape wherein true love is no longer possible. Marriage under such a social order, he writes – the cynical union of two *jaded and shopworn products* – ought to be regarded as a purifying humiliation (from the Latin *humiliare*, 'to bring low'). It is here, just before Duka's wayward essay ends and we cut back to the bedroom antics of Philippe, Valeria and Celine, that we grasp its significance in the context of Ren Duka's recent religious turn:

marriage, to him, is the spiritual path in that it humbles the self and cauterises pride, bringing us closer to God.

After the account of Ren Duka's bizarre novelistic essay, much of *Ren Duka's Honeymoon* consists of sensual descriptions of the meals Ren, Melodie and Alissa enjoy at restaurants around Montmartre, Le Marais and the Latin Quarter, and the conversations the three friends conduct over a variety of wines (whose bouquets and textures are lovingly evoked). They discuss Alissa's work as a prison psychiatrist in Milan, where she interacts with some of Italy's most perverted and violent criminals. They discuss art and music, love and desire, and the nature of jealousy. In a cosy bistro near Montmartre, Ren admits to the months of brutal retrospective jealousy he had endured on renewing his relationship with Melodie: a period he spent imagining, in exquisite detail, encounters from her past, nights of lust she'd enjoyed in numerous cities with various men ... ruminations which, even as they tortured him, he'd found terrifyingly intoxicating. Alissa replies that whenever her male lovers start up with that kind of retrospective jealousy, she immediately counters with what she calls 'exposure therapy', talking freely and in vivid detail about her many adventures. 'Besides, I've never once been able to stay monogamous in a relationship, not once, even when I've tried,' she adds. 'I'm just not able to stay faithful. Retrospective jealousy is the *least* of their worries.' As Melodie pours more wine and the coffee and desserts arrive (*macarons* for Melodie and Alissa, *tarte Tatin* for Ren), Ren tells them about the treatise on sexual politics nestled within the otherwise lightweight erotic novel he has been writing. Melodie laughs. Alissa laughs too, and tells him that his sexual politics are not only regressive, they're frankly infantile, and that he ought to publish the essay if only to demonstrate, once and for all, that men seriously need to *get over themselves*. She tells him he is doing what a certain type of male writer has always done: inflating his private wound and stunted moral imagination into a worldview he secretly wishes to impose on everyone else. 'If you want to talk about despotism,' she says, making a very Italian gesticulation, 'then there's your despotism.' Ren grins sheepishly. 'At the same time,' Alissa adds in a thoughtful voice, 'there probably *is* something to what you're saying.'

A few days before Alissa flies back to Milan, the trio enjoy a breakfast of almond croissants, coffee and orange juice at a cafe terrace on rue Ordener. Then they each take a tab of LSD and walk together in the direction of the Seine. The first, subtle hints of autumn light filter through the city. The museum they are seeking is on a quiet street named the rue de la Rochefoucauld, which prompts Alissa to quote the aphorist: 'What makes the vanity of others insufferable to us is that it wounds our own.' The house where the Symbolist painter Gustave Moreau lived and worked in the nineteenth century displays a grand array of his otherworldly, mythological and fantastical works. The acid is coming on as they pay the lady at the ticket desk and step inside. Immediately they are submerged in colour and voluptuousness. Enchanted, they fan out and explore the rooms singly. Melodie stands marvelling before the painting *The Triumph of Alexander the Great* – she feels she recognises its landscape from some dream or past life. Alissa falls into a trance while gazing at *Jupiter and Sémélé*, absorbed in its lustrous, mystical complexities. Ren finds himself looking up at a painting of wine-soaked carnality titled *La Débauche*. As he stands before the image, Melodie joins him, and the two of them gaze at its lovely vision of licentious abandon.

Ren Duka's Extinction – US Title: *Duka: End of Days* (June 2031)

In 2029, the largest climate protest in history took place in London. More than two million marchers gathered to express their fury during yet another conference at which world leaders tried to agree on a plan to avert humankind's catastrophic trajectory. The author spent four days as a reporter in the heat of the action. The novel that emerged from the experience is altogether stranger than a mere account of a historic demonstration.

In *Ren Duka's Extinction*, Ren Duka travels from Moscow (where he and Melodie now live) to report on the climate protests for *The Moscow Times*. As the protests begin, he sets up at a hotel in Piccadilly and arranges meetings with leaders of the various factions. The massive crowd's points of convergence are Westminster, London Bridge, Saint Paul's Cathedral and Trafalgar Square. During the second morning of the conference, the protests turn violent. Banks of tear-gas drift across Central London while police horses clatter through the streets, rearing up against masked youths who hurl firecrackers and fire slings into police lines. In the melee around the Cenotaph, two protestors die. That afternoon, Ren manages to gain access to the inner circle of a highly secretive fringe element within the climate movement – a mysterious and vilified group named Extinction Acquiescence.

Allegedly formed by a cohort of rogue critical theorists, artists and some of the most extreme climate activists, Extinction Acquiescence's members dress in black uniforms, their banners and flags bearing quasi-militaristic insignia. As riots bring London to the brink of martial law, Ren meets with the organisation's top-ranking members in a squat in Mile End. During the course of a cryptic and sinister conversation, he comes to suspect that Extinction Acquiescence, rather than the eccentric and minor outgrowth he took it for, is in fact the most influential faction within the climate movement. After a tense negotiation, a hood is placed over his head and he is taken to an abandoned underground train station. There he is granted an audience with the movement's leader, a slight, dark-haired woman named Masha Vasiliev. From Vasiliev he finally learns E.A.'s true agenda, which leaves him at once appalled and fascinated. Rather than hoping to save the planet, she tells him, E.A. are committed to accelerating the process of 'species-suicide' via the active destruction of the ecology, in part by aiding the institutions that are already committing the destruction. 'We – the human species – are our own judge, jury and executioner,' she says, looking hard into Duka's eyes. 'Think of it as species-level euthanasia. The human race has made it clear that it no longer wants to live. The only question is whether the end is protracted and miserable, or relatively quick and painless. Extinction Acquiescence is the midwife to this suicide. We no longer stand in the way of human destiny. We *accelerate* it.'

'But what about the natural world?' asks Ren, his voice childish and weak. 'What about all the *other* species? Don't they deserve to live?'

Masha Vasiliev regards him for a long time with an expression of wry contempt. 'What *planet* are you living on?' she finally asks. 'Look around you. Look at the continents and oceans, the mountains and deserts. Consider the many millions of senseless and brutal years that preceded our brief career. All that agony, that emptiness – an infinite screaming. Nature is nothing other than a perpetual holocaust, an incessant, churning abyss of atrocities, a vertigo of waste and cruelty. The earth is a vast extermination camp, a hell suspended in infinite space. This is what makes *us* special and it is the *only* thing that makes us special: we alone, as human beings, can apprehend the carnage, fathom the depth of the horror, the nightmare that was created when life first appeared on earth. We have seen it, and now we are taking the only honourable course of action and putting an end to it all. Don't you understand? This is the *true* final solution. Our enemy is not humankind, Gaia, or the ecology. Our enemy is *life*.' At that, Masha Vasiliev signals to someone out of sight. Two stocky men promptly appear and roughly usher Ren Duka out of the room. One of them replaces the hood over his head. Then he is led out of the underground base and driven to a neutral location.

Ren's efforts to learn more about Extinction Acquiescence's aims at the protests are frustrating. None of it makes sense. Why are they here? Whom do they really serve? Is the movement a ruse, perhaps a Saudi or Iranian psy-op to destabilise Western power structures while reinforcing the reliance on fossil fuels? After considering various hypotheses, he concludes that Extinction Acquiescence is a terrorist organisation motivated by sheer nihilistic *jouissance*. He suspects that Masha Vasiliev is a cypher, wheeled out to mislead the authorities as to the organisation's true structure. As twilight falls on a battle-scarred London, he receives an anonymous text message telling him that E.A. has placed operatives at the highest levels of government and the military; these sleeper units have long awaited the signal to put the grand plan into motion, and now the signal is going out. Over several tense chapters, Ren becomes convinced that E.A. is about to perpetrate a large-scale terrorist attack on London. Not only would such an attack decapitate the worldwide climate movement, it would decimate the community of political and business leaders who otherwise just might cooperate to save humankind from itself. Spiralling into paranoia, he runs through streets acrid with tear gas amid blaring sirens and the surge of the crowd, not knowing who to warn first. Eventually he slumps exhausted against the wall of a laneway off Baker Street. As his breath gradually slows and his thoughts cohere, he realises he has become unhinged – the capital is not in imminent peril. Weary and overwhelmed, he makes his way through the subsiding disorder to his hotel room, where he sits naked under a hot shower for forty minutes. Calmed, he puts on a bathrobe and stands on the balcony overlooking Central London. As if shaking off the residue of a bad dream, he comes to accept what should have been clear all along: Extinction Acquiescence is just a bunch of pretentious art-world pranksters, and he was their dupe. Gazing across the London skyline, he realises that E.A. rattled him because it touched a very private nerve, reawakening emotions he thought he had long moved past.

It is here that the novel turns from being a semi-journalistic rendering of a historical event to something darker and more introspective. What follows is a long digression on the subject of fatherhood and the moral weight of bringing new life into the world. At bottom, the essay nestled inside the novel addresses the question of whether or not life is worth living. A month past his forty-seventh birthday, Ren Duka reflects on his decision not to become a father – a decision he has recently come to question, at a point when it is all but too late to change his mind (for one thing, his wife Melodie is adamant that she does not want children). He stands on the balcony for hours, imagining how his destiny might have unfolded if he hadn't set his heart against the possibility of begetting new life. When the cold night air eventually drives him inside, he sleeps for a few hours. He rises before dawn, checks out of the hotel, and takes the Underground to Liverpool Street Station. There he buys a rail-and-sail ticket and boards a train that leaves London just after 9 a.m.

Through the morning and early afternoon the train crosses the English and Welsh countryside. It arrives at Holyhead a little after 2 p.m. From there, Ren boards a Stena Line ferry that crosses the Irish Sea and arrives in the early evening at Rosslare Europort, a ferry terminal at the end of the railway line on Ireland's southeastern coast. On disembarking, he exits the port on foot and walks up a concrete stairway built into the side of a cliff. On the clifftop he passes a boarded-up hotel and a forlorn fish and chip shop, then crosses a road and walks into a housing estate where most of the houses appear to be unoccupied. The one he is headed for is a semi-detached at the bottom of the estate with a line of dark trees looming behind it. After pausing at the front door for several minutes,

Ren lets himself in. He walks along a hallway and steps into a kitchen. Sitting at the kitchen table, his laptop open in front of him and a text document glowing on the screen, is the author. He looks up, startled. Ren notes the three cups on the table beside him – two are empty, one contains coffee. Also on the table are some notebooks and pens, a stack of books (including Kevin Mulvaney's autobiography *I'm Done With this Life*) and the remnants of a small meal. The author regains his composure as the two men regard each other in silence. The other man is a decade younger than him, but to Ren he seems older, dishevelled and seedy and faded, as if he is in the process of disappearing. His sallow skin and lifeless greying hair suggest irreconcilable sorrows and advanced alcoholism. Glancing around, Ren notes the two large black bags full of empty bottles resting against the sliding door to the back garden. A plastic bin overflows with instant noodle wrappings and crushed salt-and-vinegar Pringles containers.

Abruptly, Ren asks the question that has led him here. 'Why were you always so adamant you didn't want to be a father? What made you turn against life so young? You've had a *good* life, compared to the overwhelming majority of the human beings who live and die on this planet. You've known friendship, art, love, laughter. Why such torment and aloneness? Can't you see where all this is leading you?'

Rather than reply, the author simply gazes at him, as if so lost in thought he hasn't registered the question. Ren persists: 'Were you afraid to have children because you felt you had somehow failed as a son, or more simply as a man? Was your life really too filled with sadness and disaster for you to bear creating a witness? Did you believe that having a child would be a punishment? Did you even convince yourself it would be born deformed, or grow up evil, or suffer unbearably?'

The author glances shiftily around the room, visibly tense, as if expecting someone else to burst in. Finally, accepting that the encounter cannot be avoided, he looks Ren Duka in the eye. As the two men regard one another, his features soften. 'Some of that may be true,' he says, 'or at least true to an extent. But none of it was decisive.' His face now radiates empathy. 'Don't you see?' he asks the older man. '*You* are my child. I *am* a father, and a young boy and a grandparent too. I want for nothing. I have it all – thanks to you.'

Neither man speaks for a long time. Suddenly the author suggests a drink. He goes to a cupboard and takes from it a bottle of Chilean red wine with a Supervalu special-offer sticker on the label. He opens it and pours two large glasses, one of which he immediately gulps down and refills. Ren takes the glass he is handed but does not drink, only twirls the stem between his thumb and middle finger. The wine's bouquet fills his nostrils. Dusk is falling on the Wexford coast. Soon it will be autumn, and with it will come the relief he knows the author craves during these long, bright summer months. The author is already pouring himself a third glass as Ren raises his in a toast. 'To old times,' says Ren.

'To evil,' says the author.

They clink glasses and the author gulps his down while Ren Duka sips. Somewhere on the estate, a dog barks.

Excerpt from *A Cool, Dry Place*

I wished I could have gone in disguise to Isabel's funeral. I was sure that almost everyone there hated me, blamed me. But they could hardly bar her ex-husband from turning up to mourn. The graveyard was in Glasnevin in north Dublin, her Spanish relatives huddled in the cold like dark, exotic birds, the day wet and grey. Her Tipperary-born father, to his credit, shook my hand with no outward sign of ill will. Her mother, over from Seville, wouldn't even look at me. It wasn't just the family. I'd expected the gutter press to go in hard, stoking the scandal by recalling public episodes and viral meltdowns – but they'd been strangely muted. Not so the online swarms. Any time I glanced into that maelstrom in the weeks after Isabel's death I saw my name being dragged in all directions, like a human form rent apart in a black hole. They were calling me a murderer, saying I should be held accountable, that I'd driven her mad, driven her to her death (even though we'd been divorced for a year when she went into the sea). Gaslighter, abuser, misogynist – they called me these things and worse, framing the tragedy as another instance of a powerful man and his blameless female victim. An army of devotees had amassed around this shy, private woman who'd never shown the faintest desire for publicity even when she'd married me. I suspected that most of them were bots but I didn't look into it, I was too tired, too worn down by what had happened although I'd anticipated it for years. The vigilante-stans resurrected a long-deleted post in which Isabel, at a nadir in our marriage and in her psychosis, had claimed I'd got inside her mind to corrupt her will and that, 'mark my words, 100% he is going to drive me to suicide – only it won't really be suicide, it will be murder'.

There was no point debating her avengers or expressing in public what I privately believed: that Isabel's exit from this world was scripted long before I ever knew her, and all the torment she found with me she would have found with anyone. Neither of us had chosen this, any more than my one-time schoolteacher Mr Manly had chosen the course of his sordid life. I'd watched it happen like a disaster witnessed from afar: a skyscraper on fire, an aeroplane going down off the coast. At the very most I'd hastened the inevitable. At the very most.

After the burial, the mourners moved to a nearby pub with dark green upholstery and blessed little daylight. The pub seemed to me like a sea cave where you could hide out for years as the world went to ruin. I lingered near the door, swapping words with Isabel's less hostile friends as the family amassed around tables down the back of the pub. I talked for a while with a white-haired woman with big round eyes who seemed to be there on her own. She spoke in a confusing monologue that flitted about like a panicked moth – one moment she was talking about the colour of my skin ('like porcelain or marble'), the next about a painting she'd once seen of a witch devouring a baby from her own womb. The woman had an otherworldly, haunted air. I wondered if she and my ex-wife had become friends in an institution, bonding over visions of the hell behind life's paper-thin surface – but before I could ask her if that was so, she was gone. I finished my drink, then I slipped away and took a taxi to the airport.

Excerpt from *Night Taxi*

Henry K. Dillon dropped off his last fare a little after 4 a.m. He cruised aimlessly for a while, the streets empty after the Saturday night revel. A fox trotted across O'Connell Street, pausing to root inside a discarded burger carton. A bearded, homeless man walked along the traffic island past the GPO, like some wanderer through time. All was quiet. This was Henry's cherished hour, on the cusp of dawn when work was finished and he had the city to himself. He drove by the quays towards Custom House, turned north into the inner city.

Down a back street amidst Chinese businesses and dere-lict properties, he pulled up outside the all-night cinema. He bought a ticket from the indifferent usherette for the next film that was showing, *Gunfather 4: Realm of Shades*. He stepped into the small, dark theatre and took a seat three rows from the back. Solitary figures sat slumped here and there. A voice whispered. Somebody coughed.

The film depicted a limo driver who works nights in a rainy city populated by vagrants, criminals, hookers, psychotics and addicts. In a pre-credits sequence, a bald man with bags under his eyes stands naked in front of a bathroom mirror. A voiceover intones, 'They say the only way to endure the horror of being someone else's simulation... is to simulate someone else.' The bald man raises a pistol to the side of his head and pulls the trigger. We follow the passage of the bullet as it smashes through bone, flesh and cerebral matter, tunnelling into white blinding light.

Henry awoke to harsh electronic music playing over the closing credits. Amid the scrolling names were some he recognised from his own life. He saw his own name. If only he hadn't slept through the film, he thought, he might finally have understood everything. He sat there till the credits ended. Then he stood up, brushed himself off, and stepped out into the street.

In the murky blue dawn, Henry drove out of the city centre, past Dublin port and alongside the grey beach where you could walk for what seemed like miles over wet sand before you reached the sea. He drove to the end of a headland and killed the engine. A cry of seagulls ripped the stillness. He sat watching the horizon, the freighters setting out for France or England. Memories of fares, conversations, dramas he'd witnessed tumbled through his mind.

After some time, he pushed open the glove compartment and took out a green, hardbound notebook. It had lain in there for years. He opened the first page, clean and white. Then he pulled the top off a black uni-ball pen and began writing:

When he had reached the age of Zarathustra, the author who would become known to the world as the creator of Rain Dukkha returned home after many years in foreign lands. Measuring the life he had lived alongside the life he might still have left, he began to conceive of a narrative cycle, a story of stories that would transmute the horrors and wonders he had witnessed into the hard, pristine stuff of art. He would step out of the river of experience, into the flow of time. In a tattered blue notebook he wrote the first words: 'All his life Rain Dukkha had been maddened, tantalised, obsessed by the feeling that existence was a book that was writing itself through him. Then, when he was forty years old, he began to write it down.'

9. Generation

The Death of Ren Duka (December 2032)

'At a certain point I knew I had to kill off the Ren Duka persona,' the author said in an interview with the *People's Daily* that ended an uncharacteristic, three-year media silence. Many readers had believed that *Ren Duka's Extinction*, with its shock metafictional denouement, marked the end of the cycle, but the author now claimed that the unusually long wait for the true finale was simply the result of him taking more care than he ever had with a Duka novel. 'I wanted to write one perfect, culminating volume to bring it all to an end. I'd become obsessed with the idea that I might die – people do, they just drop dead without having sorted out their affairs – and if I did then he would outlive me in an aggravating way. His narrative would never be tied up in a satisfactory manner. It was crucial that he died before I did.' A few deviations into outright fantasy excepted, the life of Ren Duka and that of his author had hitherto cleaved quite closely together. In writing the final novel, the author determined to split them irrevocably apart.

The Death of Ren Duka begins with a diagnosis, followed by a spree. On an otherwise ordinary Tuesday morning, a visit to the doctor prompted by frequent migraines leads to an emergency brain-scan at an inner-city Dublin hospital. A tumour is discovered in Ren Duka's brain. He receives the news with an ostensible calm that the neurologist mistakes for stoicism – in truth, he is speechless with fear. The brain-scan images are immediately sent for testing to establish whether the tumour has turned malignant; if it has not, it might yet be successfully treated. That night Ren makes love to his wife Melodie with a tenderness and passion that has lately been lacking between them, but he cannot bring himself to tell her the grim news.

The following evening, he meets up with his friend Matt and some others before a long-anticipated techno night in the city centre, which will culminate in a set by the Detroit icon Jeff Mills. Before the event, they gather at Matt's bachelor flat opposite the Google headquarters at Grand Canal Dock. Sniffing lines of cocaine and ketamine from a glass table, they pour drinks and laugh about this increasingly rare get-together of middle-aged hedonists, stepping out from wives and families to relive the kind of night that had electrified their twenties and thirties. It strikes Ren that he has not been around cocaine since Paulie Sheehan's ordeal years earlier – the memory brings with it a fleeting sadness. For the past decade, he has kept his drug consumption to a studious minimum. But tonight, the brain-scans flash in his mind's eye, and when someone offers him an ecstasy pill he swallows it down with a gulp of rum and coke. By the time they are all seated inside a taxi heading towards the venue, he is cresting above the dread that descended the instant he received his diagnosis. The city streaks past in rainy, neon smears. The taxi driver, a bald man with a lined and pensive face, seems familiar to Ren, as if they have glimpsed one another in dreams. Matt leans over in the back seat to offer Ren a cloth pouch – Ren reaches in, fingers up a handful of dried magic mushrooms

and lobs them into his mouth. Inside the venue – a cavern-
ous, low-ceilinged techno-box on the quays – the sound is
crystalline: you can hear *inside* each beat and chord. The laser
lights and dry ice suggest the emanation of an alien vessel or
a portal of contact between dimensions. Jeff Mills is an hour
into his set when Ren collapses. The young dancers around
him signal for assistance as the beat pounds without relent.
Venue staff in black bomber jackets lift the prone body away
with fast efficiency; then the dancing crowd swallows up the
space where he had fallen. Outside, the staff shelter Ren from
the rattling rain under an awning and call for an ambulance.
They lie him on his front and connect him to a yellow drip
while swaddling his body in blankets to prevent hypothermia.
He begins to wretch, froth, and spasm as blackish blood pours
down his lips. The staff shout at one another, losing their air of
professional sangfroid. Matt and the others hover frantically
around them. The words 'Where's the fucking ambulance!' are
the last that Ren Duka hears before his consciousness clouds
over, blurs, dissolves . . .

. . . and now floats free, its link severed with the body that
lies face-down beneath it, surrounded by milling figures and
hooked up to the yellow drip. From here on in we inhabit
the disembodied viewpoint of the exhaled spirit that floats
above the scene of Ren Duka's death. Over a single night
in Dublin, the untethered consciousness drifts through the
Bardo in search of a fresh womb to enter. Before it can be
reborn, the spirit is compelled to face the conflicts it left
unresolved when Ren Duka's body perished (we see it being
wheeled on a gurney through the corridors of Hollis Street
hospital and taken into the E.R. for attempted resuscitation).

Pulled by karmic forces, the homeless spirit seeks out those among the living to whom to it owes moral debts. We perceive Dublin by night as a scrolling grid of lights, like an immense circuit board. The spirit searches for Nicole, who shared her childhood with Ren and who he loved more than any other woman. We glide over the alleys and streets of the city centre, past the coastal lights to the suburban house where Nicole is making love to her new boyfriend. For a luminous instant, the consciousness transports inside its sister's body and we too become her as she makes love with abandon, unaware that her brother's life has ebbed away on a roadside in the rain. As the spirit moves through her and within her, she orgasms more powerfully than she ever has before, a cascading pleasure that obliterates her bordered self and grants her a glimpse of infinity, the merging of innumerable minds. As the pleasure subsides, she sees a vision of her brother lying in the street with flashing lights all around. And now it is no longer Nicole's body we are inside but that of Melodie, whose sleep is stirred by strange dreams as we breach her womb, encountering a radiant orb of energy growing inside her, humming with immeasurable force. But the restless spirit leaves her, soaring out the window and once again over streets that shimmer in the rain. We pass shopfronts, casinos and nightclubs as the exiled consciousness seeks out lovers and enemies, friends and rivals, those it harmed or was harmed by. In each instance the implication is the same – it is too late. Now we float into the home of his mother and father, hovering above them as they watch television, and as we do so this last night on earth begins to fray and glitch and becomes flooded with images of the past. The drifting consciousness relives it all – the humiliations and shocks, triumphs and joys, defeats and truces; the moments of pity or hatred, nights of pleasure or desolation, acts of revenge or forgiveness that made up one human life. He experiences it in a hurtling succession of instants, becoming once more the beloved and the bullied child, the inspiring and the disappointing friend, the passionate and the selfish lover, the tongue-tied son, the hated rival, the trusted ally, the betrayer and the betrayed, the transgressor and the victim, the laughing stock and the victor, the hero of a day and the villain of another, the nobody and the everyman. As the vision dissolves we are transported far away, leaving Dublin and its island at the edge of the Atlantic, crossing oceans and continents. We glimpse again the glowing orb of energy within the generative chamber of a living womb. A dull, red smoky light fills the air ... and still the consciousness drifts on, elsewhere and elsewhere ...

Fiction, the author more than once suggested, is anticipated fact. So much of what he had ever dreamed up in novels, he insisted, was later to come true. It was for this reason, he explained in interviews, that he had for a time come to regard fiction with a respect that verged on fear. But such trepidation, he came to see, was pointless. Fiction, it seemed to him, was nothing other than non-fiction in another of its dimensions, an ultra-realism that records the unfolding of time and space across planes both visible and invisible. When an event occurs – a killing, a conception, a suicide, a transgression – it does so first as an echo, in writing, and only then (as if time is flowing backwards, a river returning us all to the womb of wombs) on the plane of perceived reality. In the wake of this realisation, he told several interlocutors, his writing had poured forth torrentially as he accepted that the story he was telling was the story of everyone and everything because he was indivisible from the fabric – the beginning and the end, the book and its author, the teller and the told, the reading and the read. In short, he was nothing.

In August 2032, when the author was halfway through writing *The Death of Ren Duka*, a routine check-up led to the discovery of a tumour growing on his brain. He scarcely had time for astonishment at this final congruence of imagination and reality because he had precious little time for anything now. The solemn neurologist informed him that the tumour had already metastasised. His brain, as he saw in the umbral and strangely beautiful images presented to him, was riddled with cancer (he later envisioned it as a shoal of small black fish eating through silver membrane). He sat in a consulting room with his second wife as the neurologist quietly told them that he had perhaps one month to live, maybe less, not more. The days that followed the prognosis were filled with a series of goodbyes – phone calls to friends scattered around the planet, last drinks at Dublin bars, a tearful meal with his parents and sister. And then, accepting that not all of his affairs were in order but knowing that the greatest freedom he had now was in choosing his priorities, he kept on writing. Begun in innocence, from its midpoint on *The Death of Ren Duka* was written in the full awareness of its author's imminent death. Just as the authorial persona had easefully shifted genres from one book to the next – from detective novel to espionage drama; prison thriller to erotic confessional – the discarnate spirit now shifts between entire metaphysical traditions. The untethered consciousness no longer floats above Dublin's rainy streets but ascends on a beam of sheer white light, passing far above the surface of the earth, climbing through a fathomless abyss. Leaving behind for ever its corporeal form, the unbound soul soars beyond the limits of the visible universe until, amid blinding light and thundering vibrations, it comes face to face with the mind that *is* all, is *within* all and is *beyond* all. What follows is a delirium of rapture, awe, and ecstatic obliteration as the ephemeral droplet finds its way back to the ocean of eternity. For page after breathless page it is as if the prose itself dissolves into pure light, a blaze of splendour in paean to the mystery and magnificence of all things: to the blue skies of earth and the starry heavens; the lakes and oceans of innumerable worlds; the deserts and tundra; the ravines and forests; the creatures and birds; the fish and flowers; the cities and machines; the planets and suns; the galaxies and supernovae in all the pasts and presents and futures, rotating perpetually on an eternal instant.

The author of the Ren Duka novels died on 20th September 2032. He was fifty years old. His funeral was a private affair, attended only by family and a few close friends. Photos were leaked on social media. While one opinion columnist crassly implied that his death was a deserved punishment for the mistreatment of his first wife, Isabel, such intrusive speculation was rare. Three months after the funeral, *The Death of Ren Duka* was published. Five months later, the author's widow gave birth to a daughter, Alissa.

Reviews of *The Death of Ren Duka* were uniformly respectful, in some cases highly laudatory, and tended to resemble obituaries. While the novel was generally received as a worthy culmination to the prolific sequence that had gripped readers for over a decade, a few wary notes were sounded not so much concerning the novel's literary merit as its moral and metaphysical implications. Almost two years would pass before an article appeared that properly explored the troubling questions that, in the period immediately following the author's death, were only hinted at. 'Seeing as the author repeatedly declared fiction to be anticipated fact,' wrote Nathalie Parillaud in *Le Figaro*, 'and seeing that he went on to imagine his novelistic persona afflicted by an ailment whose real-world existence he could not have suspected; and seeing finally that he, the author, like his literary persona, really did subsequently die from the same affliction – are we not to understand the writing of a tumour into Ren Duka's brain as ... an act of metaphysical suicide?'

Most contemporary critics chose to leave such delicate questions aside, acknowledging the novel's qualities of rapturous surrender and mystical exaltation. Regardless, the reviews did not matter much. The online forums bestowed instant canonical status on *The Death of Ren Duka*. As one commenter posted, '*TDORD* is his *least* personal book, in the sense that it's his gift to everybody. *And* it's a message from the beyond. I don't regard it as fiction, I regard it as prophecy.'

On the same thread, a year later, another commenter speculated that Alissa, the late author's infant child, would grow up to write a 'metaphysical sequel' to the saga: *The Daughter of Ren Duka*. The poster conceived of Alissa sublimating her life in a revolutionary sequence of novels that would right the wrongs of the father, speak new words to as-yet unmapped regions of the spirit, and usher in a bright dawn for the literature of the future.

Epilogue

The Last Interview

Now that you are nearing the conclusion of this major cycle of work, and having been through some remarkable highs and lows, what motivates you to continue writing?

The same thing that motivated me to begin: it beats getting a real job.

Are you joking?

No.

Earlier in our conversation, you suggested that beginning to write the Ren Duka novels was your response to an emergency. Ten years on – in a world unrecognisable in so many ways from the one you began the series in – do you feel the same sort of urgency around your work?

To quote an author I long ago stopped reading, Friedrich Nietzsche, I can say that the entire Duka series stands as a monument to a crisis. Only, the crisis turns out not to have been mine alone, as I imagined it was when I wrote the first pages of the original novel. Ren Duka is the window through which I've viewed the world's catastrophes and mutations. He's the microcosm that contains the macrocosm.

It's certainly true that the years you've spent writing the Ren Duka novels have been among the most tumultuous in human history. And yet these various events – nuclear attacks, a wave of world leaders being assassinated, the disintegration of the United States, eruptions of war across the globe, astonishing new forms of social control, the creation of virtual heavens and hells, the irreversible destruction of the environment, the emergence of a new world religion – have hardly been acknowledged in the books. Haven't you missed the real story?

It's not true that these developments aren't acknowledged, though it is true that they feature largely as a backdrop, part of the weather of my novels. I'm not about to apologise for that. What I'm up to is an investigation of Self, and that's weather resistant. Like I said, writing the Duka novels has helped me to realise that there's no clear line between the inner and the outer, between what we perceive and what we imagine, between writing and being written. Duka is the Void; the Void is Duka.

Of all the Ren Duka books you've written to date, do you have a favourite?

You and I have known each other for quite a while, so you'll know that the one I'm working on is always automatically my favourite. This time it's no different, but *especially* so. I won't say too much about it except that it's climactic. Otherwise, I've always been fond of *Ren Duka in the Third Reich*.

And a least favourite?

I don't care much for *Seventeen Suicides*, and few others cared for it either.

Naturally the Duka novels have demanded most of your time and energy in the last decade. But are there other literary projects you are working on? You mentioned a non-fiction book and a possible novel. And then there are rumours of a series of numbered notebooks...

It's true I keep a series of numbered and coloured notebooks, but all they are for is recording Ren Duka ideas. Each of the novels begins its life there, but many of the ideas never graduate and the notebooks are where they remain, as embryos. The notebooks are a warehouse of ideas – shelves of foetuses in little glass jars. My agent brought up the picturesque idea of farming out the unused Duka story outlines to other writers, getting a sort of franchise going, the way the Lovecraft estate has done, among others. But that never works out very well, and besides, I'm still alive. If others want to reboot the Ren Duka series when I'm dead in the ground, I don't have a problem with that. But not while I'm still here.

Could you tell us about some of the abandoned novels in the notebooks, the ideas that never saw the light of day?

Well, let me see. There was a potential book that was modelled on Nietzsche's *Ecce Homo*, where Ren Duka looks back over each of his own novels, briefly summarising them while reflecting on the circumstances of the books' composition. It ends with him appraising the book he's currently writing, which contains within it all the other books. But the only idea I really regret not developing further – it's too late now, it's out of sequence – is one called 'Ren Duka Throws it All Away'. I came up with it early on. It's a melancholy narrative where he decides that obscurity and failure are essential for his inner development and so he self-destructs in a highly dramatic fashion. There was a rare, gorgeous tone in the pages I wrote for that one that I haven't quite achieved before or since. A road not taken.

Do you ever read the Duka novels you've already published?

Until recently, absolutely not. I was superstitious about it and felt it was best to always be moving forward, like a shark. I somehow connected the idea of looking back with cessation, and in a sense I still feel that way. A short while ago, however, because of the stage I'm at with the series – with the end in sight – I decided it was an opportune moment to reread all of the Duka books to date. I went through them in reverse order, starting with *Extinction* and ending with *Seen a Few Things*. I read them quickly, one a day. I had the impression that he was getting younger as I read on, living his life backwards, and that if I'd been able to keep going I'd have followed him into the womb, and from there into his past lives.

Did you have any particular insights or revelations while reread-ing the Ren Duka books?

Not really. I enjoyed them. I felt I'd done a decent job. Not perfect, but good enough. Some pleasing yarns, some worth-while insights.

And would you say, now that you're coming to the end of a phase – a quite spectacular phase – of your writing life, that life as a whole has treated you well, that you're pleased with your lot?

Yes, I would. With Duka, I've done what I set out to do and it's left me cheerful. Life has given me what I've desired while at the same time showing that this wasn't much. But what can you do?

[*The interview ends in wild laughter brought on by the last state-ment.*]

Keep the laughter. You should put: 'Ends with laughter'.

Acknowledgements

Thank you to:

Susie Lopez, whose extraordinary and generous hospitality was intrinsic to this novel's creation. Alexa von Hirshberg, for faith and passion. Sam Copeland, my agent, for the right thoughts at the right time. All who were present in a beautiful house on the Wexford coast on a certain summer's night in 2021: Geoff, Simon, Andy, Roisin, Kieran. Lias Saoudi, for laughter in the dark. The Arts Council of Ireland, for awarding me two generous bursaries that enabled me to write this book. Jon Gresham and all the staff and Creative Writing students at Nanyang Technological University in Singapore who facilitated and made memorable my residency there. Antoinette and Jimmy Doyle, and my family. Roisin Kiberd, my beloved, for strength, love, belief and endless inspiration. And thanks finally to my friends and all those who helped me, too many to list but none of them forgotten.

The final lines in *Cameo* were lifted and modified from 'Self-Portrait at Seventy' by Jean-Paul Sartre, a text I read in a weathered volume borrowed from the university library in Singapore.

About the author

Rob Doyle is the author of four previous, internationally acclaimed books: *Threshold, Autobibliography, This is the Ritual* and *Here Are the Young Men,* which was adapted as a film starring Anya Taylor-Joy and Dean-Charles Chapman, and was named as one the *Irish Times'* 100 best Irish books of the 21st century and one of *RTÉ's* 21 books that define 21st century Irish literature. Doyle's writing has appeared in the *New York Times, Observer, New Statesman, Dublin Review* and many other publications. His work has been translated into several languages and nominated for various prizes. He is the editor of an anthology published by Dalkey Archive Press, *The Other Irish Tradition*, and the book *In This Skull Hotel Where I Never Sleep*. He lives where he can, in Dublin, Berlin and Rosslare Harbour.